Alberta and Freedom

Cora Sandel/Alberta and Freedom

Translated by Elizabeth Rokkan
Introduced by Solveig Nellinge
Afterword by Linda Hunt

Ohio University Press
Athens, Ohio

First published in English by Peter Owen Limited 1963
Original title, *Alberte og Friheten*
English translation copyright © Elizabeth Rokkan 1963
Copyright © Cora Sandel 1931
All rights reserved

Ohio University Press edition 1984
Printed in the United States of America.
All rights reserved.

Library of Congress Cataloging in Publication Data

Sandel, Cora, 1880-1974.
  Alberta and freedom.

  Translation of: Alberte og friheten.
  Vol. 2 of the Alberta triology; v. 1, Alberta and
Jacob; v. 3, Alberta alone.
  Reprint. Originally published: London: Women's Press,
1980, c1963.
  I. Title.
PT8950.F2A73 1983   839.8'2372   83-19322
ISBN 0-8214-0758-8
ISBN 0-8214-0759-7 (pbk.)

INTRODUCTION
A personal memoir by Solveig Nellinge

Cora Sandel's real name, Sara Fabricus, did not become known
until several years after her first book was published. She was
born in Oslo, in 1880. Her father was a naval officer and when
she was twelve her family moved to Tromsø, in the most northern
part of Norway, which is where *Alberta and Jacob* is set.

She decided early to become a painter and around the turn of
the century left for Oslo, then called Kristiania, to become a
pupil in Harriet Backer's Art School. When she was twenty-five,
in 1905, Sara Fabricus left for Paris, taking with her 800 Norwegian Crowns. Her plan was to stay for six months but her
visit was to last for fifteen years. She was determined to earn her
living as a painter and worked hard at it until 1918 when she put
down her brush, having finished her last painting, a landscape
from Bretagne. In the spring of 1970, when she was nearly ninety,
an exhibition was arranged in Stockholm of as many of her
paintings as could be gathered together. She found it very
strange to have her first exhibition so late, especially as she had
given up painting so long before.

While in Paris Sara Fabricus had sent home a few sketches,
articles and short stories in order to survive. She also admitted to
having written down ideas, sentences and words on pieces of
paper which she threw into a large suitcase. Writing never came
easily to her and that she was for so long torn between her two
major talents – writing and painting – was a continuous source of
conflict for her until she decided to give up painting. She would
never admit that both her talents were far above average but she
chose to write – or, rather, writing chose her.

Her first novel, *Alberta and Jacob*, was published in 1926. By
then she had left Paris: 'It felt like having one's heart torn out.'
Those fifteen years left their stamp for life on Cora Sandel's
personality. French taste and French ésprit always characterised
her.

She was married in 1913, while still in Paris, to the Swedish

1

sculptor Anders Jönsson and together they had one son, Erik. For his sake they tried to save their marriage but in the summer of 1926, as she wrote the last chapters of *Alberta and Jacob*, their divorce became a fact.

Cora Sandel had Swedish citizenship through her marriage and lived in Sweden before the war, moving there permanently in 1939. For several years she lived in Stockholm in the home of a good friend, a Swedish woman doctor, but later, in 1945, moved to Uppsala. She was sixty-five by then and for the first time had an apartment of her own. She lived there almost to her last years.

She was never keen to acquire lots of possessions. Cora Sandel and her character Alberta are alike in this: 'in their fear of dying of surfeit they'd rather die of starvation and are capable of running away from everything – even pension benefits.'

There is one fairly complete biography of Cora Sandel, written by her countryman Odd Solumsmoen. In this book (*A Writer of Spirit and Truth*) there is a typical footnote added by Cora Sandel who had read the book herself and approved of it before its publication in 1957. Towards its end Solumsmoen writes that Cora Sandel always followed the example of Alberta in not having too many belongings to worry about: 'Everything she owns is packed in trunks and deposited in various attics here and there.' Cora Sandel's comment (the *only* one in the whole book) states in three words: 'Not *quite* everything'. This reservation is characteristic of Cora Sandel, who always kept a certain distance. Although she was prepared to part with a certain amount of information about her private life she would never tell everything. 'I have always been of the opinion that no more needs to be expected of an author than that they should write books', she once said in a sentence which has become a classic. When asked by a literary magazine which was the most important experience in her life Cora Sandel replied: 'That I prefer to keep to myself.' The biographical data she once gave to her publisher could hardly be more concise: 'I was a child in Oslo, a young girl in Northern Norway, a grown woman in France and Sweden. I grew old during the Second World War; I had a son during the First and I live in fear that he will be sacrificed during the Second.'

When I first met Cora Sandel she was eighty-five years old. She was living in her apartment in Uppsala and made very few new

2

acquaintances. There was a myth about her reserve, many stories were told at the university among the students who studied her work of how she always refused to see people. It is still easy to remember the calm sitting room with beautiful, beloved belongings – the stillness of the room and the things themselves in such contrast to the heavy traffic in the busy street outside. She used to sit on a blue sofa, above which hung a painting of Tromsø. She cut ice cold grapes: 'Grapes, like chocolate, should be kept in the fridge.' On the small table next to an easy chair were many of the new novels or collections of poetry which authors had sent her, or new novels and books of poetry which she had bought herself. In her bookshelves were many French books in beautiful leather bindings, several by Colette, her twinsoul, whose books she translated into Norwegian but whom she never met in person. 'I considered it too presumptuous to have friends arrange a meeting – Colette was forced to meet so many people anyway – although it could have been done while I lived in Paris.'

She had no television set and when, in 1963, *Krane's Café* was adapted for television, her Swedish publisher brought a television set to her flat in Uppsala so that she could see it at home. All her life she refused to be interviewed for television or the Swedish Broadcasting Corporation. When she was over ninety her Swedish publisher and I were allowed to make a long radio interview with her. Out of respect we hid the technician in the bathroom but she immediately caught on when she saw the wires and asked him in and gave him a glass of sherry.

Animals were always most important in her life. She even called one of her books *Animals I have known*. In her study all the animals from *Winnie the Pooh* sat in a row and it was, of course, Piglet, the small and frightened one, who had most of her sympathy. One of the paintings in her small breakfast room where we used to have tea is dominated by the green colour so characteristic of her style. It shows a garden in summer and in the lush grass a black and white cat is arching its back. If one looks closely one discovers that it is a wooden toy cat. 'I don't find it all that good,' she said, 'I would have liked a real cat for a model.'

To all those who even late in life feel that they have an unborn novel inside them, Cora Sandel may represent a certain hope. She was forty-six when she published her first novel in Norway, under her pen name, Cora Sandel. Her real name was not known and no photo was to be had of the author. Her uncle wrote to her from Tromsø: 'I have just read a book by a woman who calls herself Cora Sandel. Everyone here says that it is you.' And he went on to tell her how he liked the book and how he always thought she would do something quite exceptional one day.

Alberta and Jacob is indeed an unusual book and with it she made a real breakthrough. It was to be followed five years later, in 1931, by *Alberta and Freedom* and the final volume in the trilogy, *Alberta Alone*, was published in 1939. It didn't come easily. Proofs were read and sent back to the publisher together with the next chapter – and all the time cables and letters were arriving imploring her to send more of the manuscript.

'One of the truly great woman characters in contemporary Scandinavian fiction' was how Alberta was described by the critics. The trilogy is partly autobiographical but, one wonders, can such a perfect whole be 'partly'? Cora Sandel herself says: 'In everything one writes there is woven in a thread from one's own life. It can be so hidden that nobody notices it, but it *is* there and it must be there, I suppose, if it is to be seen as a piece of living writing.'

Although the trilogy was a feat in itself several collections of short stories were written and published while Cora Sandel was grappling with her Alberta character. In 1927 came *A Blue Sofa*, followed by three more books of short stories. Her last novel, *Köp inte Dondi*, was published in 1958 and translated into English under the title *The Leech*. She did not publish much after that, only a last collection of short stories with the symbolic title *Our Complicated Life*.

Cora Sandel's own life was long. She was ninety-four when she died and she left an impressive legacy, perhaps above all, she had created Alberta. Cora Sandel said about the writing of *Alberta Alone*, the last volume in the trilogy: 'Every word came floating up from the unknown depths whence it rises anew, transformed, unrecognisable, like a dream, impossible to refute.'

Solveig Nellinge
Stockholm, 1980

4

❈ *Part One* ❈

When one's clothes drop off and one stands without a stitch on in front of a stranger, one's predominant sensation is not that of modesty, but rather of being unprotected, of disquiet in case someone should come too close and do harm, an anxiety of the flesh, so to speak. There is the sensation of solitude too, similar to finding oneself alone in a deserted part of the country. One never gets used to it, it is the same each time.

Alberta took off her clothes as if she were jumping into the sea, a little giddily, feeling that it was a matter of now or never. She undid one button here, another there, and her clothes slid down round her all at once. Before they reached the floor she seized them, stepped out of them and put them in a heap on a chair. Then she stepped on to the model's stand and faced reality boldly. She did not slouch ashamed with her hips or her head, but clenched her hands slightly and looked Mr. Digby straight in the eye, while she gradually took up her position. Then she ' stood '.

Mr. Digby gauged the distance, righted his spectacles, put his head askew. With rounded gestures he implied directions, giving orders in his incorrigible English accent: ' *Comme ça . . . comme ça.*' Finally he announced curtly but pleasantly that that was good, *c'est bien.*

And time began to creep painfully forward in the way Alberta remembered from her childhood; the way it could creep in church, for instance, or when she went out with Papa and they walked and walked and never got on speaking terms with each other. She could sense physically how it crowded slowly past her, tenacious, absorptive, exhausting, how it could be heard and felt. To stand there doing nothing else but stand, came to feel like being stretched on the rack. Her limbs ached and turned numb. But that was not the worst. The gnawing in her mind was worse, a steady murmur as if from an exposed nerve.

There was something she ought to have been doing, something besides standing there. It was only that Alberta could never find out what. She earned one franc twenty-five an hour, and managed to exist as long as it lasted, without being a burden to anyone. She should therefore have had a clear conscience.

She could see her body in the long mirror, thin and lithe, clad in spare, lean muscles which arched and curved a little here and there, not much, not more than was fitting. A controlled nakedness, without exaggeration, without any gross stamp of sex. If she had to be a woman she could not very well demand to be encumbered with less.

Out of doors it was an early, tempestuous spring; indoors the house was cold. Mr. Digby's studio, which was first-class and faced north, without disturbing reflections, was full of a stale winter clamminess. Alberta quickly turned blue and muddy, especially on the lower half of her legs. And it was not only warmth that escaped from her pores; it was life itself slowly filtering away. An insidious wastage of energy was taking place.

Mr. Digby was no slave-driver. At brief intervals he would ask pleasantly whether Alberta was tired, whether she was cold, while he strode forwards and backwards on his short legs between the canvas and what seemed to be a permanent observation point in the middle of the floor. For her part, Alberta stood for her three quarters of an hour without sagging at the knees, however much she might tremble and sway. She had some kind of foolish and unreasonable notion that the more doggedly she stood, the more would she placate certain mysterious powers which habitually force us into circumstances and situations we hate and abhor.

6

Round, honest, completely innocuous, Mr. Digby's eyes viewed her through the spectacles, relinquishing her not a moment too soon. Precise to the minute, by which time Alberta was empty-headed and paralysed, beyond hope or expectation, simply a stupefied body, he said: 'Rest yourself, Mademoiselle'. He continued to come and go, to narrow his eyes, gauge the distance and add small dabs of colour, look satisfied and hum. He had the fearful diligence of the dilettante in his blood.

Alberta wrapped herself in her coat and huddled over *Le Journal*. She finished reading the short story for the day which she had begun in the Métro, gobbled down theatre, art and literature, murders and sensations, but consistently skipped all politics. Finally she looked through the advertisement colums, noted that ' Wonderful Remedy for Wrinkles ', Pink Pills and Rubber Stockings, Crème Simon and ' Abbé Soury's Rejuvenating Elixir ' were there as usual, and that the background to existence was to this extent unchanged and completely normal. Sometimes she took advantage of her breathing-spell to complete a recently scamped meal, and chewed a little bread, fruit or chocolate.

The worst thing about it was the passing of time, the next worse the people who dropped in and stood watching, ' admirers of Mr. Digby's art '. Every time the door opened to let one of them in Alberta was on tenterhooks, wishing she could vanish into thin air. Yet again she had a secret iron in the fire, and was travelling along one of life's small murky back streets, as she had done since childhood. These intruders to whom she owed nothing at all caught her red-handed. Well-dressed, exceedingly respectable, often somewhat elderly, they belonged to a category of persons from which she hid and whom she deceived without exception.

They were dangerous. It was true that Mr. Digby lived in Passy, in a quiet, prodigiously correct *quartier*, apparently as distant as it possibly could be from the milieu which Alberta normally frequented. Nevertheless her luck could fail her at any time. The very thing one wishes to hide has a curious tendency to sift up into the daylight. Both Mr. Digby's and Alberta's associates moved about freely, could meet, become acquainted, and could in no way be prevented from doing so. The possibility of catastrophe was always there. On the other hand, one does what has to be done. She had to take the risk that went with it.

Tensely, a little convulsively, she would stand enduring the strangers' gaze, racked by defiance and antipathy. She understood the model who once, at Colarossi's, suddenly pulled a face at someone who had come in and just stood and stared. She understood the prostitute who hurls a contemptuous term of abuse in the face of the woman walking by. She felt an obscure solidarity with them.

' *Eh bien,*' said Mr. Digby. ' I thank you.' He put down his palette and rubbed his hands.

When Mr. Digby said as much as that, it meant he would not be needing her any more. There would be no more five-franc pieces to earn for the time being – solid, weighty coins that made her feel solvent; or pieces of gold, ten francs, twenty francs, that gave her the over-confidence of the rich, making her step light, her face new, her mood extravagant and reckless. It meant that she would be free and unemployed again and would have her alibi in order. It meant that she would be able to expand a little. Once again Alberta had scraped a means of existence. As far as the human eye could see, it had been brought to a conclusion without catastrophe.

' I thank you,' repeated Mr. Digby. ' I am very pleased with you. I shall be travelling in the South, in England, in Brittany. I shall be coming back to Paris in October. I may then need a model who is a little more *comme ça.*' His hands indicated generous curves and his eyes widened enormously behind his spectacles. ' I don't know in advance, I never know in advance. I am a very capricious man, very capricious. But if . . . .' And he nodded encouragingly at Alberta.

8

Mr. Digby had said almost the same thing this time last year. He skimmed the surface of this foreign language in short sentences which often petered out. It never occurred to him to speak to Alberta in English, nor was it necessary; he managed to say what was important and to imply the rest.

With short, hurried steps he went into the apartment next door, and spoke quietly to someone inside. There was a rattle of coins. Alberta thought urgently: Will it be seven or eight or nine times? Will he deduct for the time we had to stop because he was taken ill? Or the time someone arrived unexpectedly from England? Then it will only be just enough for the rent. If he does deduct it I ought to say something, but I'm stupid about things like that. I ought to say, for instance –.

Mr. Digby returned with Mrs. Digby. Jokingly he referred to her as ' my jury ', putting two new twenty-franc pieces and five francs in small change on the table. He had not deducted anything. Alberta, whose whole body was relishing the feeling of clothes about it again, appropriated the money carelessly, a little offhandedly, as if she collected such sums daily. ' Thank you,' she said.

With admiring cries Mrs. Digby inspected the picture. As always when a work was finished she appealed to Alberta: ' It's very beautiful, isn't it? Such delicate colours? Mr. Digby's a real artist, yes indeed, a real artist. I do hope you're not too tired? It must be very, very tiring. But I expect it becomes a habit, doesn't it?' She went up close, small, friendly and short-sighted, and raised and lowered her lorgnette all over the picture, inspécting it with the air of a connoisseur. It was sleek and sugary like the lid of a chocolate box, similar to the rest of Mr. Digby's production, a collection of rose-pink ladies, all more or less ' *comme ça* ', against the same background of faded lilac and iron grey. They embellished the walls from floor to ceiling.

Politely Alberta expressed agreement. She put on her hat and powdered her nose.

'And if,' said Mr. Digby, 'When I come back?'

'Just get in touch with Alphonsine. She always has my address.'

'Very well. Still Madame Alphonsine. Very good . . . I thank you.'

Alberta's hand was shaken first by Mrs. and then by Mr. Digby. And she hurried across the neat courtyard. White shingle, newly spread, difficult to walk on, forcefully accentuated its length and breadth. Budding box bushes, clipped low, framed a centre bed. Small-leaved ivy, trimmed and refined, covered the walls with an even, monotonous green, and, clipped as if with a ruler, framed handsome doors with shining brass plates and large studio windows with raw-silk curtains inside. A concierge, looking like the housekeeper of an elegant residence, appeared watchfully at her window. She nodded to Alberta, because although Alberta obviously had to be considered a questionable character, she was not the worst kind, but on the contrary looked comparatively respectable.

The wind blew in gusts. It was one of those March days when sharp, warm sunshine alternates with cold wintry blasts. Along the road, which was bordered by low walls with gardens behind them, naked branches tossed in confusion against racing clouds and sudden depths of ultramarine sky; at the edge of the pavement on a corner was a handcart full of violets and mimosa, like a festive cockade on the ragged clothing of the day.

Alberta turned another corner and found herself beneath the tall iron skeleton of the Métro, between barrack-like blocks of flats that cast clammy shadows. A train passed noisily above her head. Soon afterwards she was sitting in one herself, travelling high in the air between earth and sky over Passy bridge, across the Seine.

There was a rustle along the benches as newspapers were lowered and people looked out. Far below lay Paris, bright in sudden sunshine beneath a tremendous sky full of moving banks of cloud. People, cars, *fiacres* bustled about like toys. To the north-east above Menilmontant was a

10

coal-black shower of rain; directly beneath, the Seine like flowing metal. A tug with a string of barges behind it, working its way upstream, hooted piercingly and belched out thick black smoke, making the sharp light even sharper.

A wave of expansiveness passed through Alberta, washing away fatigue and stale cold. She felt her face changing to an expression that men found disquieting. God knows how it came about. It was suddenly there, making them turn their heads towards her, jerkily, hurriedly, as if in surprise. It was no special distinction, for it can happen to almost any woman. But at least it was a kind of guarantee that she was reasonably like other people, not remarkably ugly, not directly repulsive. And if the person in question was not himself an affront, it sometimes helped her to expand a little more.

The train rattled through the Grenelle district, alongside broad avenues with tree-lined walks down the middle. Some of the buildings were old-fashioned and squat, a bit decayed, a bit rotten with damp, some were brand new in *Jugend* style, shining like butter in the sun. Suddenly it was all gone. White tiled walls and arched roofs, variegated posters darkly illuminated, slid past. An intrusive reek of cellars and disinfectant filled the carriage. And Alberta again felt the fatigue in her limbs. Underground she flickered out.

She alighted at Montparnasse, coming up into the daylight again behind the railway station, in the shadow of the high wall and of the bridge that carried the trains out of the city on a level with the second floors of the houses. Here the pleasant parts of town ended, here the large, depressing working-class districts on the other side of the Avenue du Maine began. One was always met by a gust of greyness and narrow circumstances. Here Alberta could not help thinking of death sentences and executions. Perhaps it was because of the wall.

She paused and looked up at one of the houses in the

11

Rue de l'Arrivée. 'Hôtel des Indes' was written in huge gold letters on a balcony railing right across the façade.

From a railing several storeys higher something white fluttered for a moment, a cloth, a handkerchief, fastened up there. It was carried outwards by the wind and then slackened again. Alberta made certain it was there, then hurried away underneath the bridge where there was a blaze of fruit, flowers and vegetables on handcarts in the semi-darkness. She bought violets and a spray of mimosa, made a couple of other purchases, went into a dairy.

Then she disappeared inside the Hôtel des Indes.

* * *

To come up from the hard street. To kick off one's shoes and stretch out one's whole length on something, a bed, a divan. To relax in every limb, while the little spirit stove hums gently. To have a cup of tea, or perhaps two, some biscuits, marmalade, a couple of cigarettes – and the numbness arrives: that blessed state of indifference out of which the will towards life is born anew.

Hungry? Yes . . .

But not as when she used to come home from skiing as a child and grabbed something or other on the way through the kitchen, because she could not wait until her ski clothes were off and she was seated at table. Not that healthy, demanding voraciousness that made all food taste good and satisfying. No – now there was the eternal dissatisfaction of the body, which remained after she had eaten, which could not be quieted, only deadened and diverted. With tea, for instance, and cigarettes.

Alberta lay on her elbow on Liesel's bed, listening to the singing of the spirit stove and smoking a Maryland. Liesel came and went, fetching cups and spoons from the wardrobe, wiping them and arranging them in the sunlight on a chair with a towel over it. Her black dress, poorly cut in one piece, tended to hang askew. She pulled at it repeatedly and stuck her nose into Alberta's flowers now

12

and again as she passed them. They stood resplendent on the mantelpiece and were multiplied by the mirror behind them. ' *Reizend,*' said Liesel. ' *Wunderbar. Wie freundlich Albertchen.*'

The balcony doors were ajar. The narrow, oblong room, which obtained all its light through them, was filled with muffled noises from the street, smoke from nearby chimneys and the steadfast old bedroom smell that goes with cheap hotels. It is no use trying to air it out, it seeps back in again from the staircase.

Only now did Alberta realise how tired she was, a tiredness like disintegration. It would take at least two hot cups of strong tea to pull her together again. She exhaled small puffs of smoke and exchanged everyday remarks with Liesel. Brief as a code they dropped from them both: ' Well? ... Oh, all right .... No news .... *Gar nichts.*'

On the washstand lay a quarter of a pound of butter wrapped in paper, because, as Liesel said in her house-wifely manner, it keeps better on marble. There were also mandarin oranges and two small cream cheeses, which were Alberta's contribution. Liesel's wash-bowl bristled with paintbrushes put to soak.

Alberta looked round for the study of the Pont Neuf. It was on the floor, leaning against two chair-legs and facing the wall, a bad sign. Traces of yellow ochre along the edge of the canvas frame and on the skirt of Liesel's dress emphasized the connection between them.

Now she was warming the teapot. Tilting it with both hands she made a small amount of boiling water flow here and there inside it, while she watched it thoughtfully: ' Fräulein Stoltz makes tea with the egg water. I think that's too economical. There we are Albertchen, the butter was fresh today.'

She straightened her dress and sat down. It was one of her absent-minded days, when she would be a little round-shouldered, a little despairing and lost in her own thoughts. Today it would be no use asking how the Pont Neuf was going, someone had probably stopped to watch Liesel and disturbed her. One of the barges in the foreground had perhaps disappeared when she got there, or something unexpected had displayed itself in the motif: a fresh pile of sand, an unsuspecting fisherman on his camp stool. She had no doubt ruined her picture again and was dejected and untalented. It happened sometimes.

' Thank you.' Alberta took the cup Liesel handed her and gulped it down eagerly like a drunkard at last getting a drink. Without a word, as if following a ritual, Liesel filled it again, and Alberta emptied it a second time. Then she sat up, put her feet into her shoes, and moved nearer. The strong, hot liquid was taking effect.

' Finished with Papa Digby for the time being,' she said, buttering a biscuit. ' That's the rent, ten francs extra, five for the garçon. I'll buy those unbleached chemises from the pawnbroker's, Liesel, cut them up at the bottom and make them into combinations. That'll be seventy-five apiece. I won't get any at Bon Marché under five francs.'

Liesel's eyes focused again, returning from a great distance. She doubted whether the project could be carried out. Alberta would have to insert gores, it wasn't as simple as she thought, and it would take a long time to sew the seams by hand. But Alberta had her plans and her faith in them would not be shaken. ' Gores? Of course not. When you're as thin as I am!' As far as the seams were concerned, you could always make large stitches. She knew a concierge who took in machine sewing, five centimes the metre, but she'd rather save the money. ' And I must wear something underneath,' she said. ' Soon I shan't have a rag left to send to the laundry.'

' Nor I,' sighed Liesel, who needed a petticoat, stockings, shoes. It was fatal when it got to the point where those kinds of things had to be replaced. You *had* to have them. And the possibility of getting a new hat or a new dress vanished for an uncertain period of time. If only the five-francs man would turn up!

' Oh, it's no problem for you painters!' Alberta thought enviously of the five-francs man, who went round buying studies lock, stock and barrel, large ones and small ones all for the same unchanging average price. Last year he had bought everything Liesel had for a hundred and thirty-five francs. A painter could suddenly conjure up unprecedented sums of money. But the five-francs man was something of a mystery; he arrived unexpectedly or he did not come at all. It was useless to try to find him, write to him, ask people to send him along. He was as capricious and erratic as the weather. You might hear that he had called on such and such a one, and then perhaps hear nothing for a long time.

To have in one's possession a production that might be the object of enquiries from the five-francs man was in any case a basis to life. A quick glance round Liesel's room, where canvases were stacked one behind the other all along the walls facing inwards, ascertained that Liesel could do business in the grand manner again whenever she wished, if her luck was in. And if in addition you got a regular allowance from home, you were by no means so badly off.

' Painting's expensive,' protested Liesel. ' *Es kostet furchtbar viel, Albertchen*. Chinese white costs a fortune, let alone colours like cadmium and carmine lake.' Alberta was lucky, she needed no working capital. Liesel could not understand why she took jobs as a model, how could she, *aber gar nicht*.

' I can't do anything else,' said Alberta.

' You can. French. Writing.'

Alberta looked impatiently at Liesel over her cup. ' Can I live off the two pupils I taught last year and teach no longer? Can I, Liesel? Or can I hope to get more in this country? They all go to the French, you know that as well as I do. And write! I can't write. I'd rather be a model.' She took a large gulp and put her cup down roughly. Liesel made mountains out of mole-hills. She had not lived in Paris long enough.

Besides, Liesel herself posed. Alberta pointed this out, knowing full well that it was a lame argument. Liesel posed for Eliel. She made coffee for him and sewed on his buttons.

15

If only she could persuade him to adopt a collar and tie and stop looking like a shoemender.

' I pose for the head,' said Liesel. ' For the head Albertchen.'

' I know – and for a hand, and for a shoulder. If it goes on like this ... '

Liesel did not laugh.

Usually she shared the joke, laughing at the shoemender, admitting for goodness knows which time that, yes, she had turned down her dress one day when Eliel's model had been unable to come. She had thought she could do it for Eliel, who was so hard-working, so talented and so splendid – and she would laugh again.

It was tempting to tease her about it. Eliel had been endlessly busy with that portrait of her. Alphonsine hinted that he burst his buttons on purpose when Liesel was coming, so that she could put them on again for him, and sit there looking domestic and charming while she did it. And Liesel would laugh.

Now she supposed curtly and coldly that she had finished sitting for Eliel. As Alberta knew, some visitors were coming from Sweden, a Swedish girl to whom Eliel would be showing the sights. He wanted to have the plaster bust ready by that time, so that he would be quite free – it was understandable.

' Yes,' said Alberta. ' I suppose so.'

Suddenly Liesel smiled. There seemed to be a hint of defiance in her smile, and she looked directly at Alberta. ' Ness looks like a shoemender too, without his collar and tie.'

' Yes,' said Alberta, amazed. ' Of course he does.'

The years went by, the seasons changed. Through it all Alberta and Liesel found themselves in the same situation, monetarily and otherwise. They made no careers for themselves. Even Liesel, who had talent, was endlessly marking time. She paid her subscription to the Indépendants, but never got as far as sending in anything. She went summer

16

after summer to Brittany with the fixed purpose of submitting a painting to the Autumn Exhibition. She came home again, still without anything she thought would be suitable, still, without managing to produce anything.

Alberta considered this. She sat looking at Liesel, who was wandering restlessly about the room, a biscuit dripping with marmalade in her hand, picking up everything leaning against the wall and turning it to face the light.

Most of them were life studies, and looked as life studies usually do: one straight leg, one limp; sagging shoulders, arms and hips; stomachs like balloons; chests that cried out for orthopaedic treatment. A few were promising, most of them had been retouched too often. Except when providentially stopped, there nearly always came a moment when Liesel lost her head and changed a fresh, pure colour combination, a design that was good already, into something hard, dry and dull. Her work sometimes looked as if it had been spoilt purposely and in anger. Sudden thick, meaningless brush strokes would be drawn in, or irrelevant, alien planes of colour inserted, that did not fit in and killed everything else round them. Afterwards she would get nowhere with it.

She came from some small town in one of the Baltic provinces, Alberta had long ago given up remembering which. The Baltic provinces are confusing, rather like the Balkans. On the mantelpiece in cabinet size sat Liesel's mother, a small, round, German-born *hausfrau* with white bands round her neck and wrists, surrounded by her four daughters, Liesel among them as a little girl, sitting on a stool in front of the others. Above the bed hung a faded picture of a young, thin man with a long black beard and deep-set eyes: her Russian father, who had died a couple of years ago. He had been the one to sympathize with Liesel and take her part when she had wanted to paint. She had spoken two languages as a child, German and Russian, and often mixed her clipped, inadequate French with them both. She was still wearing out her mourning clothes.

When Liesel nodded in the direction of the mantelpiece and said: ' *Sie sind alle furchtbar gut, aber ...* ', Alberta understood to the full what she meant. Liesel seldom said anything else about them.

She was a little round-shouldered, a little slow in speech and manner, with skirts that dipped at the back. But she had large grey eyes in a pale, oblong face, skin smooth as cream and a little nebula of freckles across her nose. She had a red mouth, and a mass of smooth black hair twisted round her head in solid, shining plaits. All in all Liesel was handsome and the object of a good deal of attention. Doubtful individuals at the studios would kiss her, hotel residents tried to get into her room at night. She was less inured than Alberta to such phenomena and unable to appear icy and unmoved; her cheeks flamed and a frightened expression came into her eyes. And she was sought after more unscrupulously than ever.

Now and again, when Liesel completely lost courage, decided she was utterly lacking in talent, and made up her mind to give up painting, a rich merchant who lived in her home town and wanted to marry her, and who was favoured by her relatives, would figure in her conversation. Alberta had no patience with him. There was an air of bad novels about him and he was quite uninteresting, even perhaps an hallucination. She wished Liesel would stop bringing him into it.

Liesel continued rearranging her canvases, fetching them out from the corners and from behind the wardrobe. Soon they were all over the place, leaning against chairs and table-legs, on the mantelpiece and along the bed. She folded up her family and put them on the table to make room, and finally turned round the study of the Pont Neuf, placing it in front of all the rest. It showed a section of the quay, a couple of tall, leafless trees, some barges, and in the background the arch of the bridge, all of it basically good, with a certain heavy richness of colouring. But there were angry-looking ultramarine lines drawn criss-cross over the barges. They did not appear to belong any more, being quite out of keeping with the rest of the picture.

Alberta said nothing and watched. She was used to these sudden displays. Other painters did the same thing. In the middle of a mouthful they would be impelled to turn round everything leaning against the wall. They would be made cheerful and hum, or become absent-minded, irritable and inconsolable.

' I shall end up like Potter, Albertchen, like Potter and Stoltz.' Liesel sat down and contemplated her display despondently. ' That's all for this year. I don't suppose even the five-francs man would take it.'

' Nonsense, Liesel. You have talent. Marushka says so, Eliel and Ness and everybody say so. If only you could stop spoiling them all the time. Potter and Stoltz . . .'. Alberta shrugged her shoulders pityingly.

But she did not like her tone of habitual encouragement. And as she spoke she saw a whole series of elderly women perpetually trudging round Montparnasse. They were beyond any reasonable age, forty, fifty, even older; they had wrinkles and untidy grey hair, and they dragged themselves round with large bags full of brushes over one arm, their camp stool and easel under it, a wet canvas in each hand and their skirts trailing behind them. They sat at street corners and in parks and on the banks of the Seine and painted; fussing and wearisome, they filled the academies and life-classes, disappearing during the summer perhaps, but reappearing in the autumn, as inevitable as the season itself; they lived on nothing, making tea with the egg water, like Fräulein Stoltz. She was one of them, Potter another. Originally they came from different countries and had their own peculiarities. Now they were here, and behaved and painted more or less the same, all of them. It was they who filled the walls of the outer rooms at the Indépendants, the rooms one always hurried through to reach the new, the shocking, or simply the proficient. The thought that it was possible to go on living here like

19

that, and to be nothing more than an elderly, ugly, poverty-stricken dilettante, bred disquiet.

' You *mustn't* spoil everything, Liesel. You must put a stop to it and begin exhibiting your work. If only you could leave them alone while they're still good.'

' I *feel* colour,' said Liesel, pressing her clasped hands to her breast and staring wide-eyed in front of her. ' I feel it physically, Albertchen, it hurts me inside sometimes, but . . . ' She closed her eyes, her head sank forwards on her graceful neck ' . . . It's the *drawing*. I suddenly see how wrong it is. I want to put it right, I *have* to put it right, and then it all goes wrong. I don't know how it happens, something compels me. I haven't any real talent – I only have a little, and that's worse than none at all.'

Here comes the merchant, thought Alberta. She believed in Liesel's talent, as one believes in the earth beneath one's feet; she took it for granted and saw nothing tragic in her distress. But Liesel suddenly walked past her out on to the balcony, leaving the door open behind her, and stood out there, leaning on the balustrade with both hands. After a while she turned her back to it, supporting herself against it with her elbows. She leant her head back, and looked down into the Rue de l'Arrivée.

Like a light picture in a dark frame she was enclosed by the doorway and the open doors with their filthy curtains sticking to the panes, all of them that solid grey of the streets through which railways pass. A ray of the setting sun fell upon her in a beautiful alternation of light and shade, modelling a section of the plaiting encircling her head, the tense sinews of the neck, the breast forced upwards by her stance, the drooping wrists. A breath of wind carried her skirt a little outwards and sideways, almost wrapping it round her leg. The loose-limbed figure in the worn black dress was given a plastic gravity it normally lacked, the hair acquired an alien sheen of metal. Liesel was suddenly statuesque out there between earth and sky. She addressed the Rue de l'Arrivée quietly in her clipped French: ' My life is not interesting.'

20

Surprised by the brief, gently-spoken phrase, Alberta went on listening. Whether or not it was because Liesel was standing out there looking statuesque, the words grew in the silence they left behind them, turning into an oracular pronouncement, casting a sharp, unexpected light over the past and the future. One of those appalling seconds when one sees one's existence and is made giddy by it, had suddenly occurred. Deep down Alberta was gripped by the thought: Nor mine, nor mine. It goes on and on and is not interesting, as Liesel says. I don't even know what I want to do with it. I am like someone who has set out from land and is letting himself drift.

An uncomfortable chill crept over her, her heart became small and hard, hammering as it used to at home when she had done something wrong or something unpleasant was about to happen. She heard her voice dwindle and freeze as she said : ' It *will* be interesting, Liesel, of course it will. Wait till you start exhibiting and get properly under way. Thank you for my tea.'

She laced up her shoes and put on her coat, bracing herself as she got ready to leave, trying to find that feeling of freedom which, like an intoxication, can sometimes turn walking into a dance, reminding herself that now and again one lands on small islands of joy. Of course they would get somewhere, not just Liesel, but herself too. It was already something of a feat not to be lying becalmed in quite the wrong place – and after all, this was life, life itself, irreplaceable.

' Are you going to the evening class, Liesel?' Alberta half hoped that Liesel would consider further effort useless this evening. They could then go out together, laugh about things together, and finally laugh at themselves. Once you get as far as that, things begin to look brighter.

But Liesel was going to the course. She had paid for it, so she had better . . .

' What a reason!' she said. She suddenly slumped down on the bed and laughed despairingly. ' *Wie alles tragikomisch ist, Albertchen.*'

21

'It is indeed.' Alberta laughed with her, liberated, and at once felt immensely grateful at the thought of how much they had laughed off together, she and Liesel, through the years.

* * *

The Hôtel de l'Amirauté in the Place de Rennes looked respectable and inspired confidence: the name in enormous gold lettering across the façade, the laurel trees in green tubs at the entrance, the open vestibule with its red carpet, comfortable basket chairs, green plants. In the doorway Monsieur, as well-dressed as a dummy in a tailor's window, with waved hair and a ready smile, always and instantly at your service. Inside the office Madame, young, beautiful, irreproachable, in her white silk blouse and with her long shining nails. Into this correct establishment walked Alberta. This was where she lived.

Monsieur's greeting was unexceptionable. It was not the same as his greeting to the naval officers from Lorient and Brest, his smile was not in evidence, but Alberta had not expected it to be. Madame, on the other hand, greeted her strikingly coldly, looked her up and down and then stared at the bag she was carrying. Alberta stopped, and opened it in her direction: 'Only some fruit Madame – fruit, newspapers . . .'.

'*Ca va, ça va.*' Madame gazed absent-mindedly at the bag. Clearly she had been thinking about something else for some time. She leaned forward over her little counter, her hands clasped, and pronounced: 'You know, Mademoiselle, when one leaves bits of bread lying about on the floor . . .'.

'I do not leave bits of bread lying about on the floor.'

Madame looked at her even more coldly. 'The *garçon* reported that there were mice in your room. I went up there today to see for myself. There was bread on the floor.'

22

Alberta reddened. ' I did put some bread on the floor yesterday evening.'

' When food is left lying about in corners, you get mice. That is obvious,' stated Madame. ' The scraps attract the mice, you see.'

' I put bread on the floor so that the mice would leave me alone and stop attacking me in bed. There have always been mice there, yesterday was the first time I . . .'. Alberta's voice trembled and so did her legs, which did not seem quite real beneath her.

' Don't leave scraps about in the corners and you will get no mice, *voilà*.' Madame handed Alberta her key and turned smiling to a new guest, who was being led in by Monsieur with demonstrations of respect. The conversation was closed. Alberta, her face darkly flushed and her heart hammering, wandered past the open door that led into Monsieur's and Madame's private dining-room, a small room that obtained its meagre light from the courtyard. A rich reek of good food wafted out. A thin old lady in a light grey shawl was setting the table, picking up a table-napkin which was already in place and putting it down a little differently, judging the effect and righting it again. Her yellow hand trembled unceasingly, her head twisted incessantly on her neck. When Alberta went past she looked up with the short-sightedness of an old woman.

' It's me, Madame Firmin, the Norwegian.'

' Ah, is it you, is it you? Good evening, *ma petite*.'

And Alberta began the ascent.

The red matting continued between the flights of stairs, one floor, two floors. At the third Alberta quickened her pace, swinging round extra fast at the landing and looking stiffly in front of her. At once a door opened ajar:
' Mademoiselle Selmer!'

' Mademoiselle.'

' Always in a hurry, always busy! And I who am so much alone!'

' But Mademoiselle.'

' Come in a moment, have a cigarette with me. We could

23

go out and dine together. I should be so pleased if you . . . '

The pale, fair, somewhat rigid figure in the doorway was correctly tailored, tall and slender, dressed to go out. She stared with piercingly blue eyes at Alberta and stepped aside to allow her to pass.

Alberta gripped the banisters and made no move. She could see into one of the hotel's best rooms giving on to the street, one of the newly decorated ones for which the young Madame was responsible. Inside, the airy curtains were half drawn; they moved slightly in the draught from the door and filled the room with a subdued, rose-coloured light. Nickel taps and other modern fixtures shone. It was the kind of room one dreamed about in winter, when a small box of coal cost one franc fifty and the icy north wind chased the dust clouds down the street. Fruit, that had not been bought from a barrow, was in a bowl on the table, golden pears, blue grapes. A hat was lying there, a pair of gloves, a blue fox fur. A cubist study was on the floor, leaning against the legs of a chair.

' Come in and look at my latest work. Let me have your opinion. What do you think of it?'

' It's beautiful, very beautiful Mademoiselle . . . Mademoiselle . . . .'

' Wolochinska, Wolochinska! Is my name so difficult to remember? *Mon Dieu, mon Dieu*!'

' It is very beautiful, Mademoiselle Wolochinska,' repeated Alberta, looking at a confused puzzle of deep, somewhat turbid colours, with which Wolochinska was wandering about in order to place it in a better position. She drew back the curtains. The daylight fell palely on the thick layers of colour and on her own angular features under the smooth, close-cropped, very fair hair.

' Come in, don't stand out there. You actually look as if you're frightened of me.' Wolochinska laughed uneasily.

Alberta laughed even more uneasily. ' I'm busy – there's something I must do this evening, some correspondence – I'm sorry, I hope you will excuse me . . . . Your picture is very beautiful, very . . . good evening, Mademoiselle.'

24

Alberta was already on her way up. Wolochinska called out after her: ' You are unkind! Unkind! Don't you know what loneliness is?'

' Oh yes,' called Alberta. ' Yes, Mademoiselle.' And she fled, two steps at a time.

The red matting gave way to coco-nut. Soon this gave out too. The doors were different, the windows low and small. Finally Alberta groped her way forward in the darkness under the roof to a door that was hers, opened it, divested herself of her outdoor clothes and carefully removed two eggs and other provisions from inside her blouse. Then she sat down on the bed with her hands pressed against her heart as if to control it.

It was a small, stuffy attic room, smelling of mice. It had a sloping roof with a square skylight which was left open day and night, but it made no difference. An unchanging quantity of stale air, that seemed heavy with the dust and reek of generations remained immovable in the room, fed by suspicious-looking old armchairs, the proximity of chimneys and the collective bedroom smells of the whole hotel, stored in the upper part of the staircase.

Dusk was already falling. The lower half of the furniture disappeared in shadow, the fragment of sky had a thin sheen of gold. When Alberta had sat for a while, she heard a faint, gurgling sound from the wash-bowl. She went over and looked down into it.

In the grey soapsuds a mouse was swimming round and round; at intervals it would try to climb up on to the rim, but plopped back again. Alberta watched it without surprise. She went out on to the staircase and peered down into its murky depths.

When she had waited for a while, a white apron and a swinging feather duster came into view between two doors and disappeared again. The muffled tones of a song, uneven and melancholy, rose momentarily upwards: ' *Et le pauv' gas, quand vient le trépas ... serrant la médaille qu'il baise, glisse dans l'océan sans fond ... '*

' Jean,' called Alberta.

A hand placed a full toilet bucket and a mop out on the landing and was gone again.

'Jean!'

'Mademoiselle.'

'Would you please come up?'

Jean popped up out of the darkness, red-faced, red-haired, illuminated by the fast disappearing daylight from the sky-light. He was in shirt-sleeves, a bibbed apron, and armed with a feather duster.

'At your service, Mademoiselle.'

Jean was not in the least alarming. Alberta therefore informed him boldly that there was yet another mouse in her wash-bowl.

'Another? It's because they're thirsty. They suffer from thirst just as we do. Besides, the weather is sultry, it wouldn't surprise me if we had a storm.'

'Sultry?' Alberta remembered the restless, windy spring outside.

'Yes, sultry. I'll take it away.'

Jean commandeered the bowl and disappeared. He was back instantly.

'What have you done with it?' asked Alberta, stricken with guilt.

'I killed it,' Jean told her without visible emotion and without going further into the matter. 'Mice are vermin, as you know. I told them downstairs that they were bothering you, and Madame came up, but...' Jean gestured apologetically with the feather duster '... *vous savez*, Madame! And there was bread in the corner over there. I hadn't noticed it. Madame did. It was unfortunate.'

'Yes,' admitted Alberta and sat down, suddenly tired of it all. She could not be bothered to defend her little vagary any further; it was doubtless stupid, as was so much else that she did.

Out of habit Jean made several passes with the duster over the furniture within reach: 'The old lady would have sent up a mousetrap and perhaps the cat as well. This one

26

grimaces and says it's no use letting out rooms to artists and foreigners, they're *malpropre.*'

'*Pardon*?'

'Oh,' said Jean quickly. 'I, who look after the rooms up here, know better than anyone that it is not true where you're concerned. You are not an artist, you are very clean. You know how to behave. There are foreigners and foreigners. The Hungarian musician further down the passage, on the other hand, and his madame – they stopped up the water-closet again only yesterday. Madame had dropped a whole bunch of radishes down it, it ought to be obvious that you can't do things like that. She showed me that they were worm-eaten, as if that were any reason. She washes her paintbrushes under the tap out here. Your hands get covered with paint, just look at my apron. And this porridge that foreigners eat, she makes it in her room, in spite of the rule against cooking. It boils over. It's disgusting. If I've been up once I've been up ten times with a bucket and cloth. It's a waste of breath explaining anything to them, they don't understand a word. I shall have to report them to Madame.'

Alberta, who had once been green and inexperienced too, felt sympathy for the ethereal, pre-Raphaelite lady she met on the staircase now and again. It was she who, with a strong Danish accent and extremely limited vocabulary, initiated the couple's transactions with the outside world. 'Key, if you please; water, if you please; letter, if you please?' She had long, narrow, impractical hands, large vacant eyes, a personality full of anxious reserve. It was rumoured that she was in hiding with her musician. She would probably be scared to death if Alberta were to try to help her by addressing her in Norwegian and interpreting for her. Both of them had a way of going in and out, of opening their door just wide enough for their thin figures to pass through, of turning the key in the lock, that cut them off from all advances. Nothing could be done for this couple, whose existence was only noticed on account of the accidents they caused, and the occasional long-drawn

27

out, smooth tone of a violin that reached Alberta across the roof through her skylight.

On the other hand it was not so amusing for Jean and his countrymen to have all these helpless people from various parts of the earth in Paris, trying to make a fresh start in a life they had never attempted before.

" I know it's a nuisance,' admitted Alberta. ' But don't say anything to Madame. They'll be leaving soon, they're not the kind who stay long.'

Jean shrugged his shoulders : ' The old lady was patient, she went up to the rooms, talked to people and explained. The young one . . .

' The old lady's a good woman,' he asserted. ' But now she's finished and so are we all. The young one's turning everything upside down. Even up here under the roof she's going to have new wallpaper, and heating and electric light. Yes, Mademoiselle, and hot and cold water like the first and second floor rooms. It'll mean the end of living here for thirty-five francs a month, the end of artists and people like that. They want it to be a big hotel, as it used to be in Monsieur Grandpère's time, they want to modernize and compete with the Hôtel Lutétia. You'll see.'

I'd better give notice before I'm thrown out, thought Alberta wearily. She said : ' It'll mean richer guests and bigger tips.'

' It'll mean the end of me,' replied Jean. ' Of a country boy like me. It'll mean chamber-maids in black with white caps on their heads. Madame will throw both of us out, Mademoiselle, you as well as me. She gave Aristide the sack so that she could take on someone who had worked at the Hôtel Wagram. Yes, he's worked at the Wagram, that new fellow. As if he's any more clever than the rest of us. He looks like an advertisement for brilliantine, that's the only difference. In my opinion the old lady would do better to clear out.'

' Perhaps so.'

' The young one has taken over the till, that's only right and proper, she is the daughter-in-law, Monsieur's wife.

But she pretends not to hear when the old lady tries to put in a word, is that any way to behave? And Monsieur!' Jean gestured away from himself with his hands, hunching his shoulders: 'Poor fellow – he'll be a cuckold before the year's out. She makes up to the hotel guests behind his back, she's that sort. If she were my wife...' Jean suddenly fell silent.

A memory came back to Alberta. A clear, mild autumn day, an attractively-lighted, peaceful interior that had been like a revelation after the darkness of the stairs, an artist's attic perhaps, almost a studio, with sunshine falling from above in a flaming parallelogram on the red-tiled floor; a kind old lady in a light blue shawl, who mischievously put her hand in front of her mouth and whispered: 'No bedbugs – believe me – you can sleep here in peace.' The sensation of happiness, peace, security, given by it all, of having finished with dark, oblong hotel rooms, as narrow as corridors and lying opposite the staircase, filtering machines for noise, draughts and stale air, cheap, the cheapest there were ....

'I must go,' announced Jean. 'I can't stand here chatting. Some of the guests never leave their rooms, so you can't get in until late in the afternoon. What a filthy *métier* this is! *Oh là, là* – I had enough of it, more than enough, a long time ago. By the way, one of those gentlemen was here, the short one – I said Mademoiselle was not at home. If I may give Mademoiselle some advice, it would be best not to leave water in the bowl when Mademoiselle goes out.'

'No,' said Alberta submissively. 'I shan't do it again.'

Jean displayed his goodwill by cursorily waving his duster a couple of times over the bedhead, and retired.

Alberta was alone. She remained standing for a while, her arms hanging at her sides, as if crestfallen. The sounds from the street and from the interior of the house reached her like the last sounds from the outer world to one immured.

In the mirror above the grate, weakly illuminated by the fading twilight, she could see the contours of the unknown

29

girl whom she met in the mirrors wherever she set up house, a figure she would never be rid of and never understand, never quite succeed in getting to accord with her inner self. In this light the cast in her eye could not be seen and shadow mercifully covered much else. Only a slender apparition with her hair down around her ears stood there.

During the years down here in Paris she had learned to accept the figure in the mirror for what it was. She no longer attempted to adapt her awkward person to custom and fashion, but adapted her few cheap articles of clothing as far as possible to herself. Was she ugly? Probably. But here in Montparnasse people wandered about with snub noses and many kinds of facial faults and were quite acceptable. They thought up an outfit that suited them, procured themselves style, *genre,* a cheerful disposition, and did not look too bad. The aching wounds of Alberta's childhood, the smarting feeling that she annoyed people merely because of her appearance, had almost healed. Only when she met visitors from home was she reminded of it.

She wandered about the room, climbed up on to a chair and looked out of the skylight, arranged the flowers on the mantelpiece and gave them water, lighted the spirit stove. Soon she would only see the surfaces of things. The darkness flowed higher about them, seeping up from the corners, like the sea at home gaining slowly on the seals and the rocks. Only the front legs of one of the two ancient, suspicious-looking armchairs would remain standing for long out under the skylight, while the black marble profile of the mantelpiece became sharper.

It was time to light the lamp, to take out pen and ink, grammar and dictionaries, to fill her evening with studies or writing. There was no-one to hinder Alberta. She had studied French thoroughly, taken coaching, attended lectures, learned many long poems by heart and practised her ' r ', filled countless thick exercise books with inflections, had, most decidedly, continued to live in Paris ' for the sake of the language '. She was an advanced student; the literature was open to her.

She did not really do her reading here. She did it at the booksellers' counters under the arcades of the Odéon Theatre, at the *bouquinistes'* along the Seine, at the Ste. Geneviève Library. She seldom managed to buy a book, and those she owned she knew by heart. Her studies had not proceeded without cost, they had swallowed up whatever money there was to be swallowed, and more. She had been given help towards them, and as a result they had become a hobby-horse for those who wanted her to return to an orderly existence, a trump card in the letters from home, something she should come home and ' put to good use '.

As for writing, according to Liesel, she knew how to do that too. Moreover it kept her busy, according to what she herself had so brusquely said to Wolochinska.

Now and again, assailed by desperate shortage of money and reckless enterprise, she had recourse to it: when there was no other way of conjuring up the rent, when her shoes had become impossible or the need for new clothes glaring, when she dared not ask for further credit at the shops, and Mr. Digby was away or had no need of her. It was an alibi, when such was needed, but otherwise it was merely one of her chance expedients, something she could do because she had learned it at school, as the result of training, aptitude, and because it was expected of her. Articles about this and that, the Flea Market and the Fourteenth of July, a fête in the Tuileries Gardens, the Seine flooding its banks; things of which she needed to know nothing beyond the evidence of her own eyes, topics behind which to hide herself and her lack of knowledge and experience, a collection of words to throw in the face of the equally stupid, ignorant reader, confusing and startling him. She found a topic, stowed away impressions into a suitable number of lines and signed it A.S., doing so with reluctance and shame, feeling that she was doing violence to something in herself, and that what she had described was untrue, because it was shallow and merely superficial.

31

Sometimes she did write differently. But it was not the sort of thing that could be used by the newspapers. It could not be used for anything at all, was most unlikely to bring in a sou, would not even be accepted for printing. In other words, a form of idling. Alberta had always had many forms of idling. She frittered away her time with virtuosity.

Other people had a purpose in life and struggled towards it, or at least they had some kind of work. Their lives did not resemble an obscure path which wound round and beyond them in the darkness and which they could not reach.

Apart from the first couple of effervescent years, when everything, the language, the city, the museums, the past and the present, had surrendered of their own accord when she attacked them like a famished soul who at last sits down at a table set with food, Alberta did not yet know what she really wanted. She still had only negative instincts, just as when she was at home. They told her clearly what she did not want to do. Her whole being cringed when faced with certain situations and certain people, certain activities and certain surroundings, so that she felt it physically in the form of fever and pressure on the heart. Afterwards she was left free to reject what she did not want and without the slightest idea of what she should do with herself.

She had made one or two attempts to overcome this. A helpful Swedish lady had found her a post in the Scandinavian *pension* where she lived. Alberta would thereby avoid something she knew with certainty she did not want, and which yet again threatened on the horizon: going home. Because of her knowledge of French she was to be at the service of the guests, accompanying them to town, helping the ladies to change their purchases in the department stores, clearing up their misunderstandings with the servants; in emergencies to be prepared to wash a blouse, iron a creased dress, see people off at the station.

It had meant a heated room, three square meals a day, the chance of getting presents and tips, in fact, clover for someone like herself. On the seventh day Alberta had quietly sneaked out after having shown herself to be quite impossible, burnt holes in a silk blouse, and lost her temper with an old lady who wanted to go into Lafayette and change two small embroidered table-napkins after they had begun to roll down the iron blinds in front of the windows.

It was winter and raining in torrents. Just before dinner, when the guests were in their rooms and no-one was asking for her, Alberta had stolen downstairs in a daze, betaken herself to a sinister, but cheap hotel in the Rue St. Jacques, and gone to bed there, ill at ease and miserable.

The feeling of being abandoned and lost, that she was left alone with in that small, gloomy room, that smelt mildewed and uninhabited, the damp sheets, the candle-end that smoked and burned out, the cold dawn that eventually came, were impressions that still remained with her and always would. The next day she had written an embarrassing letter in a café, apologizing and asking for her trunk to be given to the messenger. Afterwards she had tried to avoid Scandinavians.

She had fallen back on casual and ephemeral pupils, newspaper articles, wandering about, reading. It was then that she had confided in Alphonsine who, after a certain amount of hesitation, had put her in touch with Mr. Digby. And she went and took off her clothes in front of this strange man. It was disagreeable, it was mortifying, but it was life's bitter law and no worse than much else. It was nothing to make a hue and cry about, as they would have done at home.

A violent fever of activity would occasionally possess her, a restless urge to use her energy, to use it for almost anything: to run down street after street to find places where such and such took place during the Revolution, to get up in the middle of the night and write long, effusive letters to Jacob, to begin studying something, to patch up her ignorance.

She had thrown herself blindly into one thing after another, had trudged systematically round museums for

33

weeks, sat in libraries poring over works on this and that, including anatomy, made notes and traced charts of the human body and at times derived a secret gratification from what bored her. Perhaps precisely this was necessary if one wanted to learn to work at something. Until one day she finished just as abruptly as she had begun.

She was shallow, soaking up knowledge and quickly satisfied even if the subject really interested her. The thought would occur to her that perhaps it was resistance that was lacking, friction against the disapproval of others. And she would feel more negative than ever.

For long periods she would be numb and indifferent. She only had energy enough for everyday matters. The world about her seemed like a film, comic and gripping by turns. And she was away from home, she had achieved that at least. This was the plank on which she floated, which she was must not abandon, whatever happened.

And the days would pass. Until life suddenly seized her by the scruff of the neck and gave her a good shaking. There she would be without a sou – or she would get a letter urging her to come home – or someone employed by her relatives' secret police would turn up – or somebody would say something, as Liesel had done today: 'My life is not interesting.' Such things roused her, waking her to bitter reflection. But they did not reform her.

Alberta got to her feet, put her eggs on to boil, looked at the station clock to see what time it was and curled up in bed to wait. The bells of the trams sounded shrilly above the traffic, a train whistled. She watched a little pool of water that Jean had spilled when he took the bowl away. Firmly circumscribed, it stood in low relief on the red floor, reflecting the delicate golden light from the ventilator.

After a while something happened near the pool. A nimble little silhouette scurried out from the darkness under the sloping roof, paused and sniffed the air, sitting for an instant on its haunches with its tiny forepaws lifted – Alberta could see its little nose moving – scurried forward

34

again towards the bright water, and drank. Like an ornament its tail lay curving behind it.

She watched it with composure. It was a fact. In a little while another one came, a new fact. Alberta's room was overrun with mice, but rooms can be overrun by worse creatures. Mice do not bite. They smell, but they are not alone in that. She was acquainted with animals that smelt as well as bit.

And she let them run about. It was only when she came across them in the wash-bowl that she failed to cope with the situation.

Later in the evening Alberta went out and wandered about the streets.

This was the refuge of many at this time of day: the homeless, the lonely, the disgraced, the puzzled, who do not know what to do with themselves. No-one is so impossible that he cannot feel he belongs here.

She walked down the Rue de Rennes, the greyest, hardest, bleakest of streets. There one met no acquaintances, there one was an anonymous person going by, a working girl on the way home, a prostitute on the way out, a straw in the current . . . .

Down, up, down again, first along one pavement, then along the other. The traffic was thinning out. After a while the street began to resemble an empty stage, where a rowdy drama had been played. Pieces of paper, banana-skins and cigarette stubs had been left behind in the gutters, and took on the appearance of uninviting props as the evening progressed. All the shutters high up on the houses were closed.

From the bars light shone cold and white. Silhouettes glided out and in, the clamour of gramophones came unevenly through doors that swung open and shut, snatches of music were thrown out from small orchestras. The passers-by began to look as if they were out on suspicious errands, Alberta too. Words were thrown at her from time to time, occasionally amusing, in some cases complimentary, never crude and vulgar as at home. The worst was the brief, low '*Tu viens*?', naked as an order to a slave. But if one walked quickly and pretended not to notice, the matter would lapse quite naturally. Sometimes it would be made good again with an apology: '*Pardon Madame*'. Alberta was never afraid in the street here, as she had been at Rivermouth and in the alleys at home in the small Arctic town.

It was lonely, and the loneliness rose from it all like bitter cold. No-one would hear if something happened on a deserted stretch of street, no-one would open the shutters to see who it was that screamed.

But nothing happened. And even the bleakness had something of adventure about it. Walking in the street can be like following a river. There may be plenty of traffic on it, or else it flows dark and forsaken, with scattered lights along the shore. It leads people towards each other, away from each other, there is no knowing where it can finally lead, or to whom.

The city streets, where you run to get warm in winter. Alberta had an extravagant weakness for them.

* * *

' How about going to Versailles, Liesel?'

Alberta leaned across the waxed cloth on the pavement table outside The Coachmen's Rest, a modest restaurant which she had frequented during her early, hesitant days in Paris, and where she and Liesel sometimes went in silent agreement. She watched Liesel expectantly. Absent-mindedly, in a slightly hunched position, Liesel was struggling with a tough chicken wing, muttering from time to time something about '*Uralter Hahn*'.

' We could get the two o'clock from Montparnasse.'

' No,' said Liesel. ' I have a life-class.'

' Today? But Liesel, if you haven't started by this time . . .'

The spring sky was tall and pastel blue above the city.

36

The waves of sound had a new tone, a light humming, peculiar to the season. The fresh colour of the new leaves was just as astonishing in the street scene this year as last year, as every year. The air and the light raised everything to a higher pitch, to the border of unreality. A hint of water and meadows was adrift in the atmosphere. Spring with all its happiness and sorrow had conquered the city, giving one the desire to do ridiculous things: to hire a cab by the hour and damn the expense, buy masses of flowers and beautiful things, eat outside at Leduc's every day, dine at D'Harcourt's at dusk with a lighted lamp on the table. One's old hat was an offence against the scheme of things.

At least one could go to Versailles. It cost thirty-five centimes, but lay within the bounds of possibility. Alberta already felt the warm sunny air that hung, heavy with the scent of box, above the flower beds there; already lay on her stomach in the grass, watching clouds and insects on their capricious ways, while Liesel sat on a camp stool, sighting with a brush, narrowing her eyes and painting. Blue shadows moved slowly round a piece of sculpture, across a lawn, up the gigantic pale green wall of an avenue. Patches of sunshine played over the elm trunks, the clock in the Palace chapel marked the hours, paying them out in ringing coin and with royal generosity. One had passed over into timelessness and abundance.

But Liesel wanted to go to her class. 'It's still full there,' she explained. 'And there's a new model who's supposed to be exceptional. The evening class is not enough. Besides, only dilettantes and old ladies go, not real artists. It lacks atmosphere. I must go to life-class today,' said Liesel. She looked nervous and distressed as she struggled with the chicken.

'Are you feeling well, Liesel?' The fact was that Liesel looked quite tousled although she had lowered the neckline of her dress even more this year, put the roses on her hat in a different position so that the faded parts were almost hidden, and sat equipped for the season, her Botticelli shoulders rather too bare, but with veiling over them.

37

'Well? Oh yes, thank you.' Liesel had not slept. But apart from that ...

Why had Liesel not slept? 'Is it those people next door again? You must ask for another room, Liesel.'

'*Ach*, you only move next to others who are just the same. You know how it is, Alberta.' And Liesel didn't care, *aber gar nicht*. She pretended not to hear. She spoke the last sentence vehemently, and flushed.

'No, no.'

Suddenly Alberta noticed a tear rolling slowly down Liesel's face. Liesel wiped it away, quickly, roughly as if to punish it. Another one followed.

'It's my nerves,' she mumbled in apology. 'It's because I'm tired.' She dried her tears more thoroughly and openly, looked up and attempted an embarrassed little smile. 'What will you think of me, Albertchen?'

'Why nothing.' Involuntarily Alberta put her hand on Liesel's, a rare and little used expression of sympathy, that made both of them look embarrassed. She withdrew her hand at once, regretting the gesture. Now Liesel was really crying; she sniffed and had to blow her nose. Alberta's gesture had evidently only made matters worse; she was silly about things like that.

There was nothing she could do but wait until it passed. Liesel dried her eyes, her face blotched and miserable, and tried to hide herself from the world under her big hat. When she had recovered a little she said, as if concluding a train of thought: 'Don't ever let anyone kiss you, Albertchen. I mean unless he's terribly fond of you.'

'No,' said Alberta hesitatingly.

'Once they kiss us the game's up.' Liesel sniffed and searched for a dry corner on her handkerchief. She did not look up.

Dread crept over Alberta. Had Liesel gone and got herself involved in something? It subsided at once when she heard that it had to do with Eliel. 'Of course you understand it's Eliel?' Liesel dabbed at herself with the handkerchief.

But Alberta, who for a moment had thought of hotel guests and other doubtful individuals, breathed again, relieved and a little embarrassed. ' Eliel! But he's certainly fond of you, Liesel.'

' Oh, not a bit of it.' Liesel gestured away from herself. ' The Swedish girl, Albertchen, the Swedish girl. It's now three weeks since she arrived. Potter has seen her with Eliel, they were sitting in chairs under the trees in the Luxembourg Gardens looking as if they were enjoying themselves.' And not a word had Liesel heard from Eliel during that time. If that wasn't a bad sign, Liesel didn't know what was. But she supposed men were like that.

It's mean of Eliel, thought Alberta. Cunning or mean or both. She set about comforting Liesel, pointing out that now and again the sort of people one had to look after from morning to night did come to Paris and one never had a moment's peace. It probably wasn't much fun for Eliel. Liesel would see.

Liesel wanted nothing more than to be comforted. She looked at Alberta with shining eyes, saying at intervals, ' Do you think so, Albertchen?' In between she returned to her original argument that if only she hadn't let herself be kissed she would never have got into this state. She quoted an observation made by Potter who, when asked what she thought about the situation, had said bluntly, ' Well, if he's hard up for a girl ... '.

' Don't take any notice of Potter. She's old, I'm sure she's never ... '. Alberta broke off. It was the same as with so many of Potter's bald, bitter utterances: they tore away the ground from under one's feet, making life uncertain and rough, ugly and unkind; one suddenly found one was freezing, standing unprotected in a desert of ice.

' Yes, there you are,' said Liesel. ' That's how you get if you're like Potter. One must have someone to love, Albertchen. Those who say so are right, Marushka is right.'

Alberta shrugged her shoulders, without going into the question. But she found something really consoling to say:

' I expect Eliel's trying to make you jealous, Liesel. I shouldn't be surprised.'

Wide-eyed, Liesel whispered fervently: ' Albertchen – sometimes I've almost thought so myself. And if only he comes back . . . .' She smiled. At the same time there was something defensive in her expression, she seemed ready to make an argument.

Alberta attacked neither attitude, advised neither for nor against and made no more bantering allusions to Eliel. He was no longer merely the big, good-natured blunderbuss about whom one made little jokes, at whom one laughed a little, behind his back and to his face. He had conquered Liesel. It gave him an unexpected halo.

Alberta had known him when he was making heavy weather as a newcomer who could not go to the post office alone nor come to an understanding with his concierge without help. It had fallen to her lot to help him over the worst, find him a cheap iron bedstead at the junk shop, arrange for his milk delivery, and so on. His expression, as happens when men are helped with things they are quite incapable of arranging on their own, had become dreamy and strange when he looked at her, *distrait* when they were alone together. But Alberta was on her guard. All her life the only men who had ever been in question had been those she could not tolerate, and she had finally acquired a certain dexterity in putting matters in their place with small means: a tone of voice, facial expressions, sudden formality. She carried out her mission without anything transpiring, and the constraint that she had felt fell away and was gone. What remained was a somewhat passive friendship, which found expression in occasional loans of money.

And here sat Liesel, altered by anxiety and longing because of Eliel. Alberta felt the same slightly embarrassed wonder she had felt in her childhood, when she had been unable to find amusement in the others' play, and she realised that it was due to lack of ability. Eliel – it was possible to fall in love with Eliel. Here sat Liesel who had done so. It was possible for him to be a dream hero, an obsession, a song in the blood.

He was plagued by catarrh in winter, and was in the habit of sniffing. In fact, his nose twisted round in his face. Presumably, that kind of thing had to be ignored.

Quietly, with shining eyes and a little smile that tried to hide itself, but constantly reappeared, Liesel talked about Eliel: of his talent, his industry, what he said on this occasion and what he did on that, how she had to laugh at him sometimes and how touched she was sometimes and how stupid she had been and if only she had not ruined everything. But he *was* intelligent. And he was *fundamentally* handsome. Alberta had said herself once that he looked handsome when he was at work.

'Of course, Liesel.' Alberta saw Eliel's tall, slightly stooping figure, surrounded by numerous large sculptures, which in some curious way seemed to be related to him, dragging limbs which they could not quite control, looking as if halted in the middle of a hesitating, half implied, fumbling and helpless gesture. She remembered an inner clarity, which would suddenly seem to shatter his heavy expression while he worked, the strangely intuitive life in his hands when he kneaded the clay and forced form out of it; the calm, legitimate triumph with which he would slowly turn the modelling-stand and show the world a new creation, the toss of his head as he did so, as if he had emerged victorious from a long, hard struggle : the essence of the man. And here sat Liesel, ignoring all that was unimportant and looking victorious too. Besides, she was starting to talk about her work. Nothing seemed lacking to her.

'What are you thinking about, Albertchen?'

'No – it was nothing. Go on Liesel.'

· Liesel was only going to say that she seemed to have definitely ruined the Pont Neuf picture; she had gone down to improve it, and the trees had become light green in the meantime, and then she got the disastrous idea of – well, there it was. But she was going to take her drawing

41

seriously and not think about colour any more: life-class from this afternoon on, and not just because Eliel might be there. She pressed her bosom and her clasped hands against the edge of the table and looked at Alberta solemnly.

Alberta was thinking that this afternoon there was only one thing to be done, she must get intoxicated in her own private way, and forget Eliel and Liesel and everyone who had everything she herself did not have and never would.

La Villette St. Sulpice.

Past St. Germain-des-Près, across the Place St. Michel, over the Seine; La Cité, past Porte St. Martin, Gare-de-l'Est; through broad and straight, narrow and crooked streets. Streets smelling of petrol, perfume, powder, and streets smelling of oil, chipped potatoes, pancakes. Regular, correct streets, where the houses stood looking just what they were; and others where signs, awnings, posters and advertisements of all kinds crowded each other, dissolving and displacing contours, charming away all underlying planes in a confusion of intricate pieces. Streets that buzzed with cheerful human life, while two rows of light-coloured treetops united in the far distant haze; and gloomy streets, full of clammy shadow, clammy fate, something oppressive and uneasy that kept the sun away. Small parks, paradises gay with flowers and playing children; and the obscene horror of the slaughterhouse.

To plunge into it. To drift, wander about, watch, absorb it all, with no other purpose. To take one of the old-fashioned horse-buses, which still swayed along here and there – not the bright red motor-bus, which bustled about in certain streets. To dismount and take other buses, penetrate unknown territory, buy fruit from carts and eat it sitting on benches, hear the clock strike in different ways in different church towers and know that it didn't matter, no-one knew where she was, no-one knew where she belonged. At the bar where she drank coffee and cracked a hard-boiled egg against the counter, she was someone who

42

came and went and no-one could give any information about her. It made Alberta feel something approaching *schadenfreude*.

There was an outside seat on the horse-bus, nearest the coachman and just above the horses' broad, pitching haunches. There you pitched high above everything too, you had a clear view.

Childhood tendencies are not easily escaped. They lead one further, lead one far. Alberta had had this inclination to drift since she was small. It could be roused by many things: tedium, weariness, physical unrest, a blue sky or a grey one, joy, an inexplicable impulse. It had acquired the addition of curiosity which did not make it any more permissible.

She could follow people unknown to her up and down streets, getting on and off the same means of transport with them to see where they finally went; listen intently to conversations between total strangers as if her whole existence depended on it; seek out places where she had no business to be, because some small feature gave her the feeling that something was happening there. Certain streets and houses had an inexplicable fascination for her; she drifted back to them time after time in order to stand there for a while, to watch people going out and in. Blindly, unable to give herself any valid reason for it, she absorbed impressions as a sponge absorbs moisture.

She would return home from her expeditions tired, hungry, knowing that she had yet again used money, time and shoe leather to no purpose, and yet strangely satisfied, as if deep and mysterious demands in her had been pacified for a while. Her brain teemed with fragments of the conversations of strangers. Disconnected pictures of the teeming life of the streets succeeded each other, shutting out regret and uncomfortable thoughts.

If only that were all. But one night a little while later she would perhaps be sitting up with smarting eyes and feverish pulse, scribbling illegibly on paper torn with

43

abandon out of the nearest exercise book, which would then be ruined.

Something she had witnessed had clothed itself in words in the secret recesses of her mind. Or remarks she had heard blazed up out of her memory, appearing to her like mysterious knots into which many threads of human life converged, entwined themselves and retreated into the obscurity from which they came. She wrote them down – and before she was aware of it, was engaged in a struggle with the language as if with a plastic material, trying to force life out of it as Eliel did with his clay. Reality lies hidden in outward occurrences, the words one hears are for the most part masked thoughts. But there are glimpses which enlighten, remarks which reveal. Alberta sometimes thought she had grasped something of it. And she fought with the recalcitrant words, they were like a mutinous flock tripping each other up. When they were eventually written down, conquered and in order, a lull fell in her mind after such unprofitable midnight turmoil.

In the morning something was there. It looked strange and unrecognizable, and belonged to some sequence, heaven alone knew what. It was blocked on all sides, there was no way out in any direction. To find it she had to know more about life, much about life, everything possible about life and more than can be observed from the roof of a horse-bus. As the waterfall sucks and pulls, so can the teeming streets suck and pull. A yearning would seize her to swirl with it, if only to see what would happen, and a yearning to track down its myriads of secrets.

This business with little scraps of paper in the night-watches was another sore spot on Alberta's conscience. The following day she would be dazed and incapacitated. And the pile of loose sheets in her trunk had been lying there for a long time, filling it up and making it untidy. They fluttered about in it indiscriminately. One day she would have to come to some decision about them. She could not be for ever opening it, slipping more into it, and shutting it again. But she had an unhappy weakness for this muddle of scribbled pages.

Buried in her memory there lay a fragmentary landscape. A shadow moved in it, appearing now here, now there, a naïve figure making up poetry. The background shifted. It might be as unreal as a theatrical décor, a blue and gold mountain range, illuminated from below by an unnaturally low sun; it might be eddies in the current, a river eternally flowing, deep with grey upon grey or green upon green; a bank of snow in thaw beneath a light that was neither day nor night, neither winter nor summer. And it might be almost nothing, a dull speck in infinity, shut in by mist, rain, snowstorms, as by enormous draperies. The shadow was always the same, in an altered jacket of regrettable cut and with her hands tucked up inside her cuffs.

Like a piece of reality crystallized out of it all there once had existed a battered exercise book, filled with bad echoes of mediocre poets. It had come to light in the trunk one cold, raw winter afternoon in the Rue Delambre and turned out to be something to laugh and cry over, certainly not something to be found by anyone after one's death; on the contrary. It became a hastily flaming, bright warmth, towards which Alberta held her ice-cold hands for a while, and to this extent it actually proved useful for an instant. Alberta did not like thinking about it.

One day the scraps in the trunk would have to go the same way.

* * *

' *Mon enfant* – beware of yourself – don't be too kind, too docile . . . . '

Alphonsine spoke slowly, with long pauses between her words. She had pushed the glasses and plates aside and spread out the cards, in apparent disorder, over the table. With her chin on one hand and the other planted with straddling fingers over a group of three or four, she gazed at them meditatively. She was reading Liesel's horoscope.

Liesel was sitting beside her on Marushka's divan, rather low down, on account of a broken spring. She stretched out her neck to listen, pouting with half-parted lips, while blushes and involuntary little smiles came and went in her face. Now and again, with an ironic *ach* or *doch,* she let it be known that she was by no means taking it seriously.

Beside Liesel was Alberta, uncomfortably squashed. Then the Russian, one of Marushka's numerous acquaintances who unexpectedly appeared and disappeared again. He had addressed Alberta in Russian and Italian with the same meagre result; she did not understand a word of either. Now he was being brutally and baldly offensive, pinching her arm, treading on her toes, leaning forward to stare into her face as if she were passive out of slow-wittedness.

But nothing is less dangerous than rough handling; it can quite safely be permitted. And demonstrations were out of the question as far as Alberta was concerned. If she could not escape quietly she would rely on her old weapon of silence, sitting stiff as a post, acting deaf, blind and numb, a strategy which in the long run is enough to render anyone harmless.

On the other side was Marushka, who had kicked off her sandals and drawn up her naked feet under her skirt. Her short little toes, of which she was so proud because they were not marked by shoes in the slightest degree, flexed and moved. She leaned forward with her elbows on the table and a cigarette in the corner of her mouth, watching the horoscope.

Across a muddled still life of bottles, glasses, fruit peelings and ash-trays Alberta defended herself through the tobacco smoke against several pairs of eyes. Openly amused or tensely enquiring they moved between her and the cards: Potter's eyes, screwed up into slits in her tired, ageing face; those of the Finn, Kalén, small, slanting, dimmed with wine; those of the little Swedish woman – the one who had run away from home and begun to paint, and whom Kalén was currently escorting everywhere, calling her his ' little angel ' – stiff, light blue, round with tension; Sivert Ness's eyes, strikingly clear and sober in his crooked Norwegian face; and high above them all, Eliel's. He had materialized again, in new corduroy trousers, the kind worn by workers in the street, wide in the legs and narrow at the bottom, and he seemed animated. A little way back from the table, mounted on Marushka's tall painting stool, he was enjoying the situation unreservedly, safeguarding himself by muttering: ' Huh – what a lout – an utter lout – I'd like to beat him up . . . '.

A Dane, a bespectacled, silent and random person, not an artist and quite uninteresting, was sitting low down and somewhat outside the group on an overturned chair. Eliel had fished him up in a café somewhere or other, dragged him along with him and introduced him to the company with the whispered explanation: ' Bet you anything the fellow has money, lives at Neuilly, I know that. We'll let him buy a sketch at least. One must fool the peasants when one can.' The "fellow" had been sitting looking about him with disoriented spectacles. Now he had suddenly heard something he understood and said with conviction: ' Beat him up – yes, that's what we should do.' But Eliel bent down and spoke to him quietly, and the question of beating up the Russian was dropped.

The hot weather had arrived, it was summer. The only movable pane in the big side window was thrown wide open. Pallid light fell through it from a threatening and stormy sky. They were in one of the numerous tiny studios in number nine, Rue Campagne Première.

' Here is happiness for you,' said Alphonsine. She looked at Liesel seriously, leaning her index finger on one of the cards. ' Happiness. Assuming that you don't let your heart run away with you. Beware of your heart.'

During the short pause, while Alphonsine pondered again, Potter leaned across the table and remarked quietly in English to Alberta: ' Men are like hungry dogs. Haven't I always said so?' And she switched over to her slow, tedious, incorrigible American-French and commented out

47

loud, to the whole company: ' It is woman's misfortune to think with her heart. Man thinks with something a little lower down.'

That awful Potter! A small storm blew up round the table. Alphonsine said, ' But you are shocking, Madame.' A quiet, reproachful ' Potter!' came from Liesel. Marushka called out seriously, with raised eyebrows, ' We too, we too, often, but yes.' Above it all could be heard Eliel's ' For shame – a female like that.'

' What? What did she say?' The little Swedish woman was roused from the confusing conversation she was having with Kalén, who was quite drunk, and looked round innocently. Kalén put his hand on hers: ' Never mind, never mind, my angel. It was nothing for little angels. But the old woman, so help me, ought to . . . '.

The Dane had understood nothing. He enquired politely what it was all about. And Eliel, who probably felt he had a kind of responsibility for the man, explained perfunctorily: ' Ugh, the old woman is talking through her hat, she's a man-hater. But Marushka really is damned outspoken.' Eliel appraised Marushka thoughtfully, and Liesel became restless and her gaze wandered.

Sivert Ness said nothing. He never did say much, this quiet, indefatigable boy from Eastern Norway who was incredibly industrious and incredibly poor in a tumbledown studio in the Rue Vercingétorix. He sat rolling a cigarette. When he raised his head, it was to look at Alberta, who out of habit immediately jerked her eyes away. She did not like Sivert Ness. He was a silent, self-assertive fellow in ugly thick country clothes, an admirable person of course, and a fellow-countryman. But she had no interest in exchanging glances with him.

At the same moment the Russian pinched her arm again, his foot caressed hers under the table, his knee pressed upwards. And Marushka, stretched full length on the divan behind them, whispered happily and vivaciously into her ear: ' It's obvious who he likes best, who he wants. It's you. He's an opera singer . . . '.

48

Alberta turned scarlet, spiteful, hard, merciless. She felt shame and anger written on her face. Opera singer! She was not sure why, but the fact only made matters worse, unendurable. In stinging clarity a sudden explanation presented itself to her. He and Marushka were old acquaintances from far back, something between them was perhaps over now. Liesel's relationship with Eliel encircled her like a protective aura; men have a nose for that sort of thing, they prefer not to get in each other's way. Potter was Potter and incredibly old, over forty, it was maliciously whispered. Alphonsine ...

Alberta ought to suit this opera singer on his way through. She was disengaged, suitably young, healthy, clean, undemanding, harmless, cheap in more ways than one, as good as free. She squinted in one eye, but that was of no importance in this context.

That was what the people who spoke to her in the street thought too, the ones who said '*Tu viens?*' into her ear. And those who were shy and circumspect, with a cunning will deep in their eyes. The sort of girl you can take liberties with.

'I'm going, Marushka. I'm going home.' Alberta rose to her feet and struggled to get out. But Marushka held on to her from behind and whispered in her ear: 'Now don't be foolish. You have the summer in front of you to sit alone in that attic of yours. We're eating at Leduc's. I'll pay for you.'

Above the murmur of all the voices persuading her to stay, to take no notice, and so on, Alberta suddenly heard the spectacled Dane say, earnestly and confidentially: 'Listen, if you really would rather go, will you permit me to see you home?'

She sat down at once, replying no, thank you very much, boldly and defensively. This stranger, who had the same feeling for where the line should be drawn as herself, was definitely not going to assume the role of some kind of rescue operation, sent out by the forces of respectability. She was where she wanted to be, all things considered, coarse-grained overtures included. Besides, Marushka's words had sent a gust of the bleak attic through her, a premonition of the sickening feeling of desolation that summer evenings in the city gave her. Soon enough she would be able to sit at home evening after evening and boil her lonely egg. She laughed nervously and said to Marushka: ' Well – if you'll lend it me, then.'

' *C'est ça.*' Relieved that all ill-humour was over, Marushka kissed her quickly on the cheek and spoke to the Russian in his own language. He looked astonished and deprecating, shook his head and laughed. Immediately afterwards he was there again, quieter than before, more secretive, more insistent.

Between the clipped trees in their green tubs outside Leduc's it was crowded. The Americans predominated, taking up as many as two of the long tables, young men with studio shoulders and bare heads, women of all ages with veiling on their hats and round their necks, hung about with long necklaces of amber, amethyst, greenstone. They sat with their elbows on the table and smoked with a remote expression, greeting Potter nonchalantly and absentmindedly, and Marushka, who was going from table to table shaking hands, warmly.

A short, sharp shower had fallen. There was a scent of earth and wet leaves, the air was heavy with spicy perfume from the Japanese rowan trees on the Boulevard Edgar Quinet. The evening sky hung sick and thundery between the rooftops.

Pock-marked Germaine waited on them. She was friends with everyone, moving people together to make room, laughing and throwing out swift repartee to right and left. Potter took Alberta under her wing: ' Poor little thing, come over here.'

Alberta was overcome by the weariness that was always a consequence of her incursions into social life. She sat withdrawn into herself. Mechanically she expressed agreement with the little Swedish woman, who was exclaiming over and over again: 'So charming to be out all together like this – just like this – how charming Paris always is in any case – how charming everybody is. I think everyone is so terribly kind . . . .'

'Yes,' said Alberta. 'Terribly kind.'

The Russian had transferred his attentions to Germaine. He seized her round the waist when she passed, followed her indoors to the bar, disappeared with her into a corner. Alphonsine looked after them and shrugged her shoulders: 'She's not as stupid as all that.'

Alphonsine had ordered a solid and sensible meal. *Entrecôte* with potatoes and salad, cold rice pudding with *compôte*, and that was that. No coffee. She ate calmly, with reflection, tearing pieces off her bread and chewing at it, talking no more than was necessary. Then she calculated what she would have to pay, put the money on the table, lit a cigarette and leaned back in her chair. *Voilà*, I've finished. If anyone wishes to hear my opinion on the Government or Monsieur Fallières, this is the moment. All you need do is present yourself.

Alphonsine did everything calmly and thoroughly. She was no longer young, but she was a sought-after model, because she was perceptive, punctual and without caprice. She had eaten, and now she was resting. She had taken off her hat and hung it on one of the ornamental trees. Above her short, broad face, in which the skin and muscles were stretched spare and taut across the cheek-bones, red hair jutted out in a thick wave and was gathered up diagonally on top of her head in an oblong roll. A painted mouth and two large irises, green as a cat's, stood out in violent contrast to her powder-white skin. Beneath her eyes it looked as if brownish blue shadow was eating in deep. It gave her a ravaged, battered, almost defaced look. She smiled with large, strong teeth.

Alphonsine was a friend. You could confide in her and meet with understanding. She read horoscopes and always found something to say that was encouraging, cautionary, or in some way to one's advantage. Always ready to do a

51

favour, she had found Alberta the job with the harmless Mr. Digby over on the other side of Paris and kept quiet about it. Alphonsine made one feel safe.

Now she stubbed out her cigarette and announced that she was leaving. If the others intended to finish up at Montmartre or Bullier's, they must not count on her. She had been on her feet for eight hours, she had to be at work at eight o'clock the next morning with her bed made and the bedclothes properly aired. She could not stand coming home to an untidy room. Goodnight everybody . . . .

As always when someone leaves, the conversation flagged a little. An American woman expatiating on cubism at the next table could be heard so clearly for a moment that everyone smiled. Then Marushka said, ' Lilac – isn't it?'

The light from the arc-lamps among the leaves still had the same magical effect on Alberta as when she had first experienced it. Fantastic, theatrical moons suddenly light up, and a mysterious world of green leafy cascades and black shadows, of moving circles of light and dark silhouettes, is created. People glide in and out of it as if on a stage, one feels as protected and secure as in moonlight; secure from the day with its many evil hours, from the endless summer night outside.

The American's words about cubism had taken effect, Marushka was in full feud with Kalén, who was making fun of the new theories. In his calm manner, which was further emphasized by his slow, hesitant French, Sivert Ness joined in the conversation. Usually he sat listening most of the time. Now he confessed that he was not a cubist, that he had bought Gleize and Metzinger's book. Yes, indeed, he really had. If only it weren't so damnably difficult. In the first place he didn't know the language well enough. If only he knew more French – he muttered the last sentence in Norwegian and looked at Alberta.

Kalén exulted. He was now really drunk and slapped Sivert on the thigh. ' Ha, ha, my friend, French won't help you there. Drivel, drivel, the lot of it. " Obscurely said is obscurely reasoned," has my friend ever heard that saying? A great poet said it, a very great poet, whom my friend does not know – yes – and that book is obscurely reasoned. Everything they say is obscurely reasoned, except for the place where they say that some of them are making a miserable *pretence* of being strong and deep, while others, *whom the authors do not think fit to mention* – mark that my friend – *move freely on the highest level*. What they mean by this pronouncement is quite clear – quite clear, yes – besides, if my friend is short of money, he could make better use of it. Does my friend even know what a theorem is? I can see that he does not. But these cubists demand of their readers that they meditate over certain of Rieman's theorems – it's ridiculous of my friend to embark on such a thing.'

Sivert did not say much in reply. He treated the drunkard reasonably, admitting that – yes, oh yes, of course. Kalén, who had talked himself into an angry, threatening mood, slouched over his glass again, pacified.

Marushka and Potter had become heated on the subject. And Sivert, never one to miss anything, turned his attention to them. In her circumstantial manner Potter contributed the usual argument about stove-pipes. The cubists painted stove-pipes, grey and brown ones, why? Or they took apart a coffee-grinder and placed its various sections around each other, on top of each other, inside each other on the canvas. Why? If you asked them they said that was not what they were doing at all, even though it was obvious to everyone. They entrenched themselves behind formulas and set phrases that no-one understood, themselves least of all: they were really quite at sea. ' *Yes*,' said Potter. She would not allow Marushka to get a word in edgeways, but shouted her down and insisted that she knew cubists who sat for long periods at a time holding their heads in desperation when they were painting, simply because they didn't know *how* they should do it. ' *Fumisterie* ', said Potter, blowing smoke down her nostrils. ' Hot air. Humbug.'

53

Marushka had fallen silent. She looked as she sometimes did when she spoke Russian with Russians about Russia. Her dark eyes, which normally danced in her face with vivacity, seemed to look inwards, lost in contemplation. In a low, deep voice she said, ' They are creators, seekers – they are pioneering a road . . . '.

' . . . that leads nowhere.'

' Yes.'

' No.'

That was how it always ended, in airy protestations. The antagonists leaned back in their chairs and did not address each other for a while, each convinced of the other's lack of judgment. But Liesel eventually contrived to put in her little confession of faith. ' I'm *not* a cubist. Even the cubists themselves say one is born to it or not. I'm not. You must be yourself.'

' Quite right,' cried Eliel emphatically. And Liesel blushed happily and looked about her to hide it. ' Muter-milka ', she said, and went on to talk about the Polish artist who was her ideal.

At a couple of tables put together a little further away, Norwegian voices exploded. Alberta had gradually come to hear Norwegian from the outside, as a foreigner might be supposed to hear it. It can sound musical, being securely embedded in a light, strong, slightly differentiated register and having its own clear, staccato melody. It is without evasion, going directly to the point, an honest, forthright language.

But when many people converse together, the brief sentences, the disconnected, self-sufficient words dart at each other like angry barks: ' *Nei. Jo. Javel. Ikke tale om. Tøv. Paa ingen maate. Tvert imot.*' They strike hard against the eardrum and the voices swing upwards on the final syllable as if in defiance. When women speak, it sometimes seems as if they intend to talk their opponent down, talk him to exhaustion, so that he is incapable of more. They lean forward, transfixing him with their eyes, and talk loudly, categorically, unanswerably, until suddenly a feminine voice, low, clear and flexible, darts light as a bird up and down its small, pure scale, so that one listens to it as one listens to music. And that too is Norwegian, and resembles no other voice in any other language.

The little Swedish woman had fastened on to Alberta. A stranger to the circle, really only acquainted with Kalén, who was also an outsider, she probably felt impelled to associate with the women. She had her worries, and sighed: ' If only he could leave the liquor alone! He's such a wonderful person in every other way, fundamentally so distinguished and kind. But unhappy, you see – he's tried to kill himself, oh yes, not once but many times. You think you've gone through a lot yourself, and even then it's nothing when you compare . . . . If only one could help a person like that, do something for him . . . . '

Alberta had heard the same story before. Kalén hung about, always drunk, occupied year out and year in with a drama that would never be finished, sometimes fighting and causing scandal, frequently disagreeable and quarrelsome. He always had some sighing female newcomer in tow, while his Swedish wife, who was a masseuse and led a neglected existence in the Rue d'Assas, paid his café debts and got up to make gruel for him when he came home in the small hours. One's sympathy for Kalén became a little blunted over the years, giving it expression easily became a matter of habit. ' Yes, poor fellow,' said Alberta, thinking about something else.

She was half watching the Dane, prepared to be on the defensive with him. People passing through, needing someone to pilot them round, fell all too easily to her lot. She thought she felt the spectacles directed towards her now and again.

He did not say much, perhaps because the confusion of tongues put obstacles in the way. He had a thin, irregular face which the spectacles made even more irregular; they continually caught reflections from various angles and hid his eyes. When he moved, the padding in the shoulders of his jacket was pushed upwards. His voice reminded her of

55

Rasmussen. Every time it reached Alberta, memories floated up piecemeal. She could hear Rasmussen saying, as they walked past the Galeries Lafayette, for instance, where cheap remnants were lying in heaps outside, ' That's your colour – you ought to buy that piece – then you should make it up thus and so.'

She never bought it. However cheap it was, it was still too expensive, because it had to be made up. But she learned a lot about herself from Rasmussen, as they drifted all over Paris together, on foot and by horse-bus. One day he had had to give up painting and go home, for mysterious, rather vague reasons. Alberta had the impression that he was going to work in an office, and that it was to be some kind of transition to something else. She missed him very much. He had stopped writing a long time ago.

' *Skaal*, Albertchen – where were you then?' Liesel, a little distance away, lifted her glass towards her, smiling. Liesel was no longer disintegrating and depressed, as she had been a short while ago. She radiated a kind of quiet, concerted glow, which she seemed to force back, but which kept on breaking through. As the evening wore on her eyes seemed to darken and become veiled, because of what she was drinking or perhaps for some other reason. Presumably everything was settled between her and Eliel. That very day Liesel had said : ' We are happy, Albertchen – *aber so.*'

Something had come over Eliel too. Not only had he acquired new trousers; he had an artist's cloak, which he slung round him with a single gesture, and a new, broad-brimmed hat. When one examined Eliel more closely, he was new from top to toe. Besides, he was beginning to get a tan. The summer was Eliel's best time. Then he acquired an even, warm patina, which contrasted well with his teeth and his eyes and made him look younger and as handsome as a peasant. Alberta had occasionally felt a pang when Eliel made his annual appearance in this condition. But she remembered the catarrh in winter and various other things, and then it was over.

Now, however, Eliel was really good-looking. New clothes certainly made a difference. A new love affair too, no doubt.

The Russian wanted to go to Montmartre. The little angel's eyes brightened, she clapped her hands and cried: ' Oh yes, do let's. I've not seen belly-dancing yet. I'd so love to see belly-dancing. Just to see it, that's all.' But the proposal came to nothing for lack of support. During the discussion Liesel and Eliel miraculously disappeared. Potter left too, lonely and dragging a little as she went along the pavement. Kalén was heavy-eyed and quarrelsome. He announced that the devil could take him if the angel was going to any Montmartre this evening, no. She fell quiet and did not insist, her face turning small and distressed. Shortly afterwards they too were gone.

Marushka commandeered a cab and packed those who remained into it. They drove round the Luxembourg Gardens. It had again rained a little. The wooden cobbles in the Rue d'Assas shone like varnish in the wet, reflecting street-lamps and occasional pedestrians. There was a strong scent from invisible trees in blossom.

Alberta had the Russian's knee against hers, he was treading insistently on her toes. An understanding had to be reached before it was too late. It couldn't be so utterly hopeless, surely. She sat knowing that she found herself in the cab for one reason only, fear of coming home and being alone.

She was finally accompanied by the Dane and Ness. They talked to each other about the country. The Dane was going to the country, to a married sister of his. He turned to Alberta and explained that he lived in Neuilly with the same sister. ' Really,' said Alberta, tired and empty-headed.

Outside the hotel entrance this person, so completely ignorant of the circumstances, who had nothing whatever to do with her, suddenly decided that she was still his responsibility. ' Now are you sure you'll get in all right?

57

We'll wait until we see you safely inside. Good evening, it
has been most pleasant, *au revoir*. We'll wait here, Ness
and I.'

It took some time for the door to open. Alberta
explained: 'Jean is asleep. One always has to ring several
times. Do go, please.'

Ness was standing in the middle of the pavement. He
intended to get up early next morning, as usual, and showed
his impatience. 'Miss Selmer will get in all right. Besides,
there's traffic on the street.'

But the Dane would not budge: 'We'll wait here, Ness
and I.'

Sure enough, Jean was on duty. In the circle of light
from the little pocket torch which he directed towards her
as if she were a burglar, she glimpsed his face, heavy with
sleep and warmth. He was lying fully clothed in his
stockinged feet on a camp-bed in the little room beside the
office, and muttered incoherently when she gave him her
name. And he pointed the torch at the shelves on the wall
so that she could find her key and her candlestick.

* * *

The furnishings were the depressing kind in brown-
painted wood that seem inevitable in all administration.
The light was poor and grey. There was a smell of poverty.

From old habit, perhaps from atavism, Alberta looked
furtively about her on the way in and squeezed herself
quickly through the door. Taking everything into consideration from childhood onwards, she was once more
embarked on one of the small back ways of life. Once
right in, such notions fell away as if she were throwing off
a burdensome old garment. She was quite simply herself,
and felt relieved. A failure, a little on the side-lines of
life – yes. But so were the other people who came here.
Nobody expected her to be any different, nobody was any
more successful than herself. On the contrary, a quiet

58

acknowledgement of life's difficulties, of the fact that it consists of alternatives, was in the air. The low-voiced people who gathered here recognized in each other reliable individuals, who gave guarantees, and they exchanged glances full of understanding and little smiles. No-one needed to brace himself to persuade the others of facts.

The bench under the window was Alberta's habitual seat. She was away from the light, could see all who came in, and right into the little window where a bald head with grey bristling moustaches and spectacles appeared from time to time. The head directed its spectacles towards one or another of those waiting, mentioned a sum with a not unfriendly ' *Ça va?*' to follow. The person concerned would get up and go forward.

Taking everything into consideration, it was an obliging head. It looked at one seriously, but without disapproval. It was the same to everyone, to the lady who nervously and surreptitiously took a ring out of her handbag, to the woman fumbling with trifles in a knot of cloth. It listened to what people had to say and went to the trouble of giving explanations. Not all heads in windows did that.

She could trust it. When, for instance, it said ' *Quarante francs, ça va?*', Alberta made no objection. She took its infallibility for granted in such matters, considering besides that if she did not get an enormous sum, no enormous sum would be demanded of her when it was time to come back again. And all the little things she had been given at her confirmation or which had been Mama's, the brooches, the rings, the necklace, the watch, had disappeared into the unknown – the enormous, grey complex of buildings that surrounded her and filled the *quartier*.

What is property? In the final instance a piece of paper, which renews your admittance to life for a while, a ticket to it, so to speak. If your luck is in you celebrate it with a brief reunion with something you thought you owned once. Round the corner, in the Rue de Regard, there was a door, a mysterious place, where a sparse gathering, silent as a congregation awaiting the miracle, sat on benches in rows. It was there. There you bought dearly the illusion of owning your property for a while. Putting it in was almost a more cheerful business than taking it out, for you could never really afford the latter.

Money in your pocket makes your step light. It is a sort of credential, giving one again the right to exist and look people in the eyes, to do things that increase one's well-being and self-respect: to ask about prices, choose food-stuffs, take them home and eat them, pay debts, smarten oneself up. On the way across the courtyard Alberta reacted as she usually did when she saw the word '*Matelas*' above a door: Thank God I've not sunk as low as the mattress yet. I haven't one, but even so . . . . She also noted with satisfaction that she had no intention of turning the corner into the Rue St. Placide and borrowing more money on the basis of her receipt. She was not as depraved as all that.

The municipal guard in the gateway twirled his moustache and smiled at Alberta as she passed. He did so out of good nature. Alberta did not misinterpret it either, but smiled back at him.

It was an evening in July following a completely still day. The heat outside beat down on her sickeningly and suffocatingly. The sun had gone from the street, but the asphalt gave off heavy, accumulated warmth. Thick with the reek of fatigue, dust, petrol and food, the air hung immovable between the walls.

Under the café awnings people were crowded round the small round marble tables. Blue syphons, golden, red or emerald liquids shone dully, sugar dripped glutinously into turbid absinthe, glasses and coolers were hazed over by quickly melting ice. The sight of a lump of ice sliding cool and smooth down into a vermouth reminded Alberta of a seal she had once seen at a circus. It had had a little rubber bath-tub to flop in and out of. It was immediately succeeded by another image, which floated up from hidden depths and remained for a second behind her eyes: a few small houses, half buried in snow under a grey sky, uninhabited, ice-cold.

60

Alongside the pavement the last fruit and vegetable barrows were moving slowly along under the impatient *Avançons messieursdames, avançons,'* of a policeman. A reek of decay, of things stored too long and slightly fermented, followed in their wake.

It was summer again, exhausted and cheapened, unaired and a little dirty, as it so quickly becomes in the paved streets. It breathes freely in parks and quiet residential districts; there, full of dark, melancholy sweetness it lets itself be surprised, but it yawns on the asphalt, trampled and soiled. Trees appear as if dying, animals and people half die. Alberta knew all about it, she had experienced it many times. For the first time she felt her courage flag on seeing it.

Slowly she wandered upwards, looked critically at the fruit barrows, studied the menu outside Léon's Restaurant, but left again. It was not the moment for extravagance, even though she had the rent, that nightmare of all the impecunious, in her pocket.

' Liesel!'

With her back towards Alberta, loaded with paper bags and parcels, Liesel was standing beside a late barrow, choosing from amongst the day's last squashed peaches. She started and looked up, her eyes wide in surprise, and collected the things she was carrying into one hand in order to give her hat a shove. It appeared to be losing its balance on top of her coiled-up hair. ' Albertchen! *Wie geht's*? It's close this evening, *aber so, nicht wahr*? That one and that one and that one, *ach nein*, not that one, it's rotten, but that one and that one.' Liesel picked and chose outspokenly from among the peaches. The fruitseller, a coarsely built woman with honest eyes and skin like copper, muttered something to the effect that if the customers were to take matters into their own hands trade would soon take a turn for the worse, then suddenly changed her mind and laughed: ' *Enfin*, it's the end of the day, and Madame is charming. Here you are, over a pound, *ma petite.*' She handed Liesel the bag and winked at Alberta: ' Her husband's fortunate, he has a thrifty housekeeper and a charming *amie*, he'll have a good dessert this evening. And you, *ma petite dame*? A pound for you too, *n'est-ce-pas*?'

She filled another bag quickly. ' There, thirty centimes. They were fifty. I'm honest, I admit you couldn't offer them to the President of the Republic, but they are good, they are juicy, believe you me. You'll be satisfied.' Holding the coin Alberta handed her tightly between her teeth, she fumbled in her bag for change, and then wandered on with her barrow. ' Good evening *mesdames, bonne chance*.'

Liesel blushed her pale blush. ' Did you hear what she said, Albertchen? It's just as if they can tell.'

' They say that sort of thing to anyone who's pretty, Liesel.'

' They can tell,' insisted Liesel. ' But they like it. Here it's the way it ought to be, not wrong as it is elsewhere. She saw very well that I had no ring. Look, not a single rotten one. I always got rotten ones before. *Am* I pretty, Albertchen?'

Timidly, with a shy little smile, Liesel produced this decisive question. At the same time she stopped, loaded Alberta with her bags, drew out her hatpins and stuck them in again differently, brushed dust off her dress. And Alberta, who knew what it was all about, and honestly thought Liesel was pretty besides, nodded in confirmation : ' Yes, of course you are.'

There was no doubt as to where Liesel was going. The days were past when she was on her way to Alberta's, or on her way home to light the spirit stove. Feeling a little flat, a little left behind and out of things, Alberta thought : Liesel might ask how I am. But Liesel said : ' I was looking at the hats in the window on the other side of the street. You know, the place where they're all the same price, four-ninety-five. But they're so boring, Albertchen, *so bürgerlich*. The ones we put together ourselves look better, more artistic, *nicht wahr*? There's one in Bon Marché -- Marushka said she'd help me with it. It only needs a flower or two, *fertig*. But fourteen francs just for the form, *unmöglich.* Especially now. I've done something very reckless, Albertchen.'

'You're always doing something reckless.' The words came out of Alberta's mouth unintentionally, from fatigue, half-teasingly. She regretted them instantly. Liesel's face seemed to fall for a second. At any rate she said in a thin little voice: 'It's true, I *am* reckless. Not a month goes by but I'm in torture – but in *torture*. And yet it's been no more than two so far.'

Faces she had watched turn miserable here on Montparnasse, disappear and turn up again even more miserable – or simply disappear, paraded before Alberta. Indifferent, casual words from street corners and cafés rang in her ears: ' Mm – yes – things went badly for her, you understand – she got pregnant.'

Cold alarm for Liesel gripped her. Then she thought: After all, it's Eliel, Eliel's decent and kind. And simultaneously Liesel said firmly and with intensity: ' I've only done what I had to do. It's as natural as being alive. I'm in *love* with him, Albertchen, I'm in *love* with Eliel. You see how mad I am to say it out loud in the street.'

Liesel's little confession was completely drowned by the traffic, a lorry thundering past making it as inaudible as a sigh in an avalanche. Nobody had heard it besides Alberta. Nevertheless Liesel looked about her fearfully and ascertained with relief: ' No-one we know, *Gott sei Dank.*'

It was a fact that the most incredible things, truth and untruth in confusion, leaked out from Montparnasse to the rest of the world, finding and causing alarm to unsuspecting relatives, even as far away as America, giving rise to turmoil and catastrophe. It probably would not take long for a rumour to reach Liesel's cabinet-sized family. They were quite obviously unsuited to receive news of this kind.

' They think you ought to be married *und so weiter*,' said Liesel, as if Alberta had spoken aloud. ' They might decide to come, and disturb Eliel.'

And Eliel must not be disturbed. He was so gifted.

Someone was supposed to have used the word genius once at the Versailles. Besides, he was ill-suited to dramatic conflict, it was quite unthinkable that he should be involved in any such thing. Liesel emphasized still further the gravity of the case: ' No-one knows besides yourself, Albertchen, no-one, and you will be careful, won't you?'

Of course I shall, Liesel.' Alberta was not the kind of person to give anyone away. Keeping silent was one of the things she really knew how to do. It offended her a little to have it enjoined on her. Coldly she asked, ' Where have you been?'

Liesel smiled her new, disingenuous smile: ' I told you I'd done something reckless – yet again.'

Alberta looked her up and down. She was wearing her eternal black. The dust showed up terribly on it in summer. Altogether it was ill-suited to the time of year, and Liesel was perspiring, pale with the heat. Alberta noticed that it had been cut down still more, the sleeves only reached to the elbow. Her hat was the faded violet one from last year, enormous, as fashion had then demanded, with small red roses round it. Liesel's bags clearly contained food from the barrows. But from her little finger there dangled a light little package.

' You're looking at my dress, Albertchen. Should I have left the sleeves alone?'

' No, no. What's *that*, Liesel?'

' You'll never guess.'

' Something from Bon Marché?'

' *Gar nicht, gar nicht.*'

' Then I don't know.' Alberta was suddenly tired of the joke. The money she had in her pocket no longer had any effect on her: she felt superfluous and futile. But beside her Liesel was saying: ' I *want* to be beautiful, Albertchen, I want to be beautiful now. I want to be . . . ' She looked round enquiringly and found a word that expressed her thought: ' *Troublante. Troublante,* like the Parisian women. You can laugh, *aber . . .* '

' *Troublante* is the right word. That's what we want to be. It's just that we're not properly equipped.'

' There, you see. Albertchen!' Liesel's voice assumed a confidential tone. ' I've just come from " *Cent Mille Chemises* " – *Hunderttausend chemisen*. I've bought a frilly nightie, *ganz allerliebstes,* nineteen francs ninety-five.'

Liesel nodded in the direction of the little package. But Alberta, who knew no better than that Liesel's wardrobe cried out for other replacements, and who was in addition short-sighted and stupid, exclaimed from an honest heart : ' Have you become a millionaire or completely mad?'

' Mad, Albertchen, mad, not a millionaire. I haven't the rent for the fifteenth, but still . . . ' A shadow passed over Liesel's face, then she suddenly exclaimed : ' It can't be helped, Albertchen!'

Her voice became still more confidential, filled with fervent, repressed emotion : ' I'm going to stay with him all night, for the first time. I'm not going to get dressed and go home again. We shall sleep together and wake together. It'll be more proper, more natural, won't it? I've wanted it all the time. One *wants* it, Albertchen.'

The tram to Fontenay aux Roses came into view at the bottom of the street, and Liesel set off for the tram stop at top speed. ' I *must* catch it. He *never* eats a proper *déjeuner,* only sardines *und so was.* I *must* get hold of a chop before they close out there. I've got the mayonnaise and ham and Brie and fruit here. You'll come out soon, won't you, Albertchen? Just imagine, he hopes to sell the group – the small, patinated one. Then we'll go away to St. Jean du Doigt – as long as Potter or Marushka don't decide on the same place. He wants to make sketches of me in plastolin, he says I resemble a Cranach, that I've given him an idea! For a large figure, Albertchen!' In all her busyness Liesel found time to look up at Alberta significantly. Her life was no longer uninteresting, she was everything, she was a Muse. She had the right to ask for a little assistance with nondescript everyday matters. ' Oh, would you mind taking a coupon for me, please?'

65

Alberta took the coupon, and Liesel mounted the congested tram-car, hot and flustered, her hat awry. Struggling to protect herself and her packages she stood in the crush on the platform, jostled back and forth, out of breath and radiant. Her breast rose and fell, her lips glowed as if painted. A couple of youths with cigarettes stuck in the corners of their mouths nodded at each other, and exchanged complimentary remarks: 'She's charming, *la petite,* very charming – if only it was worth the trouble of paying court to her.'

It was clear to everyone that it was not worth the trouble. A motherly old soul made room for her: 'Here you are, *ma petite dame,* you can stand more easily here with everything you've got to carry. I know what it's like to take the tram-car at this time of day, when one has done one's shopping.'

Liesel became even more radiant, in happy connivance with the whole world. She looked down with emotion at Alberta, left alone and probably looking a little pathetic. Just as the tram-car started to move, Liesel had an impulse. She leaned out and whispered at the last minute: 'You should find someone, Albertchen – Marushka is right – you should ...'

Her final words were swallowed up by the noise. Liesel was gone.

Up in her room Alberta gasped in the enclosed atmosphere that met her. Quickly and roughly as if in desperation she tore off her clothes, threw them on to the bed and rubbed herself down with a sponge. Then she lighted the spirit stove, sat down naked among her clothes and sucked peach after peach.

At first she thought about nothing at all, keeping hateful thoughts successfully at a distance. They can resemble greedy birds round carrion. They circle round you in narrower and narrower rings. You throw them off, they return once more. Finally they alight on you, flapping their dark wings and hooting in your ears. They tear at your heart with their sharp beaks, and your heart writhes in pain, and sometimes stops.

For the time being Alberta had sufficient food. After the peaches came the eternal eggs. She stuffed bread into her mouth while she waited for them to boil, then ate and cleared away, threw a kimono round herself and opened the door out on to the stairs, leaving it wide open.

The staircase windows were open on to the minute courtyard, deep as a well. It was dinner-time and the house was quiet. The sound of forks could be heard from downstairs in Monsieur's and Madame's apartment and the clink of dishes from the kitchen. Looking over the banisters she could see Jean and the new *garçon* going downstairs for their meal. They buttoned up their waistcoats on the way and smoothed down their hair with their fingers.

She sniffed towards the draught which she hoped would come. But the heavy, dead air did not move. Nothing moved, nothing could be heard, but the light scattered sounds of cutlery and the muffled noise of the street. Nevertheless Alberta paced between the window and the door as if on guard, listening, prepared to turn the key in the lock instantly.

She was used to the summer emptiness of the upper storeys and knew its dangers and advantages. These depended to a certain extent on the menservants, whose rooms were also up in the roof. But here there was only respectable Jean trudging round. She had nothing to fear from that quarter, nor from the couple further down the corridor.

But the unexpected can happen.

She remembered an evening last year, heavy, suffocating, with peals of thunder far away. The demands of the body for fresh air, dammed up in her summer after summer, had all of a sudden become unbearable. Carelessly she had thrown the door wide open and stood on a chair, naked under the kimono, with her head out of the skylight, inhaling through every pore the small puffs of wind that moved now and again across the rooftops. The countless

67

rows of yellow chimneys were pallid beneath the gathering storm. To the south, above Vanves and Malakoff, the metallic sky exploded in flash after flash of lightning, and an occasional violent gust of wind promised release. She seemed to feel how her blood drank the air in her lungs and flowed on, giving life to the dry network of veins. The draught played with the light material of the kimono, fluttering it momentarily. She was bathed in air, inside and out, and mind and body expanded to receive it. On a corner of the boulevard she could see the dry curled-up leaves, which the exhausted city trees strew about themselves at the height of summer, swarming along the pavement, all in the same direction, like scattered Lilliputian armies in flight. The whine of the trains at Montparnasse cut through the air.

Then her heart gave a jump as she realised that she was not alone. She looked down, and there the man stood, fat, bearded, in shirt and trousers, his chest bare, and dark with animal hair. In the sick, thundery twilight he looked unreal, especially as he did not speak, only stared at her. Alberta did not speak either. Dumb and tense she climbed down off her chair, and drove him out backwards in mutual silence, while her brain hammered with the realization: We're alone up here – it's a long way down – he'll get to the door first – if he shuts it, no-one will hear us.

He did not shut it. As silently as he had come, he disappeared again, in slippers or his stockinged feet. A lock that turned quietly out in the darkness was the only indication that he had actually been there.

He had been neither a vision nor a rapist. Alberta saw him again the next day on the stairs, a commonplace traveller in a top hat and waterproof. An ordinary man, who lived cheaply on top floors and sought cheap pleasures, led astray by the open door and the woman in scanty attire inside. It might have been worse.

Other memories from the top floors of other hotels lay stored up in her memory, uglier, more dangerous. She did not like meddling with them. And this last incident had been almost the most vexatious. The fact that she could not leave her door open on a suffocating evening unpunished, because she was everyman's booty, a woman, had left her bitter.

She walked a little way down the stairs and looked out of the low window. Now they had finished eating down there, only the clinking from the kitchen could be heard. At the bottom of the courtyard's depressing shaft someone was squatting, playing with the hotel cat. It was lying on its side, half on its back, striking out lazily with its paws. It was Jean sitting there. He had just hosed down the yard. A ring of small black puddles had been left round him in the depressions in the asphalt.

Someone was coming up the stairs, and Alberta drifted in again, shutting the door. She could go out walking, as was her custom, or she could go down and sit on the boulevard. She was free to do so, it was a harmless, cheap evening's entertainment, shared by thousands, by large sections of the population. The melancholy summer evening in the city, she had admittance to that: to its dying, sickly green light lingering in the window-panes high up, the suffocating atmosphere with its sudden puffs of fresher air which slap feebly at the café awnings, chase the dust upwards and die away again; to its gasp for tranquillity, which is drowned in the clamour of gramophones and the clanging of tram-cars. Tired, low-voiced or silent people sit on the benches. If they tilt their heads backwards they can see the sky, thin, clear as glass, far too light, pitched to hang whole and free above a scented landscape, drawn taut in bits and pieces above desert formations of stone and cement. Even the trees along the pavement look foreign and irrelevant, as if picked up from a Noah's Ark and set out in rows, artificial, unnaturally dark.

Alberta had experienced it summer after summer. It is then that the lonely cannot withstand their loneliness any longer, but come out from their hiding-places, and walk quietly down the street as if they had a route and a purpose. It is then that poor, elderly women get something impracticable and out-of-date from their drawers, something that suited them once, put it on and go out in it, guilty and uneasy, a little wry in the face.

There were evenings when a compulsion, an inner necessity, made Alberta seek out precisely this; when, with a kind of appetite, she inhaled the heaviness of the atmosphere, all it carried with it besides the reek of the day: human frugality, fatigue, resignation, unsatisfied longing. Something in her was nourished by it, and began to put out painful shoots. But it had to happen in freedom and according to her own choice, not as the only way out. It easily acquired a tinge of necessity and of touching bottom against which she had to be on her guard. This evening it was not worth going down to sit on a bench. It could be worse alone with herself down there than anywhere else.

Should she go to see Liesel? Look out for her when she came from her evening class? Ignore her slightly tired surprise and force an entrance to her sooty, narrow balcony, barely separated from the neighbours by a low trellis? Comfort herself with the thought that even if Liesel might perhaps have preferred to go to bed, she was at any rate sitting on her balcony enjoying this asset, a thing she seldom dared do when she was alone, because she would be accosted and pursued across the trellis.

No. That had come to an end. Liesel was with Eliel. She was no longer the rather lonely girl, who trailed her painting things and her long, black dress around between Colarossi's, the banks of the Seine and the Luxembourg Gardens, returning home untidy, dusty, dirty with paint and ravenously hungry, and who would explain despondently: ' There were four of them watching today. I can't do anything if someone's watching. Everything was different when I got there – now I've spoiled it again. I'll never be any good – my life is not interesting.'

Ever since a day last winter, when Eliel had taken her hand in his, lifted it towards the light, inspected it from every angle and asked if he might model it – ' It's so unusually beautiful and full of character ' – Liesel had gone through the usual stages in the correct order, sitting for a hand, for the head, for a shoulder, for everything, sewing on buttons and making coffee, collapsing like an empty rind, and blossoming like a rose; and had now invested half her rent money in a frilly nightdress. And all of it without Alberta really being aware of what was going on. Now Alberta was left by the wayside, while the others drove on with everything settled and a final 'You should find someone too'.

Find someone! Alberta stood up and walked restlessly about the room. Women repeated it in every tone of voice, wherever she happened to be. From old Mrs. Weyer in the little town at home, who had patted her on the shoulder and repeated ' A good husband, a good husband . . . ', to Marushka, who smiled introspectively at her memories and said : ' Why live as you do, *mes enfants*? To what purpose? Love gives happiness – what would life be without love – I'd wither up and die, I admit it frankly ', and to Alphonsine, whose green eyes studied her through and through, and who stated quietly ' *Il vous manque une affection, Mademoiselle.*'

But Alberta remembered Liesel on one occasion last winter, when Marushka had yet again been giving her variation on the theme. It had suddenly struck Liesel. She had heard it many times before, but now it struck her. Her eyes had become big and shining, like those of a child who has been given the answer to decisive questions. Something had happened to Liesel at that moment. Perhaps it was then that she had changed course and gradually steered towards Eliel, who had been tacking round her for a long time, allowing him to approach, as if testing him.

Then the Swedish girl had come – the one thing after the other.

' A good friend – two arms round you at the end of the day – that is what I wish for you, Mademoiselle.'

Alphonsine again. Her reflective and divergent answer to some comment Alberta had made about unsuccessful

71

attempts to work, the incompetence from which she suffered. No-one could, like her, strike down into one's daydreams and light on to what they were really about, whether one admitted it to oneself or not. She did not carry on insidious propaganda like the married women at home, who knew no rest until the whole world was caught in the trap in which they found themselves: food and servant worries, gynaecological troubles, Nurse Jullum the midwife like an official executioner in the background. She did not share Marushka's attitude either; Marushka, who glided from one affair to another incredibly easily and insouciantly, banishing all scruples by the device of trusting in her lucky star.

Alphonsine brought out one's weaknesses, holding them up to the light for an instant. She would shake her head seriously in denial, if one day Alberta were to broach the question, expose her wretchedness, and say: 'Who, Alphonsine? Who? The man in the street, who says *tu viens*? The hotel guest who tries to get into one's room? The fairly good-looking fellow who wanders about the studios looking for love, gratis, and whom almost anybody can have once or twice? Or the kind of person from whom mind and body shrink, one with catarrh, one with an obstinate will deep down in those cautious eyes?' She would say: 'But there are others, Mademoiselle.'

'Not for me,' said Alberta bitterly, out loud. She continued her train of thought: 'Tenderness? What about tenderness, Alphonsine? When you have lived next door to all kinds of people, and the walls are thin, you begin to find it a little difficult to believe in that. At first you are frightened, thinking of madness or confined animals, finally you understand. Groans, struggle, a smothered bellow in the darkness, a heavy silence as if death had supervened, the snoring. The snoring! Or women's tears, streams of bitter, upbraiding words. What happened to tenderness? It must have been lost on the way?'

Alphonsine would probably smile a melancholy smile and know better. And rightly so.

72

Alberta was sitting on her bed in the dark, her arms round her knees and her chin resting on them. Suddenly she got down, found a light, and dressed herself feverishly. Now the evil had reached her heart, anxiety gripped it. That vague anxiety for life as it reveals itself step by step; anxiety that in spite of everything it might slip through her fingers unused.

She ran downstairs, bought the evening papers, *Le Rire*, more cigarettes, even an expensive literary monthly, drank a vermouth at the zinc counter in the building next door, wasted a lot of money in great haste.

* * *

Gare Montparnasse. The train to Brittany, at the front near the engine, in the sun, far beyond the station building. Alberta's friends travelled third class. Anyone travelling second was likely to be someone from home and therefore more or less under suspicion, people who came to Paris to rush through the Louvre, spend their days in the big stores and their nights at the Place Pigalle, stick their noses into Alberta's affairs and say stupid things about the French and about Paris.

Her friends had uncomfortable and inelegant luggage, packets of sandwiches and bottles of wine in the compartment with them, as did Liesel and Eliel now. Liesel's rug strap bristled with dangerous easel-legs, her canvases were everywhere in the way. And when Eliel put her travelling bag down on the step of the carriage the sound of glass that came from it made her open the bag quickly and with trepidation. Its contents were swimming in red wine.

With a sigh Liesel applied herself to picking out toilet articles, paintbrushes, rolls and ham in paper, all of it saturated and dripping with wine, while the stream of travellers parted on either side of her as if round a carrier of disease. Eliel assisted her, a little stiff and piqued.

Now they were inside the compartment, quarrelling loudly as to the practicality of having bottles in hand

73

luggage. Alberta could see them in there as flushed, bewildered shadows behind other passengers. Liesel span round and round in confusion, pointing up at the luggage racks, parleying about her canvases. It was not an easy matter to dispose of them. Eliel wiped his forehead, rearranged things, and stowed them away. He repeated at frequent intervals, and his French was even more clumsy than hers, 'One does not pack glass comme ça'. Liesel: 'It was for your sake. I was thinking of you. But never again . . .'

Alberta knew what would happen. Soon, within ten minutes at the most, Liesel would beg Eliel's pardon for being stupid and for losing her temper besides. And Eliel would say graciously 'Never mind', and lose his tense expression. But only if Liesel begged his pardon.

There she was in the window. 'My poor Alberta. The rest of us are leaving. You – you stay behind.'

Alberta shrugged her shoulders: 'It can't be helped.'

'But I'm glad you're moving into Eliel's studio. It's almost the country, Albertchen. You'll have six weeks completely to yourself out there. And there are *no* bugs.'

Other passengers jostled Liesel aside. Eliel pushed his way forward instead, calling through the hubbub: 'My clay, my dear Alberta, you will remember my clay – to dampen it I mean – the syringe . . .'

Liesel: 'The flowers, Albertchen – the cat, poor thing – the key is with Madame Lefranc . . .'

Eliel: 'The syringe is on the stand – the clay in the box must be dampened too – the water bucket . . .'

Alberta pulled herself up on to the step to hear better, but the train started to move, and she was lifted resolutely down again by a passing guard. Eliel reappeared for the last time: 'The water bucket is standing in the broom cupboard – Liesel asks you to remember the flowers.' He wiped his forehead. Behind him Liesel was smiling, exhausted and happy. Alberta nodded her understanding. They were gone.

Half stunned by heat, light and noise she watched the

long train glide past her. It was overflowing with passengers: middle-class families with children; people with painting equipment; peasants; here and there a priest or a nun who, undisturbed by their surroundings, fingered their rosaries and twitched an accompaniment; English, German, American tourists. It was going to the sea, to fresh air, clean water, an open sky, quietness; it left at midday, every day. When the summer in Paris reached the point when it was reminiscent of an unaired room, Alberta accompanied one group of friends after another to this train, this year as last year, as every year.

From the tracks, which are carried into the city between two streets on a level with the second floors of the houses, she could see in through the windows in the Rue de l'Arrivée. Everything there was grey with smoke from the station. On Liesel's balcony in the Hôtel des Indes a man was standing in his shirt-sleeves, brushing his trousers. Liesel's room had been rented out again already. A vision of blue sea and white sand, of lady's slipper, white clover and ragged grass waving in the wind, that rose in Alberta's mind every year at this precise spot, was projected for a second against the background of grey houses, then dissolved and disappeared. Her legs felt suddenly heavy, the walk into the shadow of the station too long. Her steps seemed to make no progress.

In the depressing flight of steps leading from the station down to the street, there was something that almost resembled a draught, in spite of the dead, stagnant heat. It rose up from below, sickening and impure, full of vapours, but crept upwards nevertheless bringing relief to her body, then over her face and neck, making the flounces round her low-cut dress flutter, lifting her skirts a little. People walked slowly here, taking their time. Alberta paused for a moment.

A stranger's breath on her neck, a bated '*Tu viens*?' close to her ear, made her turn round. A fat man, glistening with the heat and carrying a suitcase in each hand, was regarding her genially and with expectancy. She hurried down the steps.

The square outside lay like a desert landscape in the sun, barren, trackless, full of dangers. Across broken-up tram-lines, between heaps of sand and stones, Alberta gained the pavement on the other side, went into her hotel, began the ascent.

On the landings used sheets lay in heaps. Inside a door Jean could be seen manoeuvring his brush over the mantelpiece. He was humming his everlasting ' *Et le pauv' gas, quand vient le trépas . . .* '.

On the second floor Wolochinska's door was standing ajar. Alberta was about to swing past, but the opening widened suddenly, and Wolochinska stood there, tall and slender, in a kimono. Behind her on the table were travelling bags and toilet articles, on the floor a large trunk with painting equipment round it. It was clear that she was leaving.

' Mademoiselle Selmer – you can do nothing in this heat, in any case. Come in and have a cool drink with me. I was just thinking of ringing for one. Make yourself comfortable in here for a while. Look at me . . . '

Wolochinska smoothed a large, beautiful hand over her body. Her flat figure was clearly modelled under the thin material; large, embroidered storks clung about her. Alberta halted. She had a slight pang of conscience, because she had not been more friendly towards Wolochinska. One should be sorry for lonely people. At the same time she felt an instinctive uneasiness in the presence of this Polish woman, who showed her a persistent goodwill she neither understood nor returned. ' Are you leaving?' she asked and feigned astonishment.

' Yes, you know that. Come in for a moment.'

Alberta entered, ill at ease.

Wolochinska pushed a cigarette box towards her across the table. ' Sit down. Take a cigarette. What will you have, a vermouth, a grenadine? Thick with ice? What do you say to that?'

' Thank you,' attempted Alberta deprecatingly. ' I – I must go soon. There's something I have to do.'

' Always you have to go. Always. One would think it was a disease, a nervous disease.' Wolochinska laughed her forced laughter.

But Alberta found a little formula, which she thought quite felicitous. It was also true to a certain extent. ' I have to live,' she said.

Wolochinska's face altered. She looked at Alberta with a new expression in her eyes. ' Yes, yes of course. I am stupid and insensitive? Forgive me, my dear.' The large beautiful hand sought Alberta's across the table, she was forced to take it for an instant, felt that it wished to hold on to hers, withdrew her own and smoothed it over with a smile. ' It was nothing. I hope you have a pleasant summer – that it will be pleasant where you are going. It's Normandy, isn't it?'

' Seine – Inférieure. Near Fécamp.' Wolochinska's face had stiffened again, with that tense expression that Alberta did not know how to interpret. She felt she had seen it before in a completely different place, but could not remember whose it was or where. Wolochinska was staring above Alberta's head, and said as if lost in thought: ' So you will be staying here?'

' Yes.'

' Why?'

Alberta shrugged her shoulders. ' I always spend the summer in Paris, I . . . . ' She stopped. She did not wish to explain how impossible it was to strike out into the unknown when one's livelihood depended upon the pawnbroker. ' I love Paris,' she explained.

' In August too?'

' In August too.'

Wolochinska got to her feet, strode about the room, stopped, stubbed out her cigarette against the mantelpiece, and said without looking up: ' Come with me.'

She turned and looked intently at Alberta.

Alberta was also on her feet. ' It's impossible.'

77

'It is possible. It's entirely up to you. I invite you.'
Wolochinska continued to look at Alberta, who was feeling
thoroughly uncomfortable. This was so strange. Perhaps it
was Polish.

'You are very kind,' she began. 'But there can be no
question . . .'

'Listen to me,' said Wolochinska. 'I feel affection for
you, great affection. I am alone here, without friends. We
shall be completely independent out there. I hate *pensions*,
I have rented a little house and shall have someone to
look after me – after us. You will be able. to bathe, rest,
do just as you please, and I – I am a lonely person,
Mademoiselle Selmer.'

'Yes, I know,' said Alberta, confused by the perspective
thus unrolled before her eyes, at once frightened and
tempted as if in front of a trap with a titbit. Again she saw
Lady's slipper, the wide sky, white sand, everything she had
in the course of time come to connect with holidays away
from town. And the expression on Wolochinska's face was
suddenly helpless, almost forlorn, her mouth drooped and
looked destitute. 'Yes, I know,' said Alberta again to gain
time.

Then Wolochinska came straight towards her. Alberta
extended her hand, prepared for an understanding squeeze.
But Wolochinska did not take it. She gripped Alberta by
the shoulders, looking into her eyes with her hard, blue
gaze. There was just time for Alberta's discomfort to
change to anxiety – and then she was given a passionate,
imperative kiss full on the mouth. As if stung by a wasp
she drew her head away.

'Come with me, Mademoiselle!' Wolochinska tried to
seize her hands.

'I cannot, Mademoiselle. You are very kind, but – I
wish you a pleasant summer, I wish . . .' Alberta was
already in the doorway, something seemed to be suffocating
her. At the same time she thought feverishly: That wasn't
what she meant : . . it is I who . . .

Behind her she heard Wolochinska: 'Little ninny. Cold

78

little ninny from the North. What did you think? You have a nervous disease, Mademoiselle Selmer.'

Alberta reached her own door and shut it behind her. Her heart was pounding. She rubbed her lips with her handkerchief, remembering simultaneously who it was Wolochinska had resembled for an instant. A sailor on a quay once upon a time. Like a sudden glimpse from a great hidden common life the same feeling had lit up two quite different faces in quite different circumstances. ' But on that occasion I really wanted it too,' murmured Alberta to herself and became a little calmer. Fair's fair. ' And I can't stand anything like this,' she said aloud.

Although it was nearly three o'clock the bed was unmade, the slop-bucket full, the heavy air tinged with tobacco smoke. She felt sudden violent disgust for the life she led. It smells of old bachelors, she thought, and snuffed the air in her own room with repugnance.

' Jean!'

No answer.

' Jean!'

Jean appeared from the obscurity of the staircase.

' It's nearly three,' began Alberta, still out of breath after the episode downstairs. It relieved her to have something urgent to do.

Jean admitted that he knew it was. But he had unexpected guests on the first and second floors. He had hoped Mademoiselle would be out this evening, as Mademoiselle often was. He also pointed out that the heat was trying up here in the middle of the day. If Mademoiselle went out earlier. Mademoiselle got up late.

Alberta could not deny this. She stood on the landing in the half-light outside her door and acknowledged that it was all her own fault, while Jean plodded in and out with slop-bucket and water-can, shook the sheets through the staircase window, went over the floor with his swab, and the mantelshelf, table and chairs with his feather duster. She did get up late, it was one of the things on her conscience.

'Leave the flowers, Jean, if you please.'

'But they are wilting, Mademoiselle.'

'It doesn't matter.'

Jean shrugged his shoulders as if repudiating all responsibility, made a sweep round the peonies on the mantelpiece and had a final look round the room. 'I cannot see anything more that I can do for Mademoiselle for the time being.'

Then Alberta said, and the words seemed to come out of her mouth of their own accord: 'I shall be moving out tomorrow or the day after.'

Jean's eyes became round as saucers in his freckled face. He flushed slowly, until his whole face was red. Then he said severely: 'You can't do that, you have to give a month's notice.'

'I shall have to pay for the rest of the month.' Alberta felt her astonishment increase. 'Nobody can stop me from moving. I'm going to live at a friend's house to look after it while they're away ... I ... '

Here she was justifying herself to Jean. That was rather unreasonable. It became even more unreasonable. Jean said, his face dark and his voice upbraiding: 'And you never said a word.'

'I didn't know before. It happened suddenly – my friends decided at the last minute. And since I shan't be able to stay on here in any case – it's going to be altered, you told me so yourself.'

Jean lowered his eyes. He stood stroking the end of the bed with his duster, watching its movements. 'I know of an hotel on the Avenue du Maine,' he said, still not looking up. 'A pleasant little place, simple, without restrictions. The old lady will recommend me to the owner, she knows him. It's an establishment where you can make yourself comfortable, come and go and make your arrangements as you please. Not like this place. I thought perhaps it might suit you too.'

Jean looked up and stared straight in front of him. He had an expression that Alberta had seen before on other boys, on Jacob. That was how they looked when something had gone wrong, at once offended and distressed. ' *Enfin* – with things as they are . . . '

Alberta's thoughts jumped to the Avenue du Maine. She would have to live somewhere when Eliel came back. But she did not like the hotels there, they looked mouldy and airless, and the avenue was not at all pleasant in the evenings. She said: ' You could give me the address. It's kind of you to bother about me.'

Jean fished a printed card out of a battered wallet and handed it to her: *Maison meublée Chauchard, electricité, téléphone etc.* Alberta took it. ' Thank you.'

But Jean stayed where he was, stroking the end of the bed with his duster, and said reflectively: ' One could see you were a *demoiselle* . . . an . . . an educated person, more educated than oneself – one can see it from your books. But . . . ' Jean made a gesture with his duster, his speech became more resolute and seemed more outspoken. ' On the other hand, Mademoiselle lives like this, all alone. To speak frankly, you seem to me to be a young lady who has met with misfortune.'

' But other women have lived here alone,' answered Alberta, a little confused. ' The Americans, for instance, and Mademoiselle Wolochinska. I'm not the only one. We have not met with misfortune, we . . . ' She had the word ' work ' on her tongue, but changed her mind: ' We study.'

' The American ladies were two,' explained Jean. ' They were painters and getting on in years. Mademoiselle Wolochinska is also a painter, she is not young either. You are young, and you do nothing.'

Alberta flushed deeply. His last words cut her like whip-lashes. As if from a great height she seemed to glimpse how utterly inexplicable and unjustifiable a phenomenon she was.

' I am here to study French,' she said curtly.

' You know French. You speak it very well for a foreigner. You speak almost like one of us. Why should you want to learn more?'

81

' But . . . to teach.'

' In your own country, then?'

' Yes – in my own country,' answered Alberta in a low voice.

Jean was looking past her, up at the blue of the skylight. It seemed as if he was seeing it all out there, when he replied: ' At home we live in a village, Mademoiselle. We have a cow and a pig, we have earth, potatoes, cabbages, the sardine fishing. When it is warm and still, as it is today, I wish I were there. Today the sea is as white as milk in the sun – it's market day in Pont-Croix.'

' You are homesick?' asked Alberta.

' Homesick? No. But I want to go home again, certainly.' Jean's gaze returned from the blue of the skylight. He looked at the wall behind her and swayed from the knees as he lectured her about himself: ' When I had done my military service, I thought I ought to see Paris. Later I thought I ought to stay until I had saved up enough for a boat. In the old lady's time it was all right, she is a good woman, but the house has changed. It's no use any more for a country boy like me. Besides I've had enough of it. It's a filthy *métier* running up and down stairs like this emptying slops, I'm going to leave it to the Parisians. If I get that job on the Avenue du Maine I shall take it. But in a year I shall have enough for a share in a boat, that's always something.'

' Yes, of course,' said Alberta encouragingly, vaguely relieved at the turning the conversation had taken.

' After forty years as a fisherman you get a pension,' said Jean. ' From the state.'

' Oh, really?'

Jean nodded, staring across the floor. There was something he wanted to say, and he suddenly took the plunge: ' Well it's like this – sometimes I've thought, this young lady, she is always alone, it doesn't look as if it has come to anything with the other gentlemen – perhaps she would be happy with us in the country. She must have a little – she does nothing to earn her daily bread, at least not as far as I know. She is modest, content with little, clean. Cleanliness is something I appreciate. I have always thought that if I married, it would be to a clean person. Well – perhaps I have been mistaken.' Jean looked straight at the wall again, suddenly piqued, although Alberta had not said a word.

She stood confused, embarrassed, touched, angry, thinking: He can't mean it seriously, and at the same time she had an obscure feeling of reparation and rehabilitation, a feeling that one misunderstanding in some way cancels out another. A sensation similar to the one she had had in her childhood when they said to her: ' Think how thankful many people would be to have a dish of bread and milk ', passed through her mind. The vision of a white beach and tossing Lady's slipper in ragged grass, that had haunted her today, was there again, urgent and insistent.

But she saw imitation-leather sofas and china dogs too, although perhaps they possessed neither of them where Jean came from. She felt the atmosphere of disapproval that she, incompetent that she was, always created round herself. And straight in front of her were Jean's round eyes, his freckles and sandy hair, the eternally unbuttoned waistcoat.

' You'll soon get married to a girl from your own village.' Alberta attempted a little conviviality as best she could.

' Perhaps,' said Jean. ' One must have somebody.' He looked dissatisfied, at the last moment caught sight of a little island of dust lying on the mantelshelf, wandered over to it and wielded his duster. And he withdrew with a ceremonious ' Mademoiselle '.

Alberta was left standing. Today she could have gone to the country. She could not complain that opportunity had been lacking.

Pigs and cows, cabbages and potatoes, something secure to live on, a place to belong to that was not in Norway, that was, on the contrary, so incredibly distant from all that had gone before that perhaps nobody would ever hear of her again – it was ridiculous, but part of her reached out after it. In her position she ought perhaps to reconsider it before definitely breaking off negotiations.

If only Jean had looked like some of the men she had met at Marushka's. Or at Colarossi's, when she went to fetch Liesel. Proud conquerors in Spanish cloaks, buoyant Americans, who frequented the studios. Or the sailor on the quay, Cedolf, whom she had known many years ago.

Then there had never been any talk of pigs or cows or any other kind of settled existence. Cedolf, for instance, had taken advantage of a moment of weakness and kissed her without ceremony. He had kissed someone else at the next port of call. Cedolf was like that, all those who resembled him were like that.

But Jean was Jean. And she was too shabby-genteel. At home they called it ' fine '. Too restless as well, too afraid of plain sailing, monotony, any situation that lacked possibilities. And too incompetent. She would hang about, clumsy and in the way.

Suddenly a cluster of petals loosened and fell from the pink peonies on the mantelshelf, lying on top of each other like small turned-up childish hands. Mechanically Alberta began taking the pictures off the walls. She was going to move, she had better take steps to do so.

And once again she took apart the interior she had put together up here, building it up from the possibilities at hand. The death-mask of the young girl said to have drowned herself in the Seine, the photograph of Jacob in working clothes on deck taken by an itinerant photographer somewhere in South America, the Manet and Gauguin, Rembrandt and Van Gogh reproductions, all jumbled together just as they made an impression on her and were daringly acquired, the drawings by Eliel and Marushka, Liesel's colour sketch, the books in yellow jackets. Everything had had its carefully planned place, some of them had fulfilled double roles, having pleased the eye and hidden ugly patches of wallpaper, everything had appeared to advantage in the tranquil light from above. Even the strong lustre that the earthenware jug on the mantelpiece acquired in the middle of its belly at this time of day had played its part in the whole. That corner of the room became dead when Alberta now emptied it of wilting peonies and dried it.

It had been made for flowers, and flowers had filled it, from the first moist violets in February to the cheap glory of phlox, dahlias and sunflowers in late summer. Some of them she knew from her childhood. They had come into the house in connection with some festivity, or at Christmas time. Or they had flaunted themselves, few in number and prohibitive in cost, in the window of the Sisters Kremer's shop. In certain cases, such as the roses, they had been coaxed out with endless care indoors, the object of rivalry, envy, secretiveness. Mimosa one only read about in bad novels; it was as unreal as counts and countesses, as Monte Carlo and Lago Maggiore. One scarcely believed in their existence.

Here one bought them all in heaps from the barrows, getting an armful for fifty centimes. They had glowed as never before under the skylight, kindling a festive bonfire in the room. They did not last long up here under the roof; they faded quickly and the petals dropped for lack of air, from too much stagnant heat. But there was richness and extravagance too in the quiet decline of the flower petals, in their piling up on the glossy black marble shelf. Alberta never took them away until they had all fallen.

She sat down and looked round her at the moment of departure. Here an oil stove had stood. Madame Firmin had lent it to her the first winter. It had shone red and warm, awakening a desire to sit busy with something or other, and had driven old chills out of Alberta that she had carried in her body from the sunless rooms in the Rue Delambre and thereabouts, where the autumn damp stole into one like an incessant fever and remained until the spring was far advanced.

Once she had lain ill up here. Jean had come up from below with camomile tea and hot soup. Via Liesel the rumour spread of the comfort in which Alberta lived. The ancient bourgeois hotel was infiltrated by an inflammable and incorrect public, individuals with a fantastic cut to their cheap clothes, bearing milk bottles and damp packages, and keeping blackened spirit stoves on the washstand. But Liesel had not come. She already lived five francs cheaper.

The young Madame had come one day, and she could freeze out anybody she chose with her two cold, clear eyes, her unhurried inspection of one's person, her silent nod in the direction of the regulations on the walls. She had frozen her mother-in-law out to the small rooms facing the yard and her husband out to the doorstep, where he stood like a figure in an advertisement.

Later that afternoon, when her packing was almost done, somebody knocked at the door. It was Jean. He had the clean towels for the day over his arm and therefore had sufficient excuse. With his back to her he busied himself hanging them up, draping them meticulously on the rail. His back looked piqued. Alberta felt strongly the necessity for saying a few words, something friendly and cheerful. She tried in vain to find them.

Then Jean spoke, looking past her: ' *Enfin* – with things as they are, I went down to the old lady and said, " Mademoiselle has always been *comme il faut*, always paid on the nail, she is a lodger of long standing, it would not be more than reasonable were she to be excused paying for half the month ". It's abominable, let me tell you,' he suddenly flared up, looking directly at Alberta. ' In this house they are rich, *oh là, là.* And for Mademoiselle it means throwing money out of the window. It's not right.'

' But Jean . . . ' Alberta shrugged her shoulders, a habit she had acquired down here when something was inevitable and had to be endured.

' It wasn't worth the trouble. The poor old lady said: " In my time no-one would have made difficulties. I was reasonable, I got on well with people and took pleasure

86

in it, even when they lived up in the attic, but now it is over, my poor Jean ". That was what she said, Mademoiselle, " Now it is over, my poor Jean ". It is sad.' Jean looked accusingly at the wall.

' Thank you all the same. It was kind of you.'

' At your service, Mademoiselle.' Jean again looked piqued. He turned hither and thither a couple of times, as if searching for something. He lacked the feather duster with which to wave himself out. Out he came, however. His slippers could be heard for an instant going down the stairs.

At once Alberta felt terribly lonely. Her thoughts jumped experimentally over to the hotels on the Avenue du Maine.

❋ *Part Two* ❋

Alberta woke with a start, and sat up.

The first grey light was barely visible through the curtains drawn across the large windows. The trill of a bird could be heard outside. In one of her collar-bones there was a stabbing pain which throbbed in competition with her heart.

She lighted a candle and moved it searchingly above the sheets and blankets, lifted her pillow quickly, with an accustomed, competent movement. Then she moistened her finger and brought it down with an exultant cry on a flat, dark little disk the size of a lentil, took it to the wash-bowl and dropped it in. A couple more were already lying there kicking.

And she took a bottle from the chair beside the bed, poured some of its contents out into her hand and splashed it over her smarting collar-bone. The stinging liquid ran down over her breast and was sprinkled round her. A light, round fleck appeared on the blanket – and another.

The sprinkling of ammonia rose suffocatingly in the clammy air that filled Eliel's studio. Shapeless masses of clay, wrapped in wet cloths, made it heavy with raw vapour. Only one of the many window-panes could be opened.

Alberta lay down again, tried to forget and doze off, but failed. She lay looking out at the grey dawn that slowly filled the room. Her blood beat painfully and uneasily. The bird's trill outside had become a chorus, drowning preludes.

Eliel's mattress smelt musty. It was the one she had

helped him to find last winter, when he had just finished a large work, and that atmosphere of enthusiasm, emotion and fussy solicitude that an impecunious and awkward talent periodically rouses suddenly came into being round him. After two years in Paris Eliel owned nothing, apart from his modelling-stands and his clay, besides a basket chair with a hole in the seat, an iron bedstead with uneven legs, a bare divan, a table, a stool and a couple of cups. This state of affairs had given his circle of acquaintances a bad conscience.

In the corridor at Colarossi's, among the many notices about this and that pinned up by the artists, one had caught Alberta's eye about a used, but good mattress offered for sale cheaply in the house next door. She had had one of her sporadic attacks of pluck and initiative. It was as if she wanted to rehabilitate herself now and again in her own eyes, to accomplish something. Up breakneck steps, built on the outside wall of the house, she had betaken herself to the place in question and concluded the bargain in a sickening atmosphere of uncertainty and poorly concealed male banter. The owner had turned out to be owners, a band of Swedes and Norwegians living together. All of them were at home, sitting or lying, each in his lair, on a confusion of ramshackle beds and suspicious-looking divans, all of them with faces she recognized as having seen on Montparnasse. One of them removed the pipe from his mouth and got up from the object of the sale.

The journey out to Eliel's studio with a messenger and the mattress had been long and slow. A flush played over Liesel's pale face when the door opened. She had just begun sitting for Eliel. With her finger on the lid of the coffee-pot she stood leaning over his cup.

Then she clapped her hands and called out ' *Wunderbar*!' and explained that the thing would have to be beaten.

Under protest Eliel had beaten the mattress until sunset. The cloud of dust rose from it just as thick and unaltered. Over and over again he gave it as his opinion that it *was* clean, that Liesel and Alberta were crazy about dust. When darkness fell, and the dust could no longer be seen, merely sensed as a discomfort in the air about them, Liesel resigned herself. The mattress must have been stuffed with dust, they would have to put it in place. When Alberta saw it again it was covered with an ' Assyrian ' drapery that had cost eleven ninety-five in Lafayette's bargain department.

There were bugs in it. Liesel could say what she liked. But Alberta was lying on it for nothing. In this circumstance there was a certain balance that accorded with the laws of life and prevented her from complaining. At the Hôtel de l'Amirauté there had been mice, a species to be preferred. But it had cost her thirty-five francs a month to live there.

The dawn floated slowly down from above, releasing Eliel's sculptures from the darkness, making them stand out in relief. They stood there, a strangely troubled world of plaster beings, vainly trying to lift their heavy limbs towards each other. Among them were the bust of Liesel, slightly built with sloping shoulders, pouting mouth and stylized plaits, and the block of marble that had been so expensive and was to be Eliel's first sculpture in genuine material. A brass instrument of torture was stuck into it; it had bored a sharp hook right into one nipple, which was almost loosened from the block, and another hook into the navel. These two small forms had something spontaneous and alive about them, which differed from the rest of Eliel's work. Alberta could not help thinking about Liesel, and felt tortured every time she caught sight of the hooks in the marble.

The casts on the walls showed up in relief, all the attempts at human anatomy, arms and legs, hands and feet – the inevitable young girl from the Seine, the wounded Assyrian lion dragging its hind leg.

On the clay crate stood Eliel's primus, which he had brought with him from Sweden and of which he was proud. There had been a time when the vicinity of the primus had consisted of empty sardine tins and Eliel's coffee-cup, which he had taken out and rinsed under the tap in the yard every time he used it. In the quick course of time Liesel had succeeded in leaving her mark on her surroundings. On the wall there now hung three small saucepans neatly in a row. There was a kitchen cloth on a nail and a small shelf with cups and dishes. A couple of chequered cushions were placed on the divan. Eliel's books were arranged neatly at one end of the table between two round stones – all Liesel's work.

The birdsong outside was drowned by the other sounds of day. There was the rattle of the first tram-car; there was the whistle of a train above the Parc de Montsouris; there was the yawn of the man next door. Someone was drawing water at the tap outside.

A beautiful, calm light filled the studio from above. Eliel's cat, a young black and white tom, arched its back and stretched itself, climbed with dignity out of its box, went to the door, mewed . . . .

And Alberta had to get up.

Above the door the ivy hung in cascades; on it stood ELIEL in large, black, uneven lettering. Rumour had it that Eliel was also called Svensson, a name he must have left behind him somewhere *en route*. Now he was called Eliel; on letters, on leases, on pieces of sculpture, on Montparnasse. Eliel, the sculptor.

In small flower beds beneath the ivy Liesel had, as one might except, planted flowers: nightshade and snapdragon and the delicate white flower called 'The Painter's Despair'. Against the wall grew clusters of bittersweet with their small dark violet and flaming yellow corollas. It looked pretty, brightening the grey, rather gloomy walled passage that led to the studio and only caught the sun for a short period each day. Many of the people who came to draw water or visit the privy, which was situated at an angle to Eliel's door, paused to look at the display. They were men in shirt-sleeves, with bare legs and slippers on their feet, artists from the adjacent studios, and now and again a model with her coat slung loosely round her nakedness. A few of them expressed surprise that anything could grow in there in the shade. The studio lay behind a large block of flats and the remains of an old garden. There was a scent of box in the evenings. With a favourable current of air, drifts of scent came from the park as well. It was almost the country.

There was a painful time of day – the hour when it arches over and goes downwards again. It does not correspond to high noon, but occurs a couple of hours later. The sun left the passage, the ivy turned blue. That was the time. In the hotel room it had been when the lustre died on the belly of the earthenware jug. The room had at once become strangely threatening and desolate.

Yet again she had not come to terms with herself today; she had not come a step nearer those admirable, industrious souls who accomplish something. She had promised herself yesterday that something would happen. She had been going to scrape together some material and write an article, if nothing else, earn fifty kroner. Now the day was waning and she sat there, silent and obstinate inside, with five or six lines on the paper.

Alberta got up, lit a Maryland, stroked the cat, sat down again. Nothing was improved by these measures, nor by her taking out Jacob's photograph and looking at it for a while – the one taken on the deck of a ship.

He was thin, with one of those faces so spare that the small knots of muscle on each side of the mouth are exposed and become visible. There was something brave about them, something of the indefatigable, hardy wanderer through life. For the ninth year Jacob was living on the other side of the globe, in South America, Africa, Australia, a casual and hard-working life; at sea, down the mines, on farms, now and again in factories – and then at sea once more. There were times when he did not write for long periods, and others when he reported: I have a good job now and am saving money. I think I'll stay abroad for another year.

There was never very much more in the letters from Jacob. For years he had written: I think I'll stay for another year. Behind those words lay Jacob's dream: to save enough to buy land somewhere, preferably in Norway. It seemed to have petrified into a couple of sentences, which were no longer even correct Norwegian. Heaven knew how much of the dream remained?

But Jacob remained true to himself, taking no short cuts or avoiding ordinary honest labour. One day, in spite of everything, he would perhaps succeed in the task he had set himself, quite quietly, simply and straightforwardly. It would only have taken more time than he had expected.

However it was, Jacob was not rootless and restless, without purpose, without duties, living short-sightedly for the moment, keeping himself alive from one day to the next and doing nothing else besides; someone superfluous, who might as well disappear, and perhaps it would be quite a good thing if she did.

As if looking towards the end of a dark tunnel, Alberta could glimpse a final perspective. Someone with out-stretched hand stood at a corner – a bundle of rags was lying on a bench somewhere, under one of the arches of the Louvre, where there were always people sleeping at night. The bundle was herself, had been someone like herself, paralysed and confused by her own life.

She fled. She could go out and sit on the fortifications in the worn, trampled grey grass, looking out over the infinity of small allotments outside them. The sky was wide in this part of the city, with clouds drifting across it like heaps of enormous eiderdowns. Children played, mothers sat on the grass with their sewing, simple house-wives from the back streets. As the evening wore on couples arrived and lay down in the grass close together, speaking in low voices, biting straws. Flocks of sheep tripped past. In the still afternoon light, with a shepherd boy following them, and a dog, with the ringing of bells for vespers from churches in the distance vibrating in the air, and smoke from bonfires drifting in from the gardens outside, they seemed merely an innocent idyll; until suddenly one or more of them fell, stretched their legs in the air and their tongues in the dust, turned up their silly eyes and were roughly shifted out of the way and left lying. The slaughterhouse would have them. Dead or alive, they could be fetched later. Old, rebellious agonies of childhood rose impotently in Alberta, an anger as if she herself were suffering torture. There was nothing to do but go.

She wandered inwards towards the city, drawn along in the dusk by the crowd of people as though by a stream. The thudding sound of countless footsteps on the asphalt beat soothingly round her, life unfolded about her like a teeming, many-scented twilight flower, smelling of sweat and labour, exhaustion, frivolity, all desire. But something quietly shining also emerged: the feeling of human freedom, that grows out of an honest day's work. It appears in voices, in footsteps, in numerous small gestures, is inherent in the way a napkin is tucked underneath someone's chin, wine is poured into a glass, a newspaper is spread out. It excited Alberta, making her walk faster, as if that might help her.

Up from the Métro exit pressed the mass of humanity, compact as a crawling animal, and was divided, groaning, into sub-species. There was one especially for whom Alberta had a fellow-feeling, perhaps on account of her sessions with Mr. Digby – the one who had struggled through the day standing behind a counter. They seemed to have a weakness about the knees. It made her think of the cab-horses which with pendulous lips were driven round, seemingly supported by their harness and their speed. The inexorable demands of the day must similarly have kept this species on its feet.

Silently and speedily a mysterious element glided through the swarm; they came from backyards, suburbs, goodness knows where. The stocky fellow with pomaded

94

hair and his cap down over his eyes, the hatless girl with the hard face who came after him; the one with a hair style that would stand up to anything and stay neat through scuffles and love-making. They came with the darkness like the cats, and shared the stealthy silence of dangerous and nocturnal animals. Alphonsine called them suspicious types, and she did not exaggerate.

Now the flood was in full spate, carrying Alberta along with it. Almost before she realised it she was down at Montparnasse, in her old haunts, was washed up at the Cabmen's Rest, and found calm over a plate of onion soup.

Occasionally Alphonsine came.

She made herself comfortable on Eliel's divan, blew smoke-rings at Alberta, and studied her with her green eyes while the water boiled for tea.

The door out to the passage was open. The sharp, brief afternoon sun lay like a flaming puddle in Liesel's little flower bed, shining through the broad leaves of the night-shade, igniting the snapdragon like an intense flame against the brick wall behind them, making the grass border round them bright as an emerald. Alberta loved this short moment of the day; it made up for a good deal. And today, with tea and fruit on the table, with the blue smoke from their cigarettes drifting in beautiful whorls and with Alphonsine, in white with green earrings that matched the colour of her eyes, on the divan, it gave Alberta an intense sensation of lazy, sun-filled summer days. If it were not for the gusts that wafted from a certain place from time to time! They undeniably spoiled the atmosphere.

Alphonsine talked about her ' little artists ', about everything she was doing now in their absence. She was making herself dresses, was going to re-cover her divan, would spend a fortnight in the country with her friend.

' I'm not one of your little artists,' said Alberta. ' It was kind of you to come, Alphonsine.'

' I have a kind heart,' said Alphonsine simply. ' I

happened to think about you the other day, the little Norwegian girl. I said to my friend, she is alone this *demoiselle,* I shall go and see how she is.'

She stubbed out a cigarette against the table and said in a different tone of voice: 'I am fond of my little artists and their friends, I wish them all well, I would like everyone to be happy.' She smiled her conspiratorial smile and studied Alberta, who bent her head and stroked the cat in her lap.

' Are you happy, Alphonsine?' Alberta's question made her tremble a little. It had come out so brusquely.

Alphonsine meditated for an instant. ' I am not unhappy,' she said reflectively. ' And I was happy when I was young. What do you expect? One must not be ungrateful.' And she summed up her assets: ' I have my work, my friend who is kind to me, good health – that is much. I have had my sorrows like everyone else. My poor husband died, my child too. I was young, I had to live, I became a model, what else could I do? But *le bon Dieu* let me meet good people, I have never had reason to complain. My little artists have been charming, yes, all of them. And if I was bereaved sometimes, I also found comfort. One must be reasonable and not want the moon.'

Alberta said nothing. She felt a pang of bitterness: I don't want the moon.

' But still,' said Alphonsine. ' When I think that I too could have had a little child to go and look after in the country as so many others do – he was so sweet, my little baby, he was three weeks old, he was smiling already . . . '

She flicked ash off her cigarette and sighed. Alberta looked up sympathetically, but found nothing to say. Her understanding of the loss of a child was limited. There was something distant and foreign about the whole thing.

Alphonsine did not go into it either, but changed the subject. ' It is a beautiful thing to live only for one's work, one's ideals, but a woman is a woman. And as long as she meets the right man. Mademoiselle Liesel . . . '

Alberta pricked up her ears, but Alphonsine again

changed the subject: ' Men are big children, Mademoiselle. They are easily spoilt. And when they are spoilt they are insufferable – but there . . . '

There was a sudden crunching of footsteps in the passage. Alberta nodded towards the door of the privy. ' It's only someone going there. It's a nuisance having it here when so many people use it.'

But the steps went past the place in question and stopped outside. Someone knocked cautiously on the doorpost, a voice asked in Norwegian: ' Are you there, Frøken Selmer?'

'Værsaagod,' answered Alberta without enthusiasm. Come in, Ness.'

Sivert Ness reddened slightly when he caught sight of Alphonsine. Then he greeted her with country familiarity: Good day, Madame.'

' Monsieur.' Alphonsine's tone was dry. She flicked ash off her cigarette again, a gesture she sometimes employed as if to dissociate herself, to repudiate responsibility. She edged further along the divan and smoked with a distant expression, definitely apart.

Sivert Ness took a Maryland from the yellow packet Alberta pushed across the table, lit it, put it in the corner of his mouth, and asked whether she had heard from Eliel.

She had his blue, momentarily much too glittering eyes directed straight at her. She sensed a loneliness as great as her own behind his visit, the hunger for human society that can be damned up inside one in Paris in the summer, when one cannot speak the language and all one's acquaintances are away – a hunger perhaps for female company too. She was used to Ness's occasional appearances, to his sitting there, as if defying everything, a little short, but square and thickset, a black lock of hair falling over his forehead, and eyes that did not seem to suit the rest of him – they were too pale and looked up with a sudden darting movement. There was something familiar in his little gleam of sly triumph which could suddenly wedge itself up from beneath much honest, simple uncertainty. Strength, and an

97

obstinate will lived behind much else in them and dared to believe in itself now and then. Perhaps she imagined it all. He was the only other Norwegian she ever saw.

To atone for her curtness she asked about his work, what he was doing, if he was not going to the country this year either.

' The country! I'm thankful I'm here at all. Besides, one can get out of the city now and again. To St. Cloud, Meudon, down the Seine.' His eyes held Alberta's for a second. ' It's refreshing to take a boat trip in the heat.'

What the tenacious eyes had meant and wanted on previous occasions had been uncertain. These at any rate wanted company on possible excursions. Perhaps also help in buying shirts at the Bon Marché, in abusing his concierge, in getting something translated, in obtaining French lessons. Here she was again, sitting with someone whose eyes forced themselves on her. But she would not be looked at in this way, with a glance that in its uncertainty yet had certainty behind it. She was not the kind they could get to do this, that and the other, those who did not dare set their sights higher; she was not the unassuming, suitable girl they had had the good fortune to run into, those who did not dare to dream audaciously. It was her fate to be encumbered with them.

This one was not really shy, on the contrary, he was only unfamiliar with things, a little unpolished, a little afraid of rowing out farther than the boat would carry him. He had more of the persevering leech about him than Grønneberg at home, more masculinity too.

On closer scrutiny there was a fearful strength in his hands. They were tranquil, staying in one place, never moving without a purpose. Sivert Ness did not pick at his sleeves, he had no nervous gestures. It was said on Montparnasse that he had talent. Provisionally he was accorded sympathy for his industry, his poverty, his home-made clothes, his ignorance of so much. But he was not like Eliel, who submerged himself in his wretchedness until somebody did something about it. Sivert managed somehow, in fact he was very capable of doing so when it was necessary. Self-denial came to him naturally and as a matter of course.

One must never feel that a man is touching. Alberta knew this from many years' experience. They interpret it in one way only. Then you are left, either ridiculous or encumbered.

'Another cup of tea?' she said, acting the hostess. She wanted to get away from the Seine and St. Cloud, having no desire to go to these places with him.

'Thank you very much.' Ness had really only intended to look in and get Eliel's address – he took out a notebook and a pencil – 'But if Frøken Selmer has another cup, then . . .'

He drank with his elbows resting on his knees. It looked as if he was sitting on a wooden crate in the kitchen, thought Alberta, and was in spite of herself a little touched at the simplicity of this. Finally he revolved the cup to get at the rest of the sugar, and her feelings became even more disturbed, as feelings can be in dreams, where they stream in and out uncontrolled. There had been something in Sivert's manner just then of the poor boy who must manage as best he can, of the toiler who sits down for a moment to rest – of Jacob. Yes, perhaps Jacob too sat like this, worker that he was, far away in strange countries.

But Sivert put the cup down, wiped his mouth, looked up, straightened himself, and the disturbance in Alberta subsided at once. She decidedly did not like his eyes.

Unasked, Sivert announced that he had finished the picture of the Rue Vercingétorix, the one with the four catalpa trees round a – well, a little house with posters on it, which was perhaps not worth mentioning. Would Alberta like to come in and look at it one day? He intended to try to get it into the State Exhibition at home this autumn, it would have to be sent soon.

'Thank you very much.' Alberta ignored the question. She hastened to suggest that it must be terribly distracting to stand like that painting in the middle of the street?

' Distracting? Yes, I suppose so, of course.' It seemed as if Sivert had not given a moment's thought to this aspect of it and now brought it up out of his mind for consideration. He smiled, sat leaning forward again with his elbows on his knees and looked away across the floor: ' The children at home were worse.' He remembered a time when they had hidden behind a stone wall, ten or twelve of them, and thrown burrs at himself and the picture. Well – it didn't happen again – for once he smacked his tranquil hands together, linking the fingers hard. And again Alberta had a vague impression of strength keeping silent and waiting, achieving its aim simply by being there, even though Sivert most certainly had not kept silent and waited on the occasion in question. A chill crept over her at the sight, she actually felt a little afraid of those hands. *Huff*, she thought.

Then she shook it off; after all, they were nothing whatever to do with her. She mentioned Liesel, from whom she had heard, all the time side-stepping a question that Sivert had asked as if by chance – ' Are they staying at the same place, Eliel and Frøken Liesel?' – talking about things Liesel was busy with there, a market scene with peasants.

Sivert smiled again. ' Women,' he said.

Alberta made no reply.

' But isn't it just like a woman to want to do something like that?' persisted Sivert, his eyes glittering.

' What do you know about it?' And yet again Sivert did not row out farther than the boat would carry him. ' No, no, that may be so,' he smirked.

A little later he asked, and now he seemed to have come to the point: ' Don't you find it lonely out here?'

But Alberta had changed since that first summer, when the loneliness had almost taken her breath away and she had allowed people to approach her, merely because they were people, and had had cause to regret it. With assurance, a tone too high, she replied that it was wonderful to be alone, she loved it.

There was a glitter again in Sivert's eyes as if of disbelief.

as if he had caught her out lying. He was insufferable.
Immediately afterwards he took his leave and went.

Alberta politely accompanied him to the door, and closed
it. The sun had gone, someone was going to the privy,
there was no reason to keep it open any longer. She turned
and met Alphonsine's green eyes. Alphonsine shook her
head energetically: 'Not that one, Mademoiselle.'

'But Alphonsine!'

'A specimen like that. They do not have two sous, but
to Paris they must come. They must have models, and
love, free models and free love. But both cost money here
on Montparnasse. Only the foreign *demoiselles* are naïve
enough . . .'

'Alphonsine.'

'A fellow like that needs you, I can see that. But when
you are worn out with standing for him and sitting for him,
going hungry and cold with him and perhaps submitting
yourself to all sorts of things for his and his art's sake, he
will become successful one day, and then you can pack
your bags. I've seen it happen, I've seen it happen many
times. I am old, as you know.' Alphonsine smiled, tired
and omniscient.

'But Alphonsine, I shouldn't dream of having him.
Besides, there's no question of – he's a fellow-countryman,
after all! We are Norwegians and acquainted, that's all
there is to it.'

'He wants you,' answered Alphonsine drily. 'And that
is dangerous enough, *ma petite. Attention* – it is Alphonsine
who tells you so.'

Alberta suddenly laughed out loud: 'What nonsense!
There's no danger of that, I assure you.'

'Very well, all the better.' Alphonsine flicked ash off her
cigarette. 'It looks to me as if he has something up his
sleeve, that fellow.'

*　*　*

A hundred in the shade.

The asphalt was like over-heated metal, the air out in

the sun a burning helmet. The trees died, curling up their leaves in a last painful spasm, and letting them fall. Alberta felt she knew how the roots in the tiny round patch of soil allocated to each of them sought vainly in all directions after escape and salvation.

Horses collapsed, humans too. Every day the newspapers reported many cases of prostration. The half-naked labourers engaged in the inevitable summer road repairs were reminiscent of penal colonies in the tropics, of atrocities and merciless torture. Their eyes looked dead under their straw hats, the sweat streamed off them. But their brown torsos were bronze against the dark corduroy trousers and the flaming-red scarves that held them in place. The invincible Sivert was sure to be out painting them.

In the Seine the fish floated belly upwards, dying in their thousands in the thick, slimy water, which stank of rottenness and chlorine. When Alberta crossed the bridges in the evenings on her horse-bus ride, her body pressed up against the weak, scarcely noticeable draught made by their speed, she saw them and listened to the other passengers discussing them and the possibility of epidemics. They could be brought about by less.

In front of the small shops and the house doors chairs were dragged out, forming a continuous chain through the city. Low-voiced, almost silent people sat out there, thousands upon thousands of people of small means, their faces pallid from the heat and the still air. On the benches under the singed trees there was not an empty seat. Working folk ate their supper there, tearing at their long loaves with their teeth and drinking their wine straight from the bottle.

Alberta was seized by uncomfortable longing. She was suddenly reminded of the slap of water against the piles of a jetty, long, shining breakers, the smell of salt water and the newly-ebbed tide; of sitting in the prow of a boat on a night of sunshine, turned away from the others, one hand in the water, watching the smooth, cool shape of the displaced water round the boat, the shoal of coalfish leaping

102

like silver-fish in the sun, boats further off, the oars at rest, with gold in their wake and accordions in the prow.

Or she remembered how the air had tasted sometimes when one went out of doors. Mild air with the thaw in it; air in transition, just as the cold was about to set in. It lay sparkling on the tongue, fresh and mild as water.

She pitched home again, the streets were quieter. Small stumps of conversation reached her from the pavement, settling in her mind like a sediment composed of other lives. A mother's: ' If only you had finished your soup – people who don't finish their soup . . . '. An elderly man's: ' It's the fault of the Government. France is governed by idiots. If only we had another Government . . . '. A young woman's angry ' Nothing doing tonight, *mon ami*. I shall turn my back on you, and serve you right.'

At intervals a flutter of relief seemed to go through the atmosphere, like the last gasps of a sea animal on land. From the Pont Neuf she could see the moon rising in the south-west over Charenton, a red, drunken, crazy August moon.

When she finally alighted from the tram-car at Porte d'Orléans and walked home along the fortifications it was sailing high above the roofs and the silent treetops, shining, yellow, in the company of a small star.

It was a fortnight since Alberta had spoken to a soul besides the *épicier* and the concierge. With them she discussed the temperature, agricultural prospects, their children's and grandchildren's conditions, endeavours and expectations, the occasional newspaper scandal, the behaviour of the cat, the dog and the canary since yesterday, and the blunders of the Government, which Alberta did not understand and on which she commented in the dark. Whereupon it was over for the day. The studios round her were deserted. No-one came any longer to the water-tap and remarked on the flowers.

With the window and door open, naked, her kimono slung across a chair-back within reach, she sat in Eliel's

103

broken basket chair with one of his books and a Maryland, got up now and then, poured water over herself and sat down again. The air in the room was stationary, an evil-smelling mass. The large clay sculpture in its cloths was stinking. It caught at the throat as one came in.

The cat, too, rose occasionally from its favourite position on one of the stands, stretched itself, walked round itself a couple of times and lay down again. Or it went to its saucer on the floor, where the milk quickly turned sour.

It was an effort to go out when evening came. A kind of fear of doing so began to creep over her. But she knew it of old, knew it must not get the upper hand. And she went; a little dizzy and uncertain to begin with, a little wry in the face. She sat on a bench in the Parc de Montsouris.

This was where the summer found sanctuary. Heavy and dark with maturity the trees and bushes trailed their foliage on the ground. The twilight was scented, people sat silent on the benches. A late bird flew home, the first bat flitted soundlessly past. Arc-lamps were lighted here and there, hidden behind the enormous crowns of the chestnut trees, casting large circles of greenish light over the lawns. Someone ought to have danced in that light, fauns and nymphs, the Russian ballet.

Occasionally someone would whisper, ' Are you alone, Mademoiselle?' She would reply politely and evasively, and betake herself in a little while to another part of the park.

Alberta's limbs became as cool as marble in the heat: if she put her hand into the neck of her low-cut dress her shoulder was as cold and smooth as polished stone. But it opened up sores in her mind. She came home to the stinking studio, and suddenly tears misted her eyes and she hid her face in her hands.

And the night took its course: a torturing confusion of waking dreams; a series of painful, insecure sojourns in mysterious border regions with an occasional violent, brutal jerk back to reality, splashing ammonia on stinging collar-bones, feverishly writing on scraps of paper that were thrown unread into the trunk; a painful awakening as if from the dead when the cat mewed to be let out.

There was something she should have experienced, something besides this. There was a path somewhere that she could not find. It was and it was not her own fault.

' The ignorant man watches every night, anxious about many things. He is exhausted when morning breaks, but his sorrow is the same as before.'

His sorrow is the same as before. It was written in the *Edda*, in Eliel's copy between the stones on the table. An old truth, therefore.

On a day of the same stagnant heat Alberta opened, from a sense of duty, Eliel's large, zinc-lined clay crate. Averting her face to avoid the sight of the wood-lice scurrying in all directions inside it, she manoeuvred the unwieldy syringe and rearranged the clammy cloths that were lying over the clay. Then steps approached along the gravel path and went past the privy. Ness, thought Alberta. Thank heaven the door's shut and I've got some clothes on. It might have been worse.

Someone knocked. She answered : ' Who's there?' At once the door opened, and Alberta jumped up, dropping the cloth and drawing her flimsy garment closer about her, uselessly folding her arms, and stood as if paralysed with her legs pressed together while her flush engulfed her mercilessly. She felt utterly at a loss just as in the old days at home, while the thought pounded inside her : How shall I move? I can't move.

' Er-huh, what are you doing? What's that dreadful stuff in the crate?'

It was the Dane with spectacles standing in the doorway, not Ness. To Ness she could have said a few curt phrases : Wait outside – come again later – it's not convenient just now. What was she to say to this one? Tall enough to block the sun out, he stood there with his hat in his hand, mopping his forehead with his handkerchief. His shoulder-padding was awry, his spectacles caught a green reflection from the big window at the far end of the studio. If he was a vision, an optical illusion, he was at any rate fully equipped. In great confusion she heard herself explain: ' It's clay.'

' Is it? It looks unappetizing, I must say. But I know nothing about that sort of thing. Listen, have I come at a fearfully inconvenient time?'

Now something seemed to have got locked in him as well. He said, stammering. ' You must tell me if you would prefer me to go – I . . . I . . . ' Then he interrupted himself: ' But it would not be very kind of you to let me go immediately in this heat. I'm almost dead.'

Alberta looked up, met a smile under the spectacles and found unexpected composure: ' I was about to change my dress – would you mind waiting outside –and taking a chair with you?'

' Will you come with me out of town somewhere or other afterwards? On a boat down the Seine or something like that?'

Alberta considered for a fraction of a second. Then she said: ' Yes, I'd like to.' Great relief welled up in her at once, as if she were about to be liberated from prison.

She stood immovably, while he tactfully possessed himself of the nearest stool and disappeared with it. Behind the closed door Alberta rummaged nervously amongst her two dresses, although in view of the temperature only one of them was remotely suitable – the sleeveless one.

* * *

' Have you considered staying here for good?'

The question, apparently casual, fell a little to one side of the conversation, and Alberta felt her old defensive mechanisms at the ready. Consider? She had considered nothing. Does one consider that kind of thing? One crawls up on to dry land somewhere and awaits the next possibility. She had had to escape, and she escaped here. She answered with her usual curt ' I don't know '.

' You've spent a good many summers here?'

' Seven, including this one.'

' And you've never been away?'

' No, never.'

' But why not? There's so much that's beautiful to be seen elsewhere in this wonderful country. Is it your work that prevents you?'

' I don't work,' answered Alberta with embarrassment. This was an awkward moment of half-truths and empty replies behind which to conceal herself. One leads whatever existence one can; hers was not worth displaying. As a rule she did not invite anyone to examine it either. It passed on Montparnasse, but it was not suitable for well-brought up people from orderly circumstances. Nevertheles, here sat one of them tampering with it. It was her own fault. She should never have come.

' Oh, don't you? I understood Eliel to say you wrote for the newspapers?'

' No, far from it.'

' I must have misunderstood him then. Never mind – but surely one can do nothing in the country as well?'

Nothing . . . . For an instant Alberta was about to answer irritably. Someone or other was always cropping up, finding her sore points and prodding them. She controlled herself, thinking: If the worst comes to the worst I shall have to give Ness a few lessons. Casually she answered: ' I have a couple of pupils.'

' Oh, have you? In French? Well, that's work. And teaching, I certainly know about that. And these pupils, don't they go away either?'

' No,' answered Alberta.

' Listen, you mustn't be annoyed. You are quite right, I ought to mind my own business. It's just that I think you're looking pale. And then this fearful heat, and the air in the city. It can't be good for you to stay here summer after summer.'

' But if I prefer to stay,' said Alberta, mollified but

depressed by this complete stranger's thoughtfulness for her person.

The stranger looked at her speculatively through his spectacles. He was sitting with his back to the light, his elbows on the table and one muscular, sunburnt hand resting on it. When they were not concealed by reflections his eyes were grey, observant, now and again a little distant as if in meditation. His face was decidedly irregular. It was difficult to deduce anything from it besides the fact that it was clean-shaven, tanned and bony, with a broken nose. His name was Veigaard, an ordinary name, that seemed to go in at one ear and out of the other. Combined with what he gradually revealed about himself, the total impression was one of somebody keeping in step, somebody from the ranks of the admirable, the irreproachable. She might wish she resembled them, but she was not on good terms with them.

Behind him, dark leaves and branches formed a rich pattern against the grey-green water of the Seine; in front of him on the cloth were two half-emptied wine glasses, coffee-cups. Capricious blue coils of smoke from a pipe and a cigarette rose up; he waved them away from time to time as if in impatience. They were at Bas Meudon, at a small restaurant on the very edge of the river, one of those that base their trade on fried river-fish.

Alberta, however, sat illuminated by the evening sun which shone in on her through the branches. It was one of her misfortunes that she always found herself in a bright light when others were protected by shadow. Since childhood she had had a compulsion, never entirely overcome, to hide her face and her person, and this cropped up periodically from its repressed condition. Involuntarily she held her head askew, so that the profile in which her squint could least be seen caught most of the light. She was a past master in being sensible of its play over her features.

' You're a strangely stubborn little girl, I must say. So you're here all by yourself? All your friends are away, are they not? Fru Marushka and Frøken Liesel and the

American lady, what was her name? Potter. And the Norwegian painter?'

'Ness? He's not in the country.'

'Indeed, so he's here? Hm – and of course there's the Russian opera singer.'

Alberta's colour rose with sudden fierceness, throbbing in her ear-lobes. 'I don't know him – he was only passing through.'

'Come, I didn't mean it seriously. And you must not think I was not concerned for you that evening at Fru Marushka's. The man ought to have been kicked out. But Eliel asked me not to interfere. I couldn't help being a little amused, though; he certainly didn't get anywhere, it looked so funny. Now don't get annoyed with me again. A lout like that. Has Fru Marushka many friends of that calibre?'

'One or two,' said Alberta and bravely met the spectacles for an instant. She saw a hint of amusement in them and was a little confused by it.

It was the kind of conversation that is kept going with some trouble, thanks to one of the parties. It drags itself heavily along the ground, refusing to take off and gather speed, so that the words may lure each other along. Altogether Alberta regretted the whole enterprise, although she was sitting carefree at table and had chosen the restaurant herself. An old awkwardness crept over her, an invincible inner stubbornness.

She had not brought out anything more about herself. But a couple of remarks had been unavoidable. Then the speculative eyes had looked even more speculative. Alberta had occasionally done a right-about turn as if in front of a dangerous fence which she had decided at the last moment not to take, hastily entrenching herself behind the language, her alibi in situations such as this. She could not help thinking how much more pleasant it would have been to sit here with Rasmussen. But of course that would have been out of the question; they had bought waffles at St. Cloud, their debaucheries had never amounted to more.

Occasionally the conversation fell to the ground completely. The pipe puffed on the other side of the table, it was poked and picked at, tapped out and filled afresh, the eyes above it becoming distant as if occupied with something else. But they returned. And the voice resumed with new courage, broaching quite different topics: It was warm in the country, but it was nothing by comparison with Paris. Of course everyone had warned him against coming back again at this time of year, but it had been impossible to work out there; the house was full of guests from morning to night. Then there had been this room, which a French student had put at his disposal for a fortnight. It was in such a pleasant spot, next to the Luxembourg Gardens and near the museum. He could look down into the Gardens – but there... 'And you never feel homesick?' attempted the voice again.

'Never,' Alberta assured him callously. Again she met his eyes for an instant. It seemed unavoidable, even necessary in order to vindicate her words. The pipe puffed several times.

The Seine below them became more lively towards dusk. Crowded steamers called at the quay, there was a hum of voices, singing and laughter. Rowing-boats slid past beneath the branches hanging out over the water, and an occasional canoe, manoeuvred by half-naked rowers. The little garden of the café filled up. With every boat more guests arrived and were packed together like sardines, while pleasantries were exchanged between the tables. Bombarded with good advice on all sides as to how it should be done, the proprietor climbed on and off chairs, lighting the paper lanterns festooned between the trees. They made a fantastic glow against the light evening sky, the treetops darkened to silhouettes, laughter rang out, it was no longer possible to be sure from which direction it came, the air was warm, pure, full of scents. 'Let's have some more wine,' suggested Veigaard.

The frankness and compulsion to examine oneself and one's life in detail which steals over people sooner or later when they sit on a bench in a French open air restaurant, had suddenly come upon him. They find everything falling into perspective, they check their accounts and sum them up. He leaned forward across the table, puffing at his pipe, and explained that Paris was *the* city to work in, there was no doubt about it. He must spend a year or two down here, finish writing his thesis, learn the language, get on intimate terms with the French mentality which was and always would be the salt of the earth. But he had to pay back his study loan and had other obligations as well. He had thought it over and decided he'd have to hold out a little longer at home, drudge along with the boys – yes, he taught at a school in Horsens, and gave private tuition in mathematics besides. It was by no means dull, boys were never dull, whatever else they might be, it was just that he would like a little time for himself. But there – he would probably get it one day.

Alberta listened to it all with polite attention, putting in a yes or a no now and again. Academic degrees were referred to in the course of the conversation, he also mentioned his subject in passing, the structure of pure thought. Alberta saw lines and squares in the air for a moment, and failed to connect anything with it.

He began to talk about his sister, who was married to a businessman down here, a Swede dealing in timber and pulp. They were doing well, had a large apartment on the Avenue du Roule, a country place in Calvados, an automobile, two lovely children. ' But there – of course she is well off in many respects ... ' Veigaard paused and rummaged in his pipe with his penknife.

Alberta registered that there was something the matter with his sister. She looked as interested as she could and said : ' Really?'

A melody suddenly awoke out in the dusk, played on a single violin, a waltz of the kind that break out all over Paris, are on everyone's lips for a while, and die away again, displaced by a new one. ' My word, he plays well,' said Veigaard. ' He has a good instrument too.' Alberta

111

wisely kept silent. She did not know how to talk about music. As a rule it was in some way fateful for her, passing into her blood like an animating or dissolving stream, making her sad or almost uncontrollably merry so that she had to resort to silence so as not to misbehave, causing her to see visions. Another waltz came out of the darkness. The little garden roared with applause.

A young man came into the uncertain light from the lanterns, and went from table to table, hat in hand. Veigaard put a two-franc piece in the hat, and thanked him for the music, expressing his appreciation in his awkward French and extending his hand to take the violin, holding it with care, giving it back again with a smile and a nod. The musician smiled too, introspectively and with melancholy. He remained standing at Veigaard's and Alberta's table, and played, as if directed at them, one of Chopin's nocturnes. In the brief silence that followed he wrapped his violin in a kerchief and disappeared, silent as a shadow, thin and pale, gaunt inside his clothes, while the applause roared up behind him, apparently too late and to no purpose.

To Alberta it seemed as if the undertow of the great world outside was seizing her. Hunger submerged her, flooding mysteriously and confusingly like an intoxication through her veins. With boundless emotion, a warmth that could carry her with it into any situation, she heard herself speaking hurriedly for a moment without knowing what she was saying. And when Veigaard looked after the violinist and said: ' But all the same, how sad it is!' new warmth flamed up in her at these ordinary words, something resembling tremendous gratitude.

From now on a conversation was brought into being across the table. Alberta felt her listening to be different, her brief, half-finished comments to be alive, woven into coherence. She told him something about herself too, something highly irrelevant besides. It was not quite clear how she embarked on it. It was about sensations she had had when she left home, the naïve feeling of having at last

112

thrown herself out into the effervescence of life, that had gripped her already on board the boat. It was comic to think of it now.

' Come – I don't think so,' said the understanding man on the other side of the table.

She had arrived in Trondheim in the evening. It was already dark, and raining, the cobblestones glittered wet in the lamplight along the quay. The cabs had their hoods up.

There had been something in the sound of the horses' hooves against the cobbles, in the clatter of the wheels up along the riverside that, more than the large houses and the many lights, had struck Alberta as continental, a part of the teeming world. They had no cobblestones anywhere in her small home town. It had been fearfully naïve.

' Yes, but quite natural. That was the way you should have felt. And then ... you came down here?'

' I spent a winter in Kristiania.'

' Eliel said both your parents had died. And almost simultaneously.'

' It was an accident,' answered Alberta. She side-stepped it and said something quickly about the necessity of going abroad, one could not stay at home for ever. But she had liked the tone of Veigaard's question. There had been no hint of intrusive sympathy, no attempt to probe; it had been refreshingly matter of fact.

On the other hand she now sat listening to her own voice, as if it were acting on its own account. It was talking somewhere up in the air in front of her, like someone else's. I must be a little drunk, she thought, appalled. What am I saying? Thank heaven this is a fleeting acquaintance, someone who will perhaps be mentioned somewhere or other several years from now, and of whom one says: Good Lord, I'm sure I met him once, now I come to think of it.

Herr Veigaard's face had become quite indistinct. Only a pale orange-coloured light fell on it from a dying lantern directly above his head. But his pipe glowed now and again. After a while the inadequately lighted face said: Why are you so quiet?'

113

' Am I quiet?'

' Yes. But now you're beginning to feel thoroughly tired.'

' Perhaps so,' said Alberta. And at once she felt all the fresh air she had breathed and the wine she had drunk like a compelling weight in her body and her limbs. She could have put her head down on the table and fallen asleep.

' We'd better see about getting home again. *Skaal,* and thank you for coming. It was sweet of you. But it was a good idea of Eliel's too, to write and tell me you were living out there. Otherwise I shouldn't have known a soul it would have been no fun at all.'

He accompanied her as far as Montparnasse, where Alberta took the tram-car. Veigaard repeated how pleased he was to be living on this side of the Seine. It wasn't at all comfortable to live as he had done the last time.

' It was too genteel,' said Alberta sleepily and knowledgeably. ' Precisely,' answered the Danish voice, as delighted as if she had found the solution to vital problems. A little astonished she looked up into the two spectacle lenses, which reflected the lamplight and hid his expression. ' Thank you! Thank you for coming!' said the voice again, rising from the first thank you up to the second. ' And *au revoir,*' it said, and went down again.

Even more astonished, Alberta pressed the hand held out to her, thanking him in turn. Once inside the tram-car she sank down inert. In bed at last, she fell asleep, for once, immediately.

* * *

The days undeniably held something new. Alberta admitted it to herself, if not earlier, then certainly on the morning she lied in Ness's teeth in order to keep the afternoon free for her new acquaintance. Before she would simply have said no, she did not wish to. Now she piled up untruths and covered up her tracks after her.

114

Ness had cropped up again tanned and looking as if burnt solid and indestructible by the heat and his work out of doors in the sun. He was handsome in his peasant way, and would have looked almost like a gipsy if it had not been for his eyes which were too pale, too china-blue. Blue eyes can be beautiful with black hair, but in Ness they were all wrong.

He wanted to go out of town to paint, but he was not very familiar with the surroundings. Could not Frøken Selmer show him some good motifs? They could take their food with them and have a picnic. In the woods somewhere?

Alberta assured him that she was engaged. Visitors from home. She recommended to him Charenton, Vincennes, knowing that wherever else she might be going, it would not at any rate be in that direction. Had he never been out that way? It was exceedingly picturesque.

When he left she felt a little sorry for his back, and could afford to be. It looked lonely.

And she rummaged amongst her dresses, again decided on the sleeveless one, and went out, perspiring with heat, to the Luxembourg or the Parc de Montsouris. Or she prepared the tea-table with the door open to the passage. Fifty kroner for an article, which she had long ago ceased to expect, had fallen like manna from heaven. She could entertain in style with good tea, good cigarettes, flowers on the table. It was a quiet period where the door of the privy was concerned, which also made for a certain festivity, a circumstance of which Herr Veigaard was, however, completely unaware.

Besides, he never sat down for long. He emptied his teacup quickly and was ready to go, out of the city or over to one of the parks; was, in fact, far from having a due sense of appreciation of the occasion. Alberta sometimes felt a little put out by this, a shadow of resentment on behalf of all good-for-nothings. She had put a cushion in the broken chair, nobody could see that there was a hole in it, nor feel it if they sat down. All in all, she had done her

115

best. But in such matters one noticed clearly where the frontier went.

In fact, shadows would pass through her memory. She remembered a ball to which she had gone that winter in Kristiania, at the home of one of cousin Lydia's friends who, to the general rapture, had invited Alberta, even though Lydia was married and had left home. A most unusual kindness therefore.

It had been held in large, high-ceilinged, rather empty rooms somewhere to the west of town. Alberta had sat out a great deal. She knew no-one and was a complete outsider. But occasionally someone would come and present himself.

Then she asked herself, as she circled with them, silent and stiff: Why did he do this? Was it out of pity or because he could find nothing better to do for the moment? The thought was not new, she had brought it with her from the Civic Balls at home. There in Kristiania it was presented in its extreme form, there no-one had any obligation towards her.

It was still with her. It reared up like a dragon when Veigaard remarked casually one day: 'We're like two people washed up on a desert island, aren't we?'

They can do nothing else but cling together – the thought was painfully insistent. Alberta did not show it, merely nodded and laughed a little. In the last resort of course that was what it was; all this bespectacled person from another world wanted of her was company on the island. As far as she could see he managed very well in other respects, wandering round churches and museums in the early morning ' before the asphalt begins to fry the soles of your feet ', then sitting over his studies at home, over in the Luxembourg Gardens, or in libraries, finding his own way everywhere with his halting French. He had told her that he was not going to set foot in the big stores; he had been there with his sister, it was dreadful.

The position was not without its difficulties. It was no longer a secret that Alberta did not have a single pupil. ' Well now, and what about these pupils of yours?'

Veigaard had said the second day they were out together. 'When do you have them? In the mornings perhaps?' He looked at her with amusement, puffing at his pipe. And Alberta, completely taken by surprise, blushed flaming red. She, a past master in defensive measures, had forgotten to include her pupils in her time-table. This fact, not the lie itself, embarrassed her. There was nothing for it but to laugh and give in, saying airily that oh, it didn't matter about them just at the moment.

Veigaard laughed too. 'Oh, indeed!' he said. A little later it came, however: 'But that you should simply hang about here like this – I don't understand it.'

Even the temperature led to the discussion of personal matters. Alberta and Veigaard sat a great deal, on chairs, on benches, in small cafés, all over the place. And they could not sit as dumb as fish. Neither could they talk endlessly about what they saw, had seen, intended to see. And Alberta could not say much about her experiences before Veigaard had found a thread to pull. And pull he did, speculating, puffing at his pipe, amused, then quickly turning serious again. 'Indeed, so you have . . . so you are . . . so you are used to . . . ' he insisted. He wound up the threads too, he remembered things, and, mathematician that he was, he put two and two together and made four out of them without difficulty. Since the matter of the pupils Alberta's standing had become quite insecure. Again and again she had had to abandon her position and search for entrenchments further back in time. A not inconsiderable portion of her casual and good-for-nothing existence in hotel after hotel, without aim or purpose, had already been wound up. Sometimes she said: 'I'm afraid it will get back home.' 'No, no, no – you know I'm not that sort of person,' said Veigaard.

He was not entirely irreproachable himself. He had a divorced wife at home in Horsens. He spoke of her as if he had a guilty conscience. 'Such a shame – a sweet, good little girl really – but it was a childhood engagement, and they don't turn out well as a rule, one grows up so very different. I take much of the blame for it, I should have known better. But there – she's young, she could be happy in quite different circumstances, if only the old people at home would stop trying to patch it all up again, but that sort of thing is the breath of life to them. Sometimes you just feel like running away from it all.'

Oh do you? thought Alberta, feeling almost rehabilitated at the thought that people with orderly lives could have those kinds of feelings. She surprised herself wondering what this man looked like when he was not sunburnt. A wan teacher, probably. There was no risk of her falling in love with him at any rate, not with a teacher in spectacles, living in a Scandinavian country. All her instinct for self-preservation rose against it, and present circumstances seemed to preclude such an eventuality absolutely.

One afternoon Alberta went over to Neuilly with him, to his sister's home. He had left some books there when he was last in town. Now it appeared that he needed them. No-one was home, but the concierge had the key.

It was in a large, silent house with red carpets on white marble staircases and a concierge in black, similar to Mr. Digby's. She inspected Alberta from top to toe and informed them in a tone implying that she washed her hands of them, that a couple of the servants happened to be in town: Joseph and the cook. All Monsieur had to do was ring.

Alberta thought better of it and hesitated. If there were people in the apartment it was a different matter, she would not fit in there. But Veigaard persuaded her: 'Of course you must come in. They are a charming couple, married; they've been with my brother-in-law for years, and I think they'd go through fire and water for him. They're the type of old French servant you don't find anywhere else. And you'll see how my sister lives.'

This decided Alberta. This sister, married to a kind and distinguished man who was far too old for her, who was loaded with comforts, but was not allowed to move so much as a flowerpot in the well-arranged bachelor home into which she had moved, was not without interest. Once Veigaard had let slip a nasty expression: Old man's love. He had tried to cover it up again, but what's said is said. Alberta felt she had peeped inside the troll's mountain.

Joseph opened the door. He had a round, placid face, covered with tiny, superficial wrinkles, which contracted jovially at the sight of Veigaard, but smoothed out into worried, slightly dismayed gravity, when it appeared that Alberta was a member of the expedition. It looked as if some friendly remark he was about to make suddenly withered and died on his lips. He went before them, however, showing the way into a large, dim room, where subdued light fell in stripes, threw back the shutters and opened the windows. When he left, Alberta sensed that he did not quite shut the door behind him.

Veigaard had already disappeared into his room. Alberta sat in a heavy Louis-Quatorze armchair, feeling utterly out of place. In her faded, sleeveless, rather too low-cut dress, her home-made hat and her sandals, she contrasted strongly with the furniture in royal styles, the battle scenes in heavy frames on the walls, the collection of old china in show-cases, and much else. Above all, with Joseph. Through the open windows she could see an iron railing. Beyond it the leaves of a plane tree moved lazily in an almost impercep-tible breeze, which died again immediately. The smell of good food mingled with the room's atmosphere of stale air and polish; it had followed Joseph. She felt that she was under surveillance, and jumped when a large golden-bronze time-piece suddenly began to strike six clear, vibrating strokes, as if to emphasize that this was going too far. Her instinct for flight was aroused.

But there was Veigaard with the books under his arm, suspecting nothing, naturally, just like a man. And just like a man, he had an absolutely desperate idea: ' What a good smell. Oh – she makes wonderful food. We'll get her to serve us a splendid little dinner. There may not be very

119

much of it, but what there is will at any rate be excellent, I can guarantee you that.'

' No, thank you very much,' cried Alberta deprecatingly. But Veigaard was already at the door: ' Joseph!'

Past him Alberta could see a dining-room which, with its dimensions, its dimness, its weighty baroque, strengthened even further her resolve to get away.

They negotiated in low voices through the door. Veigaard racked his brains arduously in French. Joseph replied with terrible correctitude and a shade of chill regret: ' We were not prepared for guests, Monsieur – Monsieur can surely understand . . . .'

' But you can find something surely,' insisted Veigaard. ' We don't mind waiting. Marie-Catherine prepares such wonderful food – *très bon* . . . .'

' Impossible, Monsieur.' The undertone of distress in Joseph's voice at what had taken place was the last straw for Alberta. ' I don't want anything, I want to go,' she said curtly and loudly.

The tall figure at the door turned, hitching up his trousers, which he wore belted in summer: ' I'm awfully sorry, but he won't do it. I don't understand what's the matter with them today. They are usually so ready to please, nothing is ever good enough. I went out to the kitchen to say good-bye to Marie-Catherine – she too was not her usual self.'

' Come along, let's go.'

' If only I could explain myself properly. The whole thing must be a pure misunderstanding.'

' Is this the way?' asked Alberta, wishing to initiate the retreat.

' Yes. No! We'll go another way, so that he won't have to see us out. I'm so annoyed, I'd prefer not to see him again. Come this way.'

They wandered through rooms in which all the shutters were closed. Weak light fell in horizontal stripes. Alberta saw dimly collections of furniture under dust-sheets, glimpses of gilding, chandeliers in tarlatan bags, mountains

120

of bric-à-brac. Somewhere the light caught a prism, was broken, shimmered softly and trembled, rainbow coloured, surrounded by the dimness. The floor was soft and deep underfoot.

Old repressed antipathy stirred in her. She had a rooted fear of rooms full of objects. They weighed one down and held one there, exerting force and discipline. Anyone married to all this was truly to be pitied.

She stumbled against a table and hurt herself. Something on the table tottered, but was saved at the last moment by Veigaard: ' Careful! Did you hurt yourself? It's a bit too full in here – like a bric-à-brac and antique shop. But there are beautiful old things amongst them. It's a pity everything is covered, it might have amused you to see . . . '

' Oh no, thank you.'

` There we are, here's the hall. Now let's go quite quietly and we shall have given him the slip. But there – he doesn't mean any harm . . . .'

They were almost out of the door and were about to draw it to after them, when Joseph suddenly appeared. Consternation and sorrow were written in his obliging face, as he uttered in a low voice, as if confidentially and exclusively to Veigaard, his own and Marie-Catherine's regrets. They regretted, they regretted eternally. Would that Monsieur would understand! Their only desire was to be of service. But if Monsieur wished to receive guests up here, would Monsieur then be so kind as to announce it earlier, and – Joseph's tone became almost pleading – to the master himself? If, on the other hand, Monsieur wished to live here for a few days, there was nothing to prevent him doing so; he and Marie-Catherine would be here until Wednesday, they desired nothing more than to oblige Monsieur . . . .

' What is he talking about?' asked Veigaard. ' I don't understand the half of it.'

Alberta prevailed upon herself to act as go-between and explain. ' Oh, what a lot of nonsense,' said Veigaard angrily.

121

Such hair-splitting. Tell him to go to the devil. And he'll be hearing from my sister and brother-in-law.'

Alberta reported the final sentence to Joseph. He listened without looking at her: ' *Bien, Mademoiselle.*'

She ran down the marble stairs with the red carpet, heard Veigaard explaining behind her that by Jove he couldn't make out what was the matter with the fellow, felt the enquiring eyes of the concierge at her back, and at last found herself in the street again.

The evening sun was low in the west. The plane trees drooped with every leaf and every flap of bark. The shade, which a short while ago had lain in deep pools beneath them on the pavement, crept tall and thin up the walls of the houses. Farther in above Paris hung the compact sky that a scorching day leaves behind it. The air seemed filled with golden dust.

Alberta walked quickly, irritated by the whole situation, trying to walk it off. She should have known better than to get mixed up in this, the whole thing was all her own fault.

Veigaard, however, had not finished with it: ' How extremely annoying. What on earth was the matter with them?'

' You can't improvise a dinner at short notice,' suggested Alberta.

' Food? Fiddlesticks! Of course they had a house full of food, they have plenty of everything. If I know them, they had at least a whole chicken out there in the pot.'

Alberta gave up replying and simply concentrated on walking. At Porte Maillot Veigaard insisted on having something to drink. 'I am both thirsty and furious,' he explained. And they sat down somewhere in the dust and the noise, in the used breath of the city, as it is spewed out in the evening along the big highways as if through ventilators, thick with petrol and vapour.

Still Veigaard had not finished. Somewhat mollified he said: ' It must be a misunderstanding. They are excellent people really.'

Alberta was tired of the whole question. She shrugged her shoulders: 'Yes, that's precisely why. They were right. They were defending the house they serve. They thought I came from the street.'

The words had fallen out of her mouth, a little indifferently and flippantly, a little too nakedly. One does not say things like that to respectable people from Scandinavia. Now the expression hung in the air, out of place and oppressive. She thought: When I occasionally do speak the truth, I always say the wrong thing. I ought to hold my tongue.

'You're joking, aren't you?' The spectacles were turned towards her enquiringly for a moment, giving her the impression that they did not find the joke appropriate. She tried to gloss it over: 'I mean that we from Montparnasse - we foreigners – here in these *quartiers* where they are not used to us ...'

Silence. Several puffs from the pipe. It was knocked out hard against a chair-leg, scraped inside, harshly and punitively handled, as if it belonged to the guilty party. Then he said angrily: 'I can't stand hearing you say such brutal things. It – it doesn't suit you at all. Oh – but God knows there are a great many things I can't stand, Alberta. Yes, I'm sorry, but sometimes I want to scold you like ...'

'Like the boys at home,' came provocatively from Alberta. She looked straight into the spectacles.

'Yes, like the boys. Oh – I know perfectly well you don't do anything really wrong. But you hang about here scamping life. Yes, *scamping* it. What sort of an existence is it? You don't paint, you don't write, you don't do an earthly thing. If things haven't gone wrong yet, they may do so. There are some people who hang about here just drifting, do you want to become one of them?'

Alberta winced, she saw clearly for an instant the bundles of rags lying on benches. Then she said, and she felt her forehead flushing with defiance: 'That's not what we were talking about.'

'That may be so, we are talking about it now.'

123

' What is " wrong "? Where does right end and wrong begin? Hasn't everyone the right to do what he pleases with himself? Is it wrong that I work as a model? That I earn my daily bread as best I can?'

At once she wanted to bite off her tongue. Why should she have said that? *Epater les bourgeois,* was that what she wanted to do? If so, she had failed. Veigaard did not look at all shocked. He said more calmly than before, lighting his pipe: ' That too? I'm not surprised. Not in the slightest. It fits in excellently with the rest of it.'

Alberta sat silent for a while. Astonished she surveyed this stranger, with whom she was suddenly on such good terms that they were quarrelling about her most sensitive points, and by whom she was in fact being scolded. Here she sat without defending herself.

A moment later she noticed something new in Veigaard's manner of looking at her, with quick little side-glances down over her dress and up at her hat, speculatively puffing at his pipe.

A strange and unaccustomed little sensation as if of power stirred deep in her mind.

*   *   *

' So Kristiania didn't turn out to be quite as you had expected?'

' Expected?' Alberta smiled a little wryly. How could she explain how it had been to a person like Veigaard? A stinging gust of narrow circumstances, of endless struggle to overcome fresh obstacles, arose from what he occasionally said about himself. He had given coaching, and yet more coaching, from before he matriculated and right through examination after examination, and still had some way to go in the same fashion. He and Alberta might be compared to a skilful, persevering swimmer and a hen fallen in the water. Things that for her were insurmountable obstacles, air in which she could not breathe, would seem

124

silly trifles, childish excuses for idleness, to someone like him.

They were sitting in the grass in the Allé des Marmousets at Versailles. Between them on a cloth were the remains of a meal. If Alberta craned her neck she could see the top of the enormous living green wall behind her disappearing into the slope up by the Palace. It was still warm in the sunlight. But from down below the shadow, blue and indolent, crept upwards at an angle, giving everything dimension, a liberating breadth.

The park satisfied a yearning derived from her childhood for masses of foliage and summer richness, abundance of sun and shade, warmth, scents and fruition. With the same avidity as on the first day she absorbed the spicy perfume of box and roses, the taste of hay and running water, that flowed in from the spacious countryside roundabout, the sheltered tranquillity of it all.

Now Veigaard's question awakened old, tarnished memories. She saw the grey-brown, sooty, trampled snow lying used and shallow along the pavement, shabby tumbledown façades, low decayed fences, the whole scene inexpressibly dirty and mean; remembered a strange light-shunning Sunday stillness, closed milk shops with three lonely bottles of Bavarian beer on display in the window, and one in particular that used to be open. Her mind hard and shrivelled, she stood defiantly outside and became absorbed in its poverty. Besides the three beer bottles it displayed a dish of palely baked cakes, a cardboard box with liquorice pipes in it, another with small champagne bottles made of pink sugar. The bell above the door rang from time to time, a customer slipped in or out, guiltily carrying a cream jug.

There had been something sly and suspicious about everything and everyone in these parts of town on a Sunday. The few people who went in and out of the filthy doorways gave the impression that they never emerged except when the city was desolate and abandoned. They hurried in and out, rounding the corners quickly as if afraid of being seen. Even the solitary dogs, who bustled, sniffing, in and out of the doorways, lifting their hind legs, did not do so in the same confident and officious manner as elsewhere.

The junction of Munkedam's Way and Engen Street, the small streets leading up from the West Station; all the young people were streaming up to the woods. Alberta had neither ski equipment nor friends. At home in Park Street sat Uncle and Aunt expecting visitors. In order to avoid them and to get some exercise, she had gone out. A desire to dive as deep down into ugliness as possible, since she had nothing else to dive into, had driven her down here.

The height – or the depth – was reached by going down the revolting steps between what was known as 'the bazaars', up to or down from Victoria Terrace. There was a stink of urine on the landings, great gobbets of spittle lay on the steps. Here there was no white, untouched snow or crystal-clear winter air, only filth and degradation.

Only one thing was more degrading, more tormenting: to *walk* up into the woods with Uncle and Aunt, slowly in galoshes like an old person, while youngsters on skis and toboggans swarmed everywhere; to be amongst those who halted circumspectly at the side of the road to stand and watch if someone came whizzing past. Her whole being, body and soul, felt mortified. A feeling of ignominy overcame her, undeserved and more bitter than she could bear. Better Engen Street instead.

One day when she was walking up the hill with them, attired in galoshes, a skier coming at full speed down the track leading from the Corkscrew slope suddenly swung round and stopped, came back, bounding on his skis and calling out to Frøken Selmer, and introduced himself to Uncle and Aunt. It was Frederick Lossius, an acquaintance she had made a couple of years ago in North Norway. He had heard that Alberta was down here, was happy to run into her, and so forth. Would she come out tobogganing with him one evening? Or skiing in the woods one Sunday?

Alberta said no thank you, she had no equipment. It was true. She had given away her old, worn skis with

126

the bamboo bindings to one of the poor boys from Rivermouth when she left home. She could not have appeared on them in the south, nor in her ski suit. She had supposed in her recklessness that life was going to be different.

Oh, but she would have to get equipment in any case, insisted Lossius. 'You can't live *here* without sports equipment, it's quite unthinkable.'

Aunt had interrupted: Alberta's plans were uncertain for the moment, nothing quite settled, best to wait for a little before making any purchases. Thank you very much, Mr. Lossius.

He took his leave and continued down to town. He had only meant to be kind. If he was unsuccessful, then it didn't matter, and good-bye. But for Aunt it was yet another occasion for emphasizing that Alberta would have need of every *øre*, whatever she decided to do: commercial college, cookery school or arts and crafts. There were so many things one would like to have, but .... that young Lossius was said to be a fearful radical. You could see that. Distressing for his parents – nice people.

'Where were you then? You haven't answered my question. Never mind – I can guess.'

It was Veigaard. He was lying on his stomach in the grass, leaning on his elbows, without hat or spectacles. The flesh round his eyes twitched nervously now and again, as it does in people who strain their sight. Then there would be a sudden gleam in them and his look would sharpen; it could be directed at Alberta almost piercingly at times. And again the strange little sensation of power would stir. deep inside her. She was actually something of a problem to this man. It was not entirely unpleasing suddenly to say things which made him puff at his pipe, to say, for instance, as if *en passant*: 'That was the hotel where I found an aesthete standing in the middle of the room one dark night.'

'An aesthete?' he puffed the pipe, at once disorientated.

'Yes, one of those fellows from all over the globe who hang about here. If you ask them whether they write, paint

127

or sculpt they answer, a little evasively, that they are aesthetes. Just like that. This one was Hungarian. I had forgotten to lock my door.'

' Hm.'

Usually that would be all. Alberta had only been scolded on that one occasion at the Porte Maillot. There was a little excitement in it just the same, rather like daring to go out on thin ice. It might break.

But fearful notions could occur to her. Just as now when Veigaard was lying there passing his slender, muscular hand through his hair, which was a little long and tended to fall over his forehead, a gesture he often employed, and a highly unmotivated desire came over Alberta to take his head in her hands and lay it in her lap. She was flooded with quite unwarranted pity for it. It was as if there were a double substratum to her personality, or perhaps several. Full of contradictions, she wanted and did not want. It was as well that irreproachable persons, with their emotions in order, could not see inside her.

It was late in the afternoon. People were leaving the park. Mothers with handwork folded up their small campstools, called playing children to them and trooped off, patiently carrying dolls and small buckets, spades and skipping-ropes and teddy bears. From the Hôtel des Reservoirs came the clink of crockery and slamming of cutlery, from the villas beyond the strumming of pianos and laughter of children, fragments of conversation, the thump of croquet mallets, all the pleasant small sounds of summer.

' How did you find out you were interested in French?' The grey eyes looked searchingly at Alberta, and she reflected, attempting to grope her way back to the vague ideas that had become decisive for her at that time. It had not just been Paris with all the promise contained in that short, bright name, it had been something else as well: roots that sought new and completely foreign soil, the hints, the anticipation, the scintillation that arose out of the little she knew of the country, and out of every word in the useless sentences she had learned at school: 'The cherry trees of my uncle are more numerous than the apple trees of my aunt'. 'The house of my cousin is larger than that of my brother'.

'This is where one wants to come,' she said. And Veigaard was satisfied with this profundity: 'Yes, of course it is.'

But Alberta suddenly felt communicative: at the end of that winter Aunt Marianne had invited her to Grimstad.

She came to a steep, stony little town composed of small white houses with red roofs, to the last remnant of the South Norwegian winter, to a hint of spring; evenings with a green sky behind the dark silhouettes of houses and trees, the beginnings of birdsong in the woods. The roofs did not drip, nowhere did the water go above one's galoshes, there had after all been very little snow. The landscape lay, not white, but brown, yellow and grey under the glass-clear spring sky in which a marvellously large star would blaze out and the moon hung like a sickle with a dark circle inside. An altogether new and foreign spring. And suddenly one evening something wonderful, something she had never experienced before: the flight of grey geese.

Aunt Marianne was small and thin, almost transparent, not at all as Alberta had imagined her. She had looked perplexed and anxious when Alberta decided on Paris, chafed her two thin little hands together and said: 'But alone, my child? Alone? In my time it would have been absolutely unthinkable.'

Then she must have asked Doctor Kvam for advice. He was a white-haired old gentleman who was a frequent visitor, a friend and contemporary from her youth. At any rate it was from him that salvation came, suddenly and unexpectedly. He thumped on the floor one day with his stick: 'If you're to go abroad, you must go when you're young. Let the little girl leave. The sooner the better. Times have changed, Marianne.' And he and Aunt conspired together, wrote to Uncle in Kristiania, moved heaven and earth.

Alberta was given presents, kind people subscribed, old friends of Mama and Papa, suddenly emergent distant relations, mobilized by Doctor Kvam. She left with a respectable sum of money sufficient for a year's stay. It had been kind, terribly kind, nobody was obliged to do it. Alberta was filled with the uneasy joy that results from that kind of thing. When she thanked Doctor Kvam he had slapped her on the back: ' God be with you, my child. Greet the Pont Neuf from an old Parisian.' Now he and Aunt Marianne were both dead.

Alberta fell silent. Again she felt the acrid after-taste left by gifts of money. Such gifts resemble stringent medicine; you are forced to accept them if you are to get on your feet. But they leave a paralysed spot, a dead place in the mind where nothing will grow.

Veigaard got to his feet. As if concluding his train of thought he said : ' You had to go abroad. You had to come here. But you must see about getting more out of it than you are doing. Now let's go and have coffee at that little place you told me about, down by the canal.'

They watched the sun set from the terrace of the Palace, sitting between scattered, silent or quiet-voiced people, while the Palace stood on its head in the fountains, golden-green from the vanishing day. Above the elaborately clipped trees in the beds below them the shadow crept victoriously forward. The angelus bell rang from the chapel, the scent of box was interlaced with stock and heliotrope and the breath of the meadows outside. Far off in the deep perspective above the canal hung a rusty sky, tarnished with soot and piled-up heat, splintered by an occasional distant flash of lightning.

.There would be no storm. It would come perhaps tomorrow, perhaps another day. The metallic clouds thickened, gathering into layers; above them rose enormous eiderdowns, tinted with the distant, vanished flush of sunset.

' How pleasant and fresh it is now,' said Veigaard. ' Shall

we go for a short walk along the canal before they close? And round by the circular fountain? You remember, the one where the water is coloured by the patina of the central figure. We'd have time for that, don't you think?'

Yes, Alberta thought so.

The park was teeming with night-life. Crickets sang round them, the grass and foliage rustled quietly, small dreaming birds gave an occasional pipe, and the scents were strong in the twilight. A young frog jumped out of Alberta's way, she jumped herself, both of them stopped to look at each other. A small, velvet-brown body, that stretches itself to leap and collects itself together again to sit; black eyes like pearls, intelligent, intently observant; a slightly deformed, minute person, a mysterious little fellow-wanderer on the turning earth, belonging to the evening and the forest.

Veigaard suddenly started to talk about his childhood. He recognized the sound of gravel underfoot in darkness under trees, remembered how, as a small child, he had driven home with his parents from a party on just such a warm, dusky night in August. He was sleepy, nodding on his mother's knee. But when the carriage entered an avenue, he awoke. The gravel had sounded different beneath the wheels under the trees, different from the day-time, deeper, more secretive. He must have been quite small, he remembered no more than that.

'That's how one does remember,' said Alberta. In her, too, pictures streamed up from the depths of her mind, memories of a large garden, of flowers. She saw small, round, sulphur-yellow roses, a tall tree with a broad crown in the middle of a courtyard. A walnut tree. It must have been in Flekkefjord, which she had visited once when she was quite small.

'I say, where are we exactly? And what was that we heard a while ago? That rolling of drums in the distance? Surely it wasn't ... ?'

'Oh, heavens,' exclaimed Alberta. 'The park's closed.'

Her heart turned over. She was the guide, she was responsible. She stood and looked about her, but saw only the darkness of the forest rising upwards, mysterious walls of trees stretching to the sky; a hint of light up there, an even weaker one on the path beneath their feet.

'By Jove, we must hurry,' said Veigaard vehemently. 'Are you sure of the way?'

Sure? The earth sank beneath her, she attempted to consider the possibilities. There was no way out through the Palace any more. They had walked along the canal, round the arm of the enormous cross of water it forms at the Grand Trianon, continued along it, turned into a side-path at an angle, come out into a large avenue and left it again. They had walked quickly, stimulated by the evening air, seized by the thwarted need for exercise that piles up during heat-waves. She had been listening to what Veigaard was saying, and had not paid very much attention to . . .

Everything was so terribly big too, the distances so enormous. Now in the darkness it engulfed them as sea and darkness had done at home sometimes, an enormity reducing one to nothing.

We must try to get out through one of the side entrances. The Palace is closed. God, let it be this way!

Beside her she heard Veigaard: 'Come, at least let me take your arm. It's as black as pitch. Then we must put our best foot forward. Whatever next!' He was not in a good temper. His voice seemed to be keeping his feelings under control.

The darkness thickened round them. Alberta assured him that of course it must be this way. She purposely ignored his question as to whether she had been in this part of the park before, repeating that, as far as she could tell, they would come out at the Trianon. If she remembered rightly, there were watchmen's houses there; they would have to knock.

And indeed, it was getting lighter in front of them. They suddenly found themselves out in a large, circular clearing.

132

From it avenues, black with night, led in all directions back into the darkness. Veigaard counted them. ' Seven,' he said. ' I make it seven. Can you decide which is the right one?' Alberta looked around her desperately. All seven of them seemed to be constructed out of obscurity.

She stood hesitating. Then the truth had to come out. ' I don't know where we are,' she admitted.

' This is a nice kettle of fish. But there – I had my suspicions. When does the moon rise?'

' Late tonight. Towards morning sometime.'

Alberta really did feel like the boys he scolded, and like the eternally ill-fated person she was. ' I'm exceedingly sorry – it's all my fault, I . . . we must try, it's not fenced in everywhere.'

' Oh, we're equally to blame,' said Veigaard curtly.

Inertia crept over her. If they had come out on the Trianon side they would not have been far from town. Now it was impossible to tell where they were. They might walk and walk for a long time without finding a house. Even if they got out of the park, it would be like trotting haphazardly round France. She felt dead tired at the very thought; like a criminal awaiting judgment too. If only Veigaard would say something. There he stood, coal-black and silent.

' Does nobody live inside the park?'

' There's a house somewhere near the canal. I don't know whether anyone lives there. If only I knew which direction it was.'

Fresh silence, then curt, cold words out of the darkness. ' There's only one thing to be done, wait until dawn. I can smell hay somewhere close by. We shall have to pack you down in that. The night is warm, so you shouldn't take harm, it could have been worse. Now just wait a little.'

She heard him pushing through branches, then a thud, as if he had jumped over a ditch, and grumbling. And she allowed herself to be taken by the arm and led away, acquiescent as if under arrest. ' I am more upset on your account,' she managed to say.

133

' Oh, I expect I shall survive. Just as I thought, here are some big haystacks. Be careful, there's a ditch here. Let me help you.'

' But I don't want to sleep,' attempted Alberta.

' The dew is falling heavily already. Down in the hay it's dry. Now then, down you go. We're not having any colds and that sort of thing.'

Oh – woman is in truth man's burden. Alberta felt it clearly at this moment. Had Veigaard not had her to drag along with him, he would have walked until he came to a house, and slept there, satisfied. Now he was burdened with a being who could not be expected to hold out for any length of time, who might catch cold, and so on; who, besides, was the cause of these developments, and whom his sense of honour forbade him simply to leave. Miserably she waited, while he pulled and rummaged in the hay, making a kind of nest for her. If only he would speak, but no. ' Thank you very much,' she muttered, when he laid a great armful of hay over her and roughly packed it together. ' Now try to get a bit of sleep; you must be up at first light,' came curtly out of the darkness.

There she lay looking up at the sky. Little black clouds were drifting about between the stars. The treetops stood mysterious and enormous against it, swaying gently now and then. Warm streams of air lapped her face, full of the scents of all kinds of flowers, sweet and bitter mingled. The crickets chirped as if for dear life. It sounded as if someone was incessantly shaking a large box of needles.

Sleep? She wasn't going to sleep. If she had dared, she would have talked to drown all her embarrassment in chatter. She heard a match being torn off, heard the small puffs of the pipe being lit. ' How are you over there? Are you at all comfortable? I can't tell you how sorry I am about this,' she attempted apologetically.

' Will you try to get to sleep,' came the severe reply. And Alberta fell silent, not daring to say more. Suddenly she yawned. A drowsiness that she remembered from her childhood and never experienced in her adult life came over her, comfortable and overwhelming.

She woke suddenly. High above the treetops sailed the moon in infinity, the moon of her childhood, shining and yellow.

Small, thick clouds drifted past, quenching the yellow of its light before reaching it, green as tarnished silver when they were right in front. When her eyes followed them she seemed to be sailing herself in a soft, scented cloud. It smelt of hay.

There was Charles's Wain, unnaturally large, apparently alone in the sky. It had been overturned, and was lying with the chariot-spokes sticking upwards, like a toy left by a child. There stood the enormous formations of the trees, coal-black against a colourless sky, against the grey, silent depths of space. Now the treetops caught a metallic half-light, midway between silver and gold – now they were melted, dissolved and made unreal by the moonlight. Now and again a murmur went through the wood, was drawn along close to the ground, then rose upwards and was released in quiet rocking. The night was like a dark material wrapped about her, saturated with extract of all that grows. Somewhere close by, a cricket was almost shrieking.

A sudden notion that perhaps she was dead and beyond the grave occurred to Alberta. No – she was on earth, more on earth than ever before, deeply and wonderfully united with all its life.

Something moved close to her, hay was drawn over her and tucked in. A hand, quickly withdrawn, moved over her cheek. A sweet sigh of recognition went through her, she was taken back to a time long, long ago when someone else had tucked her in. She had been woken by it, had felt safe and happy, and had fallen asleep again.

She was cold. The dampness was creeping up her, involuntarily she made a movement so as to get further under the hay. Then the attentive hand was there again,

135

tucking it up under her chin and round her shoulders. She looked up for his face, it was already gone. The sky above her was greying with something which was neither light nor darkness. A deep cooing came from somewhere in the wood. A voice said: ' You ought to get up now and move about properly.'

Not yet. Alberta stretched herself lazily down in the hay. Not just yet. She wanted to return to this dreamless sleep, the best she had ever tasted, wanted to go down again into the sheltered chasm of forgetfulness. She seemed to have been sleeping away years of restlessness and fatigue down there. And she dozed off.

' I'm not going to let you lie there one minute longer.'

Alberta looked up. The sky had a dull flush, but down on the earth the pale, greyish light which was neither day nor night, only a waiting, still lay. She was cold and a little stiff. Nevertheless these brief hours of sleep in the fresh air had renewed her, as a bath may do. She rubbed her eyes, plucked from her hair the straws that were hanging in her face and said: ' I've never slept so well in my whole life.'

' Will you please get up, and at once.'

Alberta sat up. There was Veigaard, his face grey and tired, his collar turned up and shoulders shivering. He was stamping his feet and had a homeless look about him, like a poor fellow who has nowhere to go for the night. His pipe was sticking up pathetically out of his pocket. But he was no longer angry, on the contrary he said in a surprisingly hilarious tone of voice: ' It's plain to see you've been having adventures. Straw in your hair, dew in your hair. You should always have it down on your shoulders, it suits you.' And he busied himself plucking straws off her, long ones that would not brush off.

Alberta knew very well that her hair, which did not look especially attractive put up, fell beautifully and coherently when she took out her hair-comb and let the coil glide down until it lay half undone on the nape of her neck.

136

Without answering she lifted an arm, which she also knew to be beautiful, and as if in a dream plucked out straw from his hair and his upturned collar. The grey, tired face in front of her altered at once to an expression that was familiar and intimate, that had something in it of the courageous wanderer through life, of a man's strict frugality, of Jacob, of Papa. Old and new feelings flooded into her in a confusing blend. She heard herself laugh an entirely new little laugh, sensed something she had never sensed before in gesture and movement. It streamed from within her, forcing its way out, whether she wished it or not.

– Something soft and gentle. And it was not humiliating or mortifying. It was submission for the first time to a law of life, an unfurling of herself like a leaf in the sun. Perhaps it made her, the ugly duckling, beautiful. At any rate it made her different, giving her something of the inevitability of a bird or an animal, the innocence of a life lived in the present.

She looked up, into a face so deathly serious and tense that the small muscles on either side of the mouth came into prominence. She felt a little giddy. She laughed again to cover herself.

They ran through the grass which was grey with dew. It was a struggle for Alberta, she felt stiff and distant. The hems of her skirts were wet and slapped heavily about her legs. But Veigaard was merciless, run she must.

They crept through a hedge and negotiated a ditch out on to a country road, an endless avenue. A peasant on a load of vegetables told them the way to Versailles, round the park. And they ran again, until Alberta could run no longer and declared that she was warm.

It was day. The air was already quivering with the coming heat. Along the roadside grew the plump, shaggy childhood flora of Lady's mantle and wild parsley. There is something erect, something wild and warm and invincible about them. Equipped with such strong roots that not even the thickest layer of dust from the country roads ever

137

chokes them, they grow along the roads of half the world, and stand each day dew-fresh in the morning light. It is like a greeting to walk along the road and see them coming continually towards you on either hand.

Versailles was still asleep, with hushed, empty gardens and closed shutters, when Alberta and Veigaard entered it, hand in hand like two schoolchildren. 'Now we must see if we can find something to eat,' said Veigaard. 'For we're both decidedly hungry.'

Outside the café just across from the station a yawning *garçon* was sweeping between the tables. Very tactfully he interrupted this task to go in and provide the matinal couple, irrelevantly gay and dishevelled in appearance, with something to eat. 'Hot coffee, plenty of coffee, coffee at once,' ordered Veigaard. He sat down with his elbows on the table and struck his fist into the palm of his hand, like someone who has made up his mind on a grave matter.

Tame sparrows approached them, sweeping the air with their wings, settled on the backs of the chairs around them and chirped urgently. Still cool and new, the day lay beneath the great elms on the Avenue de Sceaux.

* * *

'Things can't go on like this, Alberta. Not a month, not even a week longer. Some arrangement must be made for you.'

Alberta shifted restlessly. 'Making arrangements' could only mean wresting from her the only thing she had succeeded in conquering in her whole life. She was about to say something. Then Veigaard said: 'If you refuse to come home with me now, then you must move in with a family. I won't have you living here like this.'

But Alberta would not go home. She wanted something quite different. She kept silent, searching quietly for arguments.

'Yes, I know what you're going to say. You're going to talk about freedom again. Freedom? What sort of

138

freedom do you have? It's a miserable life, that's what it is, and you are far too good for it. You're not free, you're an outlaw.'

There Alberta sat. She shook her head now and again, said yes, of course, yes, yes. And she shut herself in again behind her obstinacy, her brief, sulky, ' If you knew how everything really was, Nils '.

But Nils had again concluded a train of thought: ' That obstinate mind of yours is worth a better cause, dash it. If only you could use it to work your way through . . . '

' Through what?'

' Good Lord, Alberta, through anything. We can all of us do something. And you – sometimes I get the feeling that something is on fire inside you. But you're certainly not going to find out what it is in this way. Here you are, here you've been for seven years. You know the language, and in spite of your ignorance you are informed about a great many things. If only I could fathom what it really is I like about you. When I examine you closely, I must say I don't understand it at all.'

He drew Alberta's face towards his, pressing his nose against hers repeatedly: ' Stubborn, stupid, ignorant.'

' Ugly,' completed Alberta.

' Ugly? Yes, hideous as the devil. A little heathen, an anti-social individual, a hopeless character. But there – on Wednesday I shall go home and marry someone else, a respectable, sensible little girl, who knows what she wants. And the little memory of Paris will become just one of those little memories one has . . . '

Alberta turned her face away, pulling away from him. What he was saying hurt her deeply. ' I know what I want,' she muttered.

' No, indeed you don't. You live in perpetual opposition and believe it to be freedom, independence. You are more stupid than I thought, Alberta.'

' Oh?'

' *Still* more stupid than I thought, and that's saying a good deal. But I'll tell you what you are doing . . . ',

139

Veigaard took her by the shoulders and turned her face towards him again: 'You are stunting yourself and freezing here too, you never do anything else, dash it, only in a different way from up there at home. You are stagnating, that's what you're doing, destroying yourself for lack of all sort of things, from food and air and proper clothes to ... to affection and care. You must get out of this, out of this sordid existence in seventh-rate hotels.'

Yes, said a little voice inside Alberta. Yes, yes, yes, it's true, all of it. She found escape in the new element within her, what in her innermost mind she called being 'different towards Nils'. It consisted of an indeterminable number of small cadences, gestures, expressions, a way of snuggling into her clothes and laughing, a low, clear sparkling laugh – a laugh that she herself listened to with amazement and which made her think of the chuckling of the decanters at home, when good wine was poured from them, a festive and superfluous little sound. 'You'll come down here again soon, Nils. You'll apply for the grant and get it. Then we'll rent a room in the house where you're living now, one of those with a view of the Gardens. There are no bugs there. And you have no idea how cheaply one can live down here. Or how practical I am. We could be so happy. Like many other people here. And no-one would need to know, no-one.'

Each day was a fight about the same thing. Veigaard would arrive brandishing his pipe and armed with new arguments. He would brush Alberta aside and begin at once: 'You're longing to go home, Alberta.'

'Am I?'

'Your face went so small that evening we were sitting at Lavenue's and the violinist played "I Gaze on the Sun". I saw it clearly. And you're not just longing to go home, you're longing *for* a home, like – like all homeless people. For a place to belong to.'

But Alberta shook her head and denied it. 'I shall never be of any use doing that,' she said quietly.

140

The pipe puffed: ' I wish I knew what you think it would be like. I have a sofa and a few chairs left me by my mother, an old-fashioned Pembroke table, books; a couple of rooms all told. I kept no more than was strictly necessary after the divorce. And I don't intend you to stand over a cooking-stove. We could be together, each doing his own work, quite simply. I haven't the slightest interest in all this business of running about with newly baked cakes on a dish and pulling down curtains and hanging them up again. If I did, the old marriage would have sufficed. It was perfect from that point of view, I suppose.'

But Alberta knew better. She pictured to herself washing day and the Christmas house-cleaning, felt all the critical small-town eyes pressed up close against the window-panes, saw herself, the good-for-nothing, going from defeat to defeat. And she attacked him in turn: ' *You* long to get away. You long to come here.'

' I shall come here. It's just that I can't run away from everything there at home on the spur of the moment.'

' Don't *run* away from it. Go home and make your arrangements and come back again.'

' My arrangements might take a year, perhaps two. Even if I get this grant, which you think is hanging on a tree all ready for me, I shan't be able to leave immediately. But let's leave the matter there. You'll have to stay here, and we'll just have to find something for you.'

Alberta sighed. She too had her life, that she could not run away from on the spur of the moment; it was just that it was so difficult to sum it up in words or discuss it matter-of-factly: immense, chaotic possessions for which she had fought and held out, the streets, the throngs of people, the flowers, being outside it all; the vague certainty that it was here, in spite of everything, she should seek and find the way she should go. Her way.

Mists of doubt clouded her mind. This chance traveller passing through, what had she to do with him? The loneliness had played her a trick. Was she not behaving as if ready to cling to anybody? Once he had left, would she forget him in, let's see, how long?

Nothing is incurable, everything passes. From the first stab that gives warning of danger, right through the fever of restless dreams, one most certainly reaches freedom again. One day the whole thing has dropped out of one's thoughts, and is left behind, forgotten.

His eagerness to take her with him made her feel at times like a pawn, to be played against another pawn. She remembered things he had said: 'We had been married a year, then I simply couldn't go on. When a man can't, then it's no use. There's nothing he can do about it. Well, then it all became tragic, and so it still is in a way.'

His observations on these matters were few and brief. But Alberta glimpsed a face, a contour, blonde and passionate, continually blotched with tears and continually telephoning. She thought: I won't get mixed up in all that, I won't.

Marriage – the very word dragged, it sounded compelling and burdensome. She remembered her friends who had married in the small town at home. The church would be packed, the town dressmaker almost dead with exhaustion. The next day the new bride would be standing in Schmitt the butcher's or at Ryan's, feeling the meat with her finger to see if it was tender; then she would call at Holst's to ask them to send home such and such, taking with her a good piece of cheese for supper, while people asked each other all down the street whether they had seen her, and went a different way in order to get an opportunity of doing so.

No, none of that. There were four days until Wednesday. Then the worst would be over.

But she longed for him every minute he was away from her. He lived in her, possessed her. The French call it having someone in the blood. Nothing is closer to the truth. And when he unwillingly muttered one day, under his breath: 'If only I had you, I'd know how to hold you, that's all there is to it.' anxiety and sweetness quivered

142

confusingly through her. She felt a slow cajoling call in her body to submit and give herself, to be humble and serve.

Then she would go to meet him as light-footed as if she were flying. She laughed her new laughter. In her were gestures she had not known about, as natural as the swaying of branches in the wind, cadences she listened to with astonishment. There it all was one day and nothing could be done about it. For long periods at a time all their difficulties seemed to be forgotten. Alberta felt the new element in her being play like a spring of water that has finally found its way out into the sun, bringing liberation and deliverance. She would search his face with her index finger, looking for the two small knots of muscle on either side of his mouth: ' You haven't put them on today. That's not fair, you're cheating. You will please put them on every day.' A calm certainty grew in her: It will work out all right, it will work out in some way or other. Until suddenly Veigaard would be cold and distant, although not a single word of disagreement had been spoken. He would shift his position, lead the conversation on to quite irrelevant matters, raise a wall of correct, ordinary words about him.

And the daylight would lose its brightness. Alberta would sit numbed, searching for what she had done wrong, finding nothing. And would herself shortly become a little cold and stiff, paralysed by what was unexplained, and by an old, painful thought: Perhaps there was something repulsive about her after all.

* * *

The days passed. The enormous gladioli of late summer were already in flower round the circular fountain in the Rue Soufflot. The beds in the Luxembourg Gardens were full of dahlias. The mornings were a little misty, as if carrying the autumn in wraps.

A chill would go through Alberta at the thought of being alone again. Then she would suddenly feel relief at the

143

idea of putting the whole thing in perspective. It had come so close that it was tomorrow morning.

She was sitting in the red armchair by the window. Veigaard was packing. He had acquired new books and a new trunk, had bought some knick-knacks for his relatives at home and a ring for Alberta in an antique shop in the Rue des Saints-Pères: an old ring, a dark amethyst with tiny pearls round it. He had found it and bought it on his own. Alberta got a lump in her throat and felt heart-sick when she looked down at it.

Neither of them said very much. Veigaard's face had that tense expression that made Alberta think of life's hard journey. She felt strongly the necessity to steel herself now towards the end. Nevertheless there were words that seemed to be lying on her tongue, ready to pop out now and then. She would not say them. She might regret it terribly, and fail to keep them in the long run. Now it must be left to fate.

Veigaard suddenly turned round, putting down a pile of books that he was taking to the trunk. He half sat on the edge of the table and slapped his knee with a paper-knife: ' For the last time – are you coming with me?'

' Give me a little time at least,' said Alberta yieldingly, feeling a hypocrite. She would never want this. She got up and sat close to him on the table and stroked his hand, outlining yet again a provisional plan that she had conceived: first, he would be coming back for Christmas, for the whole month. She would book a room here in good time, arrange everything so nicely. He should sit undisturbed the whole day, make enormous strides with his dissertation, no telephone would ring, here no-one ever used the telephone, the table would stand exactly like this one so that he could look out over the Gardens. But at dusk they would fan the coke fire in the grate so that it glowed and cast its light over the whole room, they would have chestnuts with freshly churned butter. On Christmas Eve, midnight mass at St. Sulpice – turkey at D'Harcourt's afterwards. It was always full of students there, gay and lively.

' Yes,' said Veigaard wearily. ' I'm sure it would be nice. And then?'

' Then?' Alberta faltered a little. ' Well – then you'll stay perhaps?'

Veigaard looked even more weary. ' And supposing I can't? Supposing I have to leave again, leave the ... the coke fire and all the rest of it?' He suddenly had the ravaged expression that she remembered from the morning at Versailles, that look of the toiler who must keep going and has no other pleasures in life. And he looked at her strangely wide-eyed. Alberta was reminded of a poor man watching sumptuously dressed rich folk. She was greatly moved.

But Veigaard said, and his mouth curled up bitterly as he did so: ' So we must arrange something for you, Alberta. I suppose it is too much to expect you to come with me on the spur of the moment. I need someone there at home, I expect it's that that makes me unreasonable. It's not good for a man to be alone, and in my situation it's terrible.

' Well – then I saw you sitting there at Fru Marushka's that evening. You sat as if alone amongst the others and you were – different. I had a strange feeling that I had always known you. And that morning at Versailles I had the ... the impression that you felt the same. But you do not, and I cannot expect you to so soon. I thought it would be so natural for you to come home with me, because of the way you live down here, with your roots groping about haphazardly in the air, so to speak. I thought we might be able to help each other as best we could. I meant well in my fashion. But there – now we must find some arrangement, you must get something out of the winter, and then ... '

Alberta was on her feet. Waves of emotion went through her, appearing as flecks before her eyes. She could hear her heart beating loudly as if measuring a moment of destiny, felt her eyes widen in her face, heard herself say

145

in a deep, slow voice: ' I mean well too. I want you to be free and ... happy and ... have everything you wish. There's nothing I couldn't do for you. I'll tell you everything I've not told you before, not even mentioned – do whatever you want .... '

She saw his eyes, wide and dark like her own. When she put her arms round his neck he drew his face back a little, but continued to look at her, as if trying to see into the depths of her mind. She thought: If I must I shall even conquer the innermost, shining white fear of anyone coming near me, I shall do it now. And suddenly these dark eyes which continued to look at her sent the blood flooding through her veins. She felt her own expression altered by it, as if it were sinking back, turning inwards. She heard Veigaard say, his voice trembling, ' Alberta '. He seized her wrists. But she forced herself up against him, tensing her body like a spring – and suddenly had his arms tightly about her.

* * *

It had rained for the first time for weeks and a smell of fresh leaves came from all the trees. The air was spicy and as buoyant as in spring when Alberta and Veigaard jogged up towards the Gare du Nord in a cab.

Alberta was wearing an old, white embroidered petticoat under her dress. She caught herself sitting thinking about this ridiculous circumstance. Nobody wore such petticoats nowadays, they were antiquated and a little comic, and it had worried her yesterday and this morning. Now it would show when she climbed out of the cab. It looked terrible with her dress, giving the effect of a country woman dressed up in her Sunday best. But sometimes you have to wear whatever you possess.

Veigaard was holding her hand in his, thumping it up and down as he recapitulated: ' Now – a week today my sister comes back to town. I shall write to her as soon as I get to Copenhagen or on the ferry. Then she will help you, Alberta. – Yes! To find some respectable lodgings and whatever clothes you need. I will not have you going round looking like this. I may like you as you are, but no-one could call you well-dressed exactly. Something radical must be done. And those old sandals of yours, I don't ever want to see them again.'

Alberta flushed, again remembering her petticoat and the episode with Joseph. Here she sat, tamed, with her wings clipped for all time, strangely bound to Veigaard and dependent on him. She did not know whether this was a good thing or not, but was simply compliant to the extent of apathy. For an instant she saw clothes, beautiful clothes such as she had passionately wanted to own, clothes that suited her. But deep down in her mind lay something resembling a little ball of mist, an immovable nothing. It was by no means certain that it would not start to swell and hide what was uppermost in her now.

'You must discuss your journey home with her as well, Alberta. And then come when you wish. When you are quite certain you want to. Not before.'

Alberta pressed his hand in reply. It was gradually borne in on her: Now you are sure of me, quite sure.

They were halted by the traffic. Veigaard looked at his watch and his small gesture made Alberta think of executions, the moments just before. They were probably like this. Perhaps they contained the same microscopic amount of curiosity as to how it would feel when it was all over. She sat drinking in all her impressions of the life about her in quite a new way: the air, the sounds, the light murmur of the city on a clear, beautiful morning. There it was still, she had not left it, nor let it slip out of her hands. In a short while she would be alone with it again.

Then warmth and tenderness filled her mind. She pressed his hand hard, spoke about freedom, the grant, the peace he would at last have down here when they finally got as far as that, the libraries, the freedom from everything that was tying him down.

Veigaard suddenly sighed. 'I've been thinking,' he said,

147

that perhaps I ought to apply to get into a school in Copenhagen. It wouldn't stop us going abroad when we had the opportunity.'

But Alberta started as if stung. Uncle and Aunt went there every year. Cousin Lydia came through on her journeys to and from England. There the whole thing would be displayed to the public gaze in the most fearful way. She heard her own voice, shocked and mortified: ' Copenhagen! That would be ten times as bad, Nils,' and regretted it at once. He had been sitting thinking this out. She pressed his hand with all her might: ' Of course you'll get your grant. Why should we want to go to Copenhagen?'

But Veigaard's voice sounded tired and a little cold when he replied: ' Well, well, I expect I shall apply.'

The painful astonishment that follows the breaking of something precious by mistake, came over Alberta. He was out of humour, it was dreadful. There was no opportunity here in the street to use the kind of argument which had proved to be more successful than talk and reasoning. Anxiously she looked up at him, watching his face for signs that it would clear. And thank God, now he was squeezing her hand again! Yes, she was indeed a different person today, overflowing with gratitude for a mere smile.

He took out his notebook: ' Have I got it correctly? *Poste restante* Alésia? Since it is so important to keep Eliel out of it. Though I must say I'm glad he'll be back in a couple of days. It's always somebody, and you can't really have anything to do with Ness. You shall hear from me from Cologne. And you are to be a good little girl, no more sessions out there with that revolting old Englishman, no more aesthetes in your room at night.'

He suddenly threw his arm round her and held her tight: I have a strange feeling that I ought to take you with me now, this very minute, just as you are and whether you want to or not. I don't like leaving you behind alone at all. But you will stay at a decent hotel for these few days until my sister comes, won't you?'

' Yes, of course,' Alberta assured him. She knew of one

up on the Boul' Mich' which was excellent. She would stay there. She kissed him quickly and passionately on the cheek. His jaw was crooked with emotion.

At once the traffic began to move, the cabman whipped up the horses, and they rolled on at a gallop. There was no time to spare.

Afterwards everything happened in fast tempo; it was impossible to collect herself or to think about anything. There was the trunk that had to be weighed, the difficulty of finding a porter, the crush at the entrance to the platform. When they finally reached the train Veigaard scarcely had time to kiss her once and squeeze her hands in his. A conductor, who was slamming the doors, parted them : ' If you wish to leave, Monsieur, into the carriage with you.'

Alberta stood on the station platform. The train was already moving. Then suddenly something seemed to give way, something forced itself up, she had not said – she wanted to say that –

But she was already drowned by the noise. She saw a last smile, a wave of his hat from the rear platform. And Veigaard was gone. She was blinded by her tears.

Two days later Alberta was sitting in the Parc de Montsouris. There had been nothing in the post yesterday, nothing by the first post this morning. But it would come by a later post, the more certainly so, the longer she had to wait. Much could happen to hinder one on journeys. She felt a secure anticipation, a calm joy, which included the next moment, and the next, and the next.

A child threw its ball to her. A little surprised at herself, she caught it and threw it back.

Then they were in full swing. Alberta had never really played in her life. She had been awkward and ignored. Now she played and laughed aloud with the child. A little way off, its mother looked up from her sewing, let it fall in her lap, and watched them with smiling eyes.

❊ *Part Three* ❊

Her hand trembling, Alberta put the book down and did not pick it up again. Some words in it had hurt her, stinging like salt in a wound. Hard, merciless, true, they had reached their target unswervingly. The words of a man, thought by a man, written by a man. They sank into her mind with painful gravity. Her heart stopped for an instant, as with all of life's shocks.

She took out other books, changed her place among the readers, turned over the pages for a while, read a few lines. They danced up and down, she did not take in their content. It was no use pretending it didn't matter. The dreadful words already lay like stones in her soul.

She started to shiver, raw cold attacked her through her coat between her shoulder-blades, a gust of the falling darkness and the lonely evening. It was closing time. A desolating stir was produced by the banging of cupboard doors, the rattling of bunches of keys, hurrying steps on the stone floor. Along the counters all the many-coloured volumes were piled up in heaps and disappeared as if by magic. The librarians' long grey coats fluttered behind them in the draught of their haste.

In a trice it was all empty, grey, deserted. Once again life had taken her by the scruff of the neck and she found herself defenceless against it. With her freezing hands clenched inside her cuffs Alberta hurried out of the Odéon arcades towards the railings of the Luxembourg Gardens and continued alongside them. The pavement glistened damply; it felt cold and glutinous through the soles of her shoes.

A bluish mist filled the Gardens. Behind the strong silhouette of the railings the tree-trunks appeared one behind the other as in a dissolving water-colour. A last remnant of yellow was left in the treetops, a hint of vanishing sunset-red hung in the air above them, light fell from a row of windows at the Senate. Untouched by trends, sentimental and traditional, the day died its quiet, natural death above the lawns. Out in the streets it was killed by the newly lighted lamps.

There was a smell of roast chestnuts and rotten leaves, petrol, perfume and damp soil. The last gladioli shone hectically under the arc-lamps round the fountain at the Rue Soufflot. Red in leaf and stem, a dark, muddy colour that contrasted violently with the clear flame of the flower, they looked as if they blossomed in fury and defiance.

People had the haste of autumn in their step, hurrying from something, to something. They seemed relieved and expectant, renewed and rejuvenated. Or they ran because they were cold, like Alberta.

Only the blind newspaper-seller fumbled slowly along the railings as usual, his back against them, holding on with one hand and stretching out the other. Quietly he mentioned from time to time the few papers he offered for sale, this year as last year, as every year. He held his head a little askew, his extinguished eyes mirrored the lamplight. No season would alter him now.

Alberta halted, looking for a tram-car. Then somebody stopped short in front of her, a small, buoyant person, who rose up on her toes as she did so: Marushka. She was dressed for autumn in new clothes. A long-stemmed rose was pinned to the white fox fur round her neck, her fur hat was set at an angle on her boyish head: ' Mademoiselle Alberta! Where have you been? What are you doing, where do you live? At Montrouge? A side-street off the Rue d'Alésia? *Mon Dieu*, what an idea! With whom are you hiding all that way out there? But you don't look well.

You're pale, you've become thinner. You're not ill, are you? You're blushing? Why are you blushing? You don't look happy. Surely there's nothing the matter? Seriously?'

' No, of course not,' said Alberta.

And Marushka went on to talk about something else, but Alberta still felt her eyes on her face like two small sympathetic searchlights. 'And Liesel? *La petite* Liesel? No-one sees anything of her any more either. But there, she's lost her heart to Monsieur Eliel, oh but of course, everybody knows that.' But Marushka had heard that she was going to Colarossi's again, and it was madness, sheer madness, after that picture of hers at the Autumn Exhibition. It was just what Marushka had always said, Liesel had been wading about in old impressionism until she did not know what she was doing. Now she had managed to shake that off this summer, and had achieved comprehension, simplification, expression: three preliminary sketches, three colours more or less, brown, green, black, the whole well concentrated, a little thin perhaps. Marushka had taken several of her friends over to see Liesel's work, people with a critical sense who understood these things, there had been no disagreement, she has a fine talent, *la petite*. Just the fact that she got in without any support whatsover, just that! And then she goes back to Colarossi's again, to that fearful dilettante milieu, among a lot of old maids. Marushka herself had joined up with Russians, Frenchmen, Americans, Scandinavians around a studio down on the Boulevard des Invalides, in an old monastery there. She would willingly try to get Liesel in there, although it was crowded. There was comradeship there, a really artistic atmosphere, earnestness. Everyone would certainly do their utmost to find room for Liesel. If Alberta would tell her so? Marushka had gone out to Eliel's place one day, but nobody was at home, nobody had opened the door at any rate. Liesel's picture had been hung well, didn't Alberta think so?

But Alberta had not yet been to the Autumn Exhibition.

' Not yet? But it closes tomorrow, the fifteenth. So you

haven't seen my work either, a still life, a landscape, both of them marvellous? *Mon Dieu*, what will become of you?' Marushka shook Alberta's arm, looked at her even more searchingly, stood on tiptoe, high on her elastic insteps, strong as a dancer's: 'Listen to me! My little finger tells me there's something wrong. Don't go fretting and getting thin blood. Come up one day and we'll have a talk. It's not nice of you never to come. I'm engaged this evening, but one day soon, you will, won't you? *Au revoir, courage!*'

And Marushka was gone. Together with an athletic American-looking man she disappeared quickly down the Boul' Mich'. She turned once and waved to Alberta.

Somewhat stunned, Alberta mounted a Montrouge-Gare de l'Est. The poverty-stricken feeling she already had increased to the point of hollowness. She shrank into the woollen human warmth of the tram-car as into a shelter, and sat for a while thinking about Liesel, as one thinks about somone half forgotten. She saw her seldom, only knowing that she lived with Eliel and that it was ' *reizend* ' but difficult because it had to be kept secret. It had come about quite by itself. On their return from Brittany late one evening Liesel had driven home with Eliel to stay the night, and had been there ever since. She had spoken of the sun and the sand in Brittany, of swimming in the clear, salt water – green and translucent so that every stone could be seen on the bottom – of her picture, which had suddenly come to her, she was not quite sure how, of Eliel's sketches and of the acquaintances they had made out there, with the same over-excited brightness in her eyes, the same nervous haste. Her face had gone thinner under its freckles. They had spread from her nose in all directions this year, as last year, as every year. They disappeared in the winter. Her busy, slightly encumbered figure, weighed down with food parcels and bags of paintbrushes, stood for an instant, wide-eyed and sloping-shouldered, almost frightened-looking, before Alberta's inner eye. How was Liesel really? Then she thought: Liesel has Eliel. As long as she has Eliel . . . . And the malicious man's words that she had read at the Odéon were there again, gnawing into her further.

But when Alberta left the tram-car at Montrouge Church, there was Liesel, carrying out some kind of transaction across a cart with fish, snails, sea-urchins and crab, slow, creeping animals fighting against death. She was as usual laden with purchases and in addition was eating something which on closer inspection turned out to be a slice of Swiss cheese. Absently she looked up: 'Oh, it's you, Albertchen. I haven't seen you for ages.'

It was a crab that the fishwife was weighing in her hand. She was holding it out towards Liesel, praising its qualities. Lying on its back, its claws crumpled together over its deathly-pale stomach, it immovably awaited its fate, as the fishwife swung it up and down, assuring her: 'Heavy, full, all alive. Look!' She prodded it with spirit, making its claws stretch and crumple, stuffed it into a bag and handed it to Liesel. Then she turned to Alberta: 'And you, Madame?' A fresh crab was being weighed in her hand.

'No thank you,' said Alberta deprecatingly. 'Not if you gave it me,' she exclaimed.

'You are mistaken, quite mistaken, Madame. Crab is excellent food, nourishing food, healthy food.' The fishwife turned to another customer.

'But Liesel! What are you going to do with a crab?'

'Cook it, Albertchen. Cook it.' Liesel pushed her hat straight and took a bite of cheese.

'But we don't cook *crabs*,' said Alberta in sudden revolt. There was something unprecedented, almost degrading about this crab, there ought to be a limit to one's submission to the laws of nature.

'Ach,' said Liesel, 'We cook anything, Albertchen. Just you wait until your turn comes. Eliel loves crab. I bought a cooked one *chez* Hazard the other day, but it gave him stomach-ache. This time I thought...'

'Is that cheese you're eating, Liesel?'

Liesel stuffed the rest of the cheese quickly into her

154

mouth and laughed a little self-consciously. Yes, just imagine, she got an absolutely irresistible urge to eat some *Gruyère*, couldn't help buying it and eating it at once. It was a good thing it was dark and that this was Paris. All in all she had been very well in the country and now had such an appetite that it was quite embarrassing. Eliel thought it was still the effect of the sea air. But there was always something to bother one. Now Liesel had toothache, such a nuisance. She hadn't slept all night. The Austrian medical student they met at St. Jean du Doigt had written a prescription for something to hold on the tooth, but it had not helped. Perhaps Liesel would have to go to the dentist, and it was so expensive here. Could Alberta see, she was swollen on the one side?

' Be sure to go in time, Liesel,' advised Alberta somewhat mechanically. She had caught sight of a large piece of octopus amongst everything else on the handcart. The thought struck her: Yes, yes, I would have cooked crab; I would have cooked octopus if I'd had to. She felt bitterly alone beside Liesel, who was on her way home to cook crab for Eliel. She was listening through everything Liesel said for something Liesel did not say; she had been doing so throughout the autumn each time she had met her. And she listened for the same thing when Eliel spoke, and complete strangers. No-one mentioned what she was thinking of, no-one ever said they had heard anything. Once, immediately after Eliel had come home, he had asked whether that Dane had called on her, whether he had been friendly? And Alberta had answered as calmly as she could that, yes, they had gone out together a couple of times, he wasn't at all bad. Since then there had been nothing but silence. Sometimes Alberta felt as if there were a conspiracy against her, as if the whole world were in agreement not to say a word. A foolish desire to shake people – But speak out, can't you – would come over her. If she did not do so, it was because we really can remain on the verge of action for a long time without doing anything.

She remembered her conversation with Marushka and reported it. But Liesel rejected the idea. What was Alberta thinking of? Scandinavians and Russians? And Liesel, who was by no means good at hiding things, blushed and was overcome with embarrassment, giving herself away completely. Incalculable catastrophes might occur in Sweden and in Russia if rumours began to circulate. Eliel could not marry, however much he wished to. There were big Swedish grants for which married men could not apply, and naturally his art had to come first. Of course it was dilettantish and boring at Colarossi's, especially now when she really had got to grips with something, but there was no choice for the time being. It was no good working at home in the studio. Eliel never stopped turning the stand, he walked about the whole time. However Liesel placed herself, he intruded into the motif. Besides, they were in debt for yet another piece of marble, so there could be no question of renting anything. But worst of all were the days when she had to lie up in the loft.

And Liesel explained. It was if anyone came so early that she had not had time to get dressed. Eliel had many acquaintances now. Some Swedes had come to Paris this autumn, who were interested in him and thought he might get a grant. And Liesel was so tired in the morning, even though she had felt so well in the country. She could not understand why. Perhaps she had over-exerted herself with too much posing out there, at any rate it was difficult for her to get out of bed, sometimes she wished she could lie there all day, just for once. But the food had to be cooked. Some cleaning had to be done. Eliel didn't think it mattered, but Liesel could not bear it to be so dirty. The floor seeemed to dissolve into dust, breed dust. Well – so there would be a knock on the door before Liesel was up, and then she would have to *stay* there. But it was such a strain. She had to be as quiet as a mouse. She was afraid, afraid of sneezing, for instance. Sometimes they would stay for hours. Once a whole crowd came, decided they would fetch a model, and sketched from nine to twelve. That was one of the days when Liesel had had toothache. She couldn't say anything, it wasn't Eliel's fault, after all. Besides, he would only suggest that she move back to the hotel again, that it would be best for them both. But Alberta would understand that she didn't want to do that. She looked up eagerly: 'It seems more devoted when we *live* together, more natural, don't you think?'

'Yes,' said Alberta.

In spite of Liesel's tribulations she felt infintely poor by comparison. When Liesel, with a final, somewhat uncertain, 'You'll come and see us soon, won't you, Albertchen?' collected her paper bags more firmly about her and went, the street at once took on a hostile and evil appearance, and all the passers-by seemed rootless and homeless.

Alberta's street looked sinister after dark. There was only just sufficient lighting; but it was not dangerous. The people who lived here were not bad people. It was simply that none of them had been successful.

Madame Caux looked searchingly out of her window. She had enteritis and the swollen stomach that accompanies it. There was always a half-empty milk bottle in her vicinity, and her eyes were gentle and long-suffering. She had had a kind of liking for Alberta from the very first, treating her obligingly and with kindness, in spite of the fact that she demanded of her a certain amount of equanimity where the unavoidable dispensations of providence were concerned, bugs and draughts, for instance. Madame Caux had a couple of standard answers for those who complained: 'Well, even if there are a couple of creatures here, we can't very well tear the house down. You must be more careful about shutting the window, *ma petite.*'

On every landing there burned a naked gas jet. It flickered forlornly, spreading a light as wretched as charity. It did not conceal that the jute on the walls was torn and flapped in the draught, but seemed placed precisely in order to illuminate the gravest damage. At every turn of the stairs one was met by it as by a symbol of grudgingly shared out goods.

The air thickened on the top floors. It was stored up here as in all houses and had received an additional contribution of the stronger exhalations of working people. As soon as Alberta came up she had to open the window. In a favourable wind the autumn fog streamed damply up towards her from the fortifications and the country beyond. If it was less favourable, the smoke from adjoining chimneys was blown in, thick and visible as at a railway station.

She reached her small, ugly room.

The tablecloth was green, a piece of thick woollen material Alberta had bought cheaply at the Bon Marché together with the table, the chair, the mattress on legs. To avoid the junk shop she had foregone all hint of elegance. The objects stood reduced, so to speak, to their original idea of simplicity. But in the evening the green tablecloth acquired an unexpected significance one would not have believed possible. When the candle was lighted ·in its candlestick, its scanty gleam included scarcely anything besides this; it seemed unable to reach any farther. And the objects on the table which could not be put anywhere else, the inkwell, the blotter, the box with writing paper in it, acquired an uncomfortably predominant aspect.

She would find herself sitting looking at them. There was nothing else at which to look. The window-panes were full of darkness. The walls enclosed her at a pace's distance, dark brown, heavy in colour, as if they were trying to force the eye back to the table. The framed reproductions that Alberta had hung up only reflected the candle-flame. Nothing singled itself out, everything was too close. The pottery jug stood empty and desolate in a corner on the floor for lack of space.

So it usually ended in Alberta sitting at this green table, as if taken by the scruff of the neck and placed there. She assembled lines, crossed them out and tore them up. Letters she would not think of sending materialized under her hands, a confused collection of words, which tumbled over one another on their way up from hidden places in her mind. And brief, bitterly polite notes, a mere couple of sentences, an address, a greeting, an initial below.

She never sent them. She had sent two. First, a letter, then a brief note. She had felt faint when she posted them. It had seemed to her that she was writing to a complete stranger, or to a figment of her imagination, or that she was perhaps a little mad. No reply had come to either of them. Nothing ever came. She could equally well stand up and call out of the window, out into the night. It would be just as effective, and less bitterly humiliating.

Every day the time came when she had to go home to all this. The Odéon, the museums and the libraries closed. She could not continually sit in churches. The street became damp and raw. And even if she still considered all possible eventualities, sickness, catastrophes, lost letters, and did foolish things as if under hypnosis, running to the *poste-restante* window time after time, even though the woman behind it had long ago started to look at her sympathetically as at someone deranged, taking the Métro over to the Avenue du Roule, sitting on a bench there staring up at a row of windows, the evening set a limit even to this. She sat there feeling a stab each time she caught sight of a sign of life up there. A hand would draw the curtains across, the electric light would be switched on here, switched off there, someone's shadow glide behind the panes. Or a lady would come out of the street door. She might be anyone from the large building. She might also be . . .

Alberta struggled with a desperate and stupid desire to run after her, speak to her, *take hold of her*. A fearful and mysterious attraction seemed to emanate from her. And yet she did not even look the same all the time, being sometimes fair, sometimes dark, sometimes young, sometimes old, now and again elegant, now and again simply dressed like a servant. One day she was holding a child by the hand, another, two small dogs on a leash. Once Alberta was compelled to hurry past her and run back again in order to see her face, but she was wearing a veil, and it was already dusk. One day two ladies came out of the door together, and Alberta felt the same about them both, searching hungrily for something in the walk, in the stature of both of them.

Whatever the appearance of this lady, when she vanished from sight, took a cab, mounted a tram-car, went into a shop or down the Métro, she took Alberta's vitality with her. She felt she could not be bothered to drag herself home again. For her too, she had words on her lips, which died unborn, lay in her mind and turned to poison.

Sometimes Alberta would feel that the concentrated agony she continually carried within her must be able to work miracles. The thought that now, in a second, something would happen, that the whole thing was really only a delusion and a nighmare, obsessed her. In a waiting attitude she would raise her head, hold her breath, stare as if magnetized towards the door. But the door did not move. Nothing came fluttering in underneath it, no gliding square of paper, rustling a little as it did so.

And the pain would be there again, like a sword along the spine. Mortification and anxiety and regret crept interlaced through her mind like cold snakes. She wept painful, tearless sobs, wretched and smarting, a grimace merely; a caricature of the liberating stream that cleanses the mind and from which one rises assuaged, even perhaps born anew.

In all her veins there beat an urgent, all-embracing hunger for warmth. The words forced themselves up towards her lips and insisted on being spoken, she whispered them, dry as if from thirst. Memories lay in her, a kind of futuristic picture. She saw a chin, a slightly crooked mouth, two eyes, a hand, a hat. A hat! She saw it out in the darkness and was not always quite certain how far the limits of reality went.

Occasionally footsteps would approach down the passage outside, and stop outside her door. They were no miracle.

They belonged to Sivert Ness. He was the only person who had come to see her since she moved there.

He would sit on the divan, broad-shouldered and squat, looking across the floor as he spoke, with one composed, loosely-clenched hand lying on his knee. His thick country clothes smelled of homespun cloth in the autumn rain. Now and then he would look up, and the gleam would come into his eyes, a gleam Alberta scarcely noticed any more. He sat there, at any rate, and helped her through an hour of miserable loneliness; and she had to give him his due and listen to him abstractedly.

Sivert was always tackling something or other. With a small phrase-book sticking up out of his pocket he used all the free time he allowed himself for seeing the sights. He did not wander round in a desultory fashion, like Alberta, but went nosing after all kinds of museums and collections, including those that artists seldom visit, coming from the Hôtel des Monnaies, the Musée de la Marine, or the motor and machinery collections. The latter had been an accidental discovery. ' I couldn't believe my eyes,' said Sivert. ' I suddenly found myself in the middle of a lot of boats. Splendid things. Models of everything you could think of, from three-masters under full sail to ironclads, old and new all mixed up together. I must admit I didn't know such things existed in the Louvre. I'm going there again. If there's anything I enjoy looking at, it's ships.' Pleased with himself, he struck his fist into the palm of his strong hand.

Sivert's other news was that he had sold pictures at the State Exhibition at home that autumn. It had made him even more composed, and a little more prosperous-looking, but not much. He still wore his home-made clothes and affected no Spanish cloak. But he admitted that he was thinking about a winter coat. And he had bought himself a stove, had got it cheaply from the junk shop down the street. It had been there all last winter too, but then he had not been able to consider it. Now he was busy walling it in. It would be a nice bit of work when it was finished, it would be pleasant to get up in the morning even when it was cold outside. Otherwise it was awful in winter in these studios built directly on to the earth, he had thought he would rot last year, it had rained so much.

It began to dawn on Alberta that Sivert was really a sailor. She could clearly imagine him in blue shore-leave clothes and a cloth cap, imagine him jumping from thwart to thwart in a boat, casting off, applying himself to a pair of oars so that the water boiled round them. It seemed all wrong that he should be here in Paris, wearing a hat and occupied with painting. However, it was easy to imagine him sitting in his leisure hours like sailors on ocean journeys, patient, infinitely strong in his patience, making elaborate sailing ships inside bottles, or embroidering blankets and cushions with two crossed flags and flowers. Everything about him that was practical and self-supporting, the underwear and socks that he told her he mended and washed himself, his thickset, four-square shoulders, the short, strong legs, all were those of a sailor.

His clothes were confusing, wrongly giving the impression that he was a countryman. But these too were explained. One evening Sivert took out a little photograph to show Alberta. She saw an ordinary white country house with attics and a veranda. It had been taken a little crookedly. An elderly man was standing at the bottom of the steps, on which two women were sitting. Sivert pointed: ' That's Father, there's Mother, there's Otilie.'

Alberta politely attempted to distinguish the faces, but gave up. The picture was so small. She could see that his father had a long beard and both women smooth, parted hair, the older with a kerchief tied under her chin. The farm was called Granli, explained Sivert: ' Quite an ordinary name. But there are in fact some fir trees about that didn't get into the picture. Father was a sailor before he started farming. Mother comes from farther up country, from Land.'

The homespun clothes, thought Alberta.

' They're a bit pious at home,' said Sivert apologetically, putting the picture back in his wallet.

' Oh?' said Alberta.

They talked besides of Liesel and of how she had got into the exhibition. Sivert could not believe this was anything more than an accident. Yes, the picture was good, he would never have believed Liesel could have produced it, but now we'll see, he said, ' Ladies . . . '. Besides, Sivert had to admit that he thought it must be a bit strange for Eliel. Liesel's picture had been very well hung, but Eliel's sculpture was hidden away in a corner.

Alberta suggested somewhat indifferently that Eliel might be sufficiently gallant to be pleased about it. ' He ought to be,' she said.

' Yes, I suppose so. Of course. But all the same . . . ' Sivert stared thoughtfully across the floor as if trying to put himself in Eliel's place.

He left early. He had to go and wall up the stove. As soon as it was ready he would begin working with a model. ' It's hellishly expensive, but there's no help for it.' And he was gone. And there was nothing for it but to go to bed.

But when the noise of the street died away, a new world seemed to come alive around her. From every joint in the large house came noises she had not heard before, which awoke with the darkness. Through the thin walls, beneath the badly-fitting doors, they filtered out unhindered, collecting in the stairwell as in a canal and vibrating further in one's every nerve. Scolding, and the cries of small children, sudden flickers of conversation, the anguished moaning of women caressed by men and sometimes struck by them, the creaking of beds. An occasional loud comment, meant to be heard : ' And in the presence of children ! People ought to be ashamed ! '

Alberta attempted to hold on to the flickering patterns that form behind the eyeballs when one shuts one's eyes hard. The patterns shift, growing out of each other, colour within colour, whorl within whorl, figure within figure. She glimpsed landscapes, animals. Strange, unearthly flowers

163

exploded in the darkness, the one out of the other, snakes writhed about each other. It was beautiful or frightening, according to how it turned out, a fantastic primeval world, hidden within reality, visible when one looks inwards.

Until all of a sudden she sat upright on the divan, her heart hammering, staring hungrily at the door.

* * *

' I don't know what else to do, Alphonsine.'

Alphonsine removed her pince-nez, rubbed the lenses, and sat holding them between two fingers, with one elbow leaning on her knee, staring in front of her.

Pince-nez did not suit Alphonsine, they seemed irrelevant to her person. Alberta was never convinced that Alphonsine's were anything more than a toy made of ordinary glass, an amusing little object she happened to possess. They were, however, real. She also had a case, in which she placed them with care. Now she tapped with it thoughtfully: ' To be frank, it's no life for you, *ma petite.*'

' But Alphonsine, I must live.'

' Of course you must live. That's exactly what you ought to do, *live.*' And Alphonsine got up, suddenly put her hand under Alberta's chin and turned her face up towards her: ' Do you know that you are of an age when one is supposed to be happy, *ma petite*? All this is stupidity. You live in a hole.'

' I beg your pardon, Alphonsine?'

' A hole. I don't at all like the way you live. Why have you left Montparnasse and your friends? Only yesterday Madame Marushka asked: " Have you seen anything of the little Norwegian girl?" She had met you at the Luxembourg Gardens, and you had promised to go and see her. But you don't go. She asked after Mademoiselle Liesel too. I said nothing. I never say anything. But Marcelle, you know, my friend Marcelle, was out at Monsieur Eliel's one day to find out if he needed her. She posed for him last year. Well, she knocked, she heard someone run up the

164

steps to the loft just as the door was opened. She came in, Monsieur Eliel was alone. But that brooch was lying on a chair – you know, the one Mademoiselle Liesel always wears, a cameo – and on the steps up to the loft there was a garter! And in the middle of the floor a clay figure, an enormous contraption, the kind Monsieur Eliel always does, female, with shoulders *comme ça*, like a Botticelli. And Marcelle, she is a tease, Marcelle, she can never leave anyone alone, she said: '*Eh bien* Monsieur Eliel, you are managing without a female model at present. You are satisfied with small details that remind you of women, small hints, so to say. That's clever.' She pointed at the brooch and the garter. And Monsieur Eliel, who is not very quick-witted, went as red as a turkey-cock. It was a little unfair of Marcelle, but Madame Marushka laughed heartily when she heard about it. But there, we all hope she is happy, *la petite* Liesel, since she loves Monsieur Eliel. But you! You wouldn't hear a whisper from me if you were living with a man. But to go and install yourself like that among working folk – oh, I know they're good people – but all the same, a milieu that is not yours. Why on earth do you want to live out there?'

'But,' began Alberta. 'In the first place it's cheap. Twelve francs a month, Alphonsine, twelve. Then it's not far from Eliel and Liesel. And I have nothing against seeing different aspects of life.'

'You don't need to look there for the aspects of life that should interest you first and foremost at your age. You have education and a good upbringing. Yes, yes, yes, anyone can see you come from a respectable home. I don't know much, but at least I understand that. And among those people out there . . .'

'But I have nothing to do with them, Alphonsine. I only live there.'

'But you ought to have something to do with someone. I've been saying so for a long time. Another cup of tea?'

Alberta looked up from the Oriental pattern of one of the cushions on Alphonsine's divan. She was lying on her elbow tracing the same whorl with her finger, a whorl that again and again led her back to the beginning, continually growing out of and back on itself.

'Yes, please.'

Alphonsine poured it out of the big silver plated teapot, put three lumps of sugar in it, which she knew Alberta liked, and pushed the biscuits closer. 'Get some strength. You look as if you need it!'

Alberta already had the winter's lurking sensation of influenza in her body. It came with the autumn fogs. She was perpetually cold and could never swill down enough cups of tea, as hot as possible. She took several large gulps, then raised her eyes and met Alphonsine's above the cup. And suddenly the tears were flowing down her face, silently, without a sound or a sob, but impossible to hold back. Embarrassed she fumbled for her handkerchief.

'*Voyons!*' said Alphonsine. '*Voyons!*'

But Alberta was at the point when the barricades fall. Smiling bitterly through her tears she quoted : '*Les femmes s'attachent aux hommes par les faveurs qu'elles leur accordent. Les hommes – guérissent – par les mêmes faveurs.*'

Alphonsine had put her head on one side. Amazement was written in her face. Alberta's tears still flowed copiously.

'What's all this?' asked Alphonsine at last. A quotation?'

'It's from La Bruyère.'

'La Bruyère? Is it now? He is not so stupid, Monsieur La Bruyère.' Alphonsine strummed with her fingers on the table as if to gain time. Then she said : 'Has someone made you unhappy, *ma petite*?'

'He never writes, Alphonsine.' Alberta twisted her sopping wet handkerchief round her fingers, feeling as if she were tearing something to pieces, something secret, holy, flaying it and throwing it away in shreds. But she could not stop herself.

166

'And what about you? Do you write?' Alphonsine seemed to be searching. Her voice was cautious.

'No – I mean, I have written.'

'Hm. Perhaps you should do so again.'

'No, Alphonsine.'

'And there was no misunderstanding, no disagreement?'

That was the good thing about Alphonsine, she kept to the point and asked no more than was absolutely necessary. It was as if she knew all life's alternatives and only needed small clues to clarify them. She did not assume that one had no brains and did not give advice at random. Now she seemed to hesitate: 'Are you sure the fault does not lie in yourself? Men take offence easily, they have much self-esteem. If their masculine dignity is hurt...'

'There was no misunderstanding at the end,' said Alberta. 'That was only at the beginning. He wanted to take me back to his own country...'.

'And you did not want to go?'

'No, yes, of course, I mean... we could have been so happy here, Alphonsine. But finally I nearly agreed to...'.

'Was it America?' asked Alphonsine.

'No. Not as far away as that.'

'Well, well, console yourself, *ma petite*. If he is fond of you...'

'He has been married before, Alphonsine. He was divorced.'

'Oh,' said Alphonsine, and became serious.

Then Alberta felt her face shrink. Something inside her was just as ready, in spite of everything, to crumple up and wither as to unfurl itself and blossom. It must have been hope, imperishable hope. Now it suddenly became microscopic, and Alberta shrank with it.

Alphonsine patted her on the cheek: '*Courage*! If there's anything to him, he'll turn up again. Besides, we don't know what's the matter, it might be any one of a number of things. And if he doesn't, then another will. That's life, *ma petite*, that's how it is.'

No-one will come, insisted a voice inside Alberta. Life

is over, death is all that's left. But Alphonsine continued:
'One does not die of an unhappy love affair. *Bon Dieu*, I
should have died many times! It is hard while it lasts,
but it passes. Well, well, so you are abandoned and
penniless. It is much all at once.'

'Yes,' said Alberta.

Alphonsine flicked the ash off her cigarette: 'Mr. Digby
is not in Paris. You don't want to go on the streets or
turn on the gas, and you are right. What about your
fellow-countrymen?'

'Ness is the only one I know.'

'You avoid them. There's a whole crowd of them on
Montparnasse. It is not wise of you to keep away like that.
Look at the Russians, they stick together, they help each
other. None of them go about lonely as you northerners do.
I know types . . . '

'Yes, I know,' said Alberta, a little fatigued. 'It takes so
long to explain, Alphonsine, how small Norway is, how
careful you have to be to avoid rumours getting home, how
one loathes the way one lived there and would rather put
up with anything than be forced back into it again.'

'And you can't work? Put something together for the
newspapers?'

'Not now, Alphonsine. I can't think. It's as if I were
dead,' said Alberta with sudden candour.

'*Pauvre petite.* I shall have to find something for you,
since you insist. A respectable type, with whom you will
run no risks. To start with we shall have to cheer you up
a little. You are alone too much, go out too seldom.
Tomorrow evening you're coming with me and my friend
to the Gaité Montparnasse. It's not like the Folies Bergère,
but the artistes can be good. And my friend is a good fellow.
You will be doing us a pleasure if you come.'

Alphonsine always spent Saturday to Monday with her
friend. The rest of the week he worked in an automobile
factory at the other end of town. He was a mechanic. 'A
mechanic,' said Alphonsine. 'You know where you are with
him. The artists, they come and go, they love here and

168

love there, believe it is necessary for the sake of their art and call it temperament. They are nervous and difficult, they have even more self-esteem than the rest of them. I've finished with artists in that respect. There are good types amongst them, I don't deny it, *mais enfin . . .* '

Alberta hesitatingly expressed her fear of being a nuisance. She was given the same unaffected reply as always: ' *Que voulez-vous,* Mademoiselle? I have a kind heart.'

* * *

Alphonsine's friend smoked a pipe. This made Alberta a little miserable from the start. His nose looked as if it had been through some accident; it looked like a boxer's. But he was sedate, dependable and dressed in his Sunday best, with hair that lay in little curls on the nape of his neck.

Alphonsine introduced Alberta as ' one of my little artists who needs a bit of starch '.

Monsieur Louis took the pipe out of his mouth and laughed genially: ' One must not take life too seriously and let oneself get thin blood.' And he gave a little lecture on this calamity.

Alphonsine supported him. ' There, you see, Mademoiselle. Learn from the men, they know the art of taking life easily.'

The Rue de la Gaieté smelt of pancakes, potatoes in oil, chestnuts. Hissing fat spluttered, cinematograph bells chimed, gramophones buzzed. A continuous stream of faces came towards one along the pavement, looking hard under the sharp lights of the bars and the *variétés*: red, white, black, tired eyes, brazen eyes, against a restless background of variegated posters. A tram-car advanced slowly, ceaselessly ringing its bell, through the noisy, nervous Saturday evening crowds.

Alphonsine had booked seats in the pit. Cramped and confined between her and Monsieur Louis, who unceasingly did his best, smiling at Alberta at every witticism, having evidently promised himself that she was not to be allowed to sink into melancholy for an instant, Alberta struggled against a boundless feeling of loneliness. Wherever she looked in the packed little theatre in which the air hung stiff with powder, dust and tobacco, and the smell peculiar to old theatres, people were sitting in pairs. When she caught sight of a woman who looked as if she were sitting by herself a few seats in front of her, all female loneliness seemed to engulf her. The reserved, slightly discouraging, unaccompanied lady, the one whom nobdy meets when she alights from a train or goes down a gangplank, who looks round her for a porter when others are surrounded by expectant friends – she who, in a railway carriage or a tram-car, cannot take her eyes off the babbling, laughing child on a strange mother's knee, who bends down to pat an animal on the road because her hands never receive caresses, and are restless from their vain search for something to enfold – oh, Alberta recognized her now, knew who she was, distinguished her without difficulty from the others. She had never seen her before.

Simultaneously the performance on the stage seemed to be ploughing deep furrows in her mind. The sentimental singer in evening dress, who sang of moonshine and couples walking two by two, the innocent young girl who attempted burlesque and was whistled off the stage because she irremediably descended into vulgarity, the man who imitated Polin and sang soldiers' songs, and the one who imitated Chevalier and sang topicalities : behind it all, the good as well as the bad, life's tragedy lay bleeding. Alberta would have preferred to weep when the laughter rang round her.

The star turn was the woman who sang about the apache in a deep, slightly rusty alto. She had a simple black dress, hair hanging about her ears, a large red mouth, slanting eyes. A sigh of expectation went through the audience.

The apache's tricks in deceiving the police, his slave-owner relationship with his sweetheart, his bloody deeds in poorly lighted suburbs, his meeting with the guillotine one morning in the dawn outside the La Santé jail. The prostitute's contempt for the men who pay her, her hatred of the lady who passes by, her savage tenderness for the man who comes home with blood on his sleeve knowing that all is up with him, her loneliness the morning his head falls, and she sees nothing, only hears the roar of the crowd. Brutal and naive romanticism, anything but original, the period's species of cheap romance. But it expressed simply and truthfully human defiance and human passion, tenderness and boldness, rawness, sentimentality and fierce, primitive philosophy. When the singer, her hand on her hip, finally slung out her last refrain, ' *Je m'en fous, de tout* ', it came from the heart and went to the heart. The audience stamped in ecstasy and the dust rose.

Monsieur Louis leaned over towards Alberta and Alphonsine: ' *Eh bien* – either you like this *genre* or you don't. Some people lap it up.'

Alberta had lapped it up. Her mind was like a ploughed field, utterly uncritical. Anything whatsover with a message from life was accepted by it as by fertile soil, but now it affected her differently from before, as new and fearful tragedy.

On the way home Monsieur Louis offered them a drink at the big café on the corner. The violent white light made their faces hard and lined, as if harrowed. In the mirror-lined walls around her Alberta could see various versions of herself, full profile, semi-profile, full-face and from behind. They all looked pathetic and windblown. She could not let herself look like that, so cowed and miserable. Involuntarily she straightened her back, talked, smiled and drank a toast with Monsieur Louis.

' There, you feel better now, don't you? It gives you something to think about to come out, even though it isn't the opera?' Monsieur Louis left no stone unturned in his attempts to cheer her up, telling her stories about his military service and discoursing to her on the disadvantages of living alone. It was not natural, as she perhaps knew and could easily imagine, not good for the health, not salutary: correct, simply stated facts with which Alberta had to agree. Alphonsine nodded approval. She sat with one elbow on the table, sipping the drink she was holding, looking round her with calm, green eyes that seemed to have seen through everything, understood everything and forgiven everything. She looked surprisingly bourgeois in a big skunk collar and she was not smoking.

Both of them accompanied Alberta to her door. It turned out that the staircase light had been extinguished long ago, and Alphonsine decreed that Louis should accompany Alberta with his torch. She would wait in the doorway. She kissed Alberta good-night on the cheek: 'Now you will sleep, won't you? Right through till morning? Like a good little girl.'

Making cheerful conversation, Monsieur Louis escorted Alberta upstairs, exclaiming *zut* and walking on tiptoe on the landings to emphasize his consideration for the sleeping inhabitants of the house, remaining with the light while Alberta searched for the keyhole.

He shook her hand heartily in farewell and assured her that it had been a great pleasure, then swung down the stairs in great leaps. Alberta heard the door open and shut behind him and Alphonsine. And nothing could alter the bitter fact that they were leaving together and were two, while Alberta was only one. Small and cold at heart she fumbled for the matches.

Everybody was two: Alphonsine and Louis, Liesel and Eliel, the apache and his girl, Marushka and – someone or other.

Alberta sat down on the divan. From old habit she tucked her hands up into her sleeves and remained sitting thus, hunched and drooping, lacking the energy to undress. Refrains flooded through her, entered her blood, danced witch dances in her brain, mingled with the noises of the house which were gradually reaching her, and resulted in a bitter brew of defiance, dejection and desperation.

Since La Bruyère's hurtful words had settled in her mind she had not written a line, not even in order to tear them up again. An empty paralysis could seize her for long periods at a time, spreading into her arms and hands. Her limbs would turn to lead, her brain to fog behind her forehead. In a kind of dull amazement she remembered times when adversity had cut into her as sharply as toothache, becoming an aching spot, localized and fierce, or a throbbing fever throughout her body. She had had small childish worries: something she had done wrong, the rent that hung over her head, the *épicier* who had reminded her of what she owed him, anxiety for the morrow. And further back in time the worries of others, the sorrows of adults that can devastate a child before the skin has formed on its soul. It had all expressed itself as something frightful and acute. But beneath the dreadful thought had existed others, which sooner or later would push it aside and come to the top. Hope, the untiring, again put out surface roots into nowhere, in spite of everything. The pain could not go on for ever, nor did it.

This evening she seemed to recognize that everything comes to an end, even pain. It burns itself out finally. One dies of it, or it passes out of one's system like an ache that is over. All that is left is a calcification in the mind, a hard scar, that cannot be affected again.

For the first time for a long period Alberta supposed she had better see about doing something, pulling herself together, quite apart from what Alphonsine could find for her.

Suddenly she stiffened. Someone was outside her door, close up against it. She felt rather than heard the proximity of a person who was standing, then noiselessly shifted his position and went on standing. Clothes brushed almost unnoticeably along the wall. Appalled, Alberta seized the key, holding it tight with both hands. The large, hostile house around her was at once frighteningly full of dangers against which she felt herself to be powerless.

Then a furious whispering began outside, the voices

173

threatening time and again to break out into normal speech, and again dropping to a whisper. Then they exploded into a noisy exchange of violent abuse:

' Old criminal!'

' Old camel!'

' Pig!'

' Cow!'

A door was hurriedly closed, a key turned in the lock. A moment of deep silence followed this most wicked and extreme of all French terms of abuse. The person who had said it was already in safety. Now the other party called with all her strength on heaven and the inhabitants of the house to witness that the fearful word had been spoken.

Farther down the corridor doors opened and shut. Assurances that the old idiots would be thrown out, that the scandal had gone on long enough, that it was someone's intention to inform · the watchman, the manager, the commissioner of police, rent the air. A woman's voice called out emphatically: ' Old shit. Garbage!' A man's exclaimed with dignity: ' Be so good as to be silent, Mesdames. It is almost midnight.'

Alberta opened her door a crack.

On the opposite side of the corridor stood a man in his nightshirt, trousers and slippers, shielding his candle to protect it from the draught. In the room behind him someone was coughing lengthily and tearingly. The commotion was subsiding with an after-swell of scandalized muttering behind the doors farther along.

The man gave Alberta a melancholy smile: ' It is your neighbours to the right and left, Mademoiselle, two poor old women who are a little . . . ' and he pointed significantly at his forehead. ' They compete with each other in listening at your door and peeping through your keyhole, this evening it has been really shocking. It's nothing to be afraid of, but it's very annoying. They've woken my wife too, and I had just got her to sleep. She is not well, unfortunately.' The tearing cough came again from behind him.

Alberta murmured something sympathetic, expressing

the hope that Madame would be able to sleep again and that she would get well. The man gave her the same melancholy smile, and Alberta suddenly shivered as if chilled by frost.

But once behind her closed door she felt something brace itself in her mind, a furious reluctance to go under, to perish in filth, cold and loneliness. In our innermost being there is a tough sinew that binds us to life. In the last resort everything depends on that. It can fairly beckon to us, flash in the darkness. Alberta was sensible of it now. She *would* have warmth and joy and find them for herself, as best she could.

* * *

Alberta was woken by the water-tap farther along the passage. There was a shuffling of slippers along the tiled floor, the tap was turned on violently for a moment. There was a shuffling again. In a little while the tap started running once more.

Madame Bourdarias was fetching water in a bucket; the jet of water slammed against the bottom of it. The old women on either side of Alberta fetched theirs in a scoop or a jug, something that filled quickly and overflowed. The doors banged continually. There was a succession of hurried footsteps going to a certain place. The plug was pulled, but it never worked properly the first time. It was pulled with increasing irritation. Finally the water crashed down.

Through the mansard window Alberta could see the sky. There you are,' Madame Caux had said, when she threw open the door for the first time. ' Look at the view, breathe the fresh air. This is much better than the lower floors. I'd much rather live here than on the first or second floor, *si* Mademoiselle.' And Madame Caux threw out her breast and inhaled eagerly. ' Much better than downstairs. And nobody above your head, no clattering heels when you wish to sleep, no piano late at night. Only quiet people who have their work to do and go to bed early. Twelve francs a month, almost gratis.'

Under the window stood her trunk with her books on top of it, difficult to get into. A closed coffin.

The sloping roof was so low that she could only stand upright close to the one wall; but if she absolutely had to stand, she could do so. Tired of looking for the cheapest possible room, Alberta had taken it.

Outside it was pouring with rain. A raw wintry draught was blowing between the window and the crack under the door. Shivering, Alberta plucked up courage and splashed herself with water while the spirit stove whistled.

There were the concierge's footsteps along the passage. She paused. Yet again she looked through the pile of letters. There was a rustling down by the floor. Something was being put under one of the doors, a voice called, Thank you, Madame Caux '. The footsteps advanced, and again stopped. From unbroken habit Alberta held her breath, her coffee-cup trembling so much that she had to put it down. But the footsteps continued, heavy, slightly dragging.

So Alberta did what had to be done if she did not want to fall into utter decrepitude and become like the old character who had had the room before her, and of whom legends were told in the house. He never made his bed, the room was a nest of fleas. He was lonely and suspicious and allowed no-one in until one day Madame Caux reported him to the Poor Relief, and they came and took him away.

Alberta aired and tidied, fetched water to wash the tiny floor, pretending to herself that it was important.

The usual bloodstains led from Madame Bourdarias's door to the water-tap. It hurt Alberta to see them; she felt as if stabbed with an awl in her sensitive parts. A person could be as destroyed as Madame Bourdarias and still stay alive. The first time Alberta had noticed the red drops on the floor she had thought: Someone has cut his finger; the

176

second time: it must be someone who suffers from nose-bleeds.

The third time she drew Madame Bourdarias's attention to the horrible stains; she was the only person she knew, and she had just arrived with her bucket. A quick flush had spread over the thin face with the kind, patient eyes, the voice begged indulgence: 'It is I, Mademoiselle, it is I. I assure you I do what I can, but as soon as I take hold of anything, lift something, it happens just the same. At the hospital they say I must stay in bed, they want to keep me there. But what would happen to my children, Mademoiselle?'

Alberta stood rooted to the spot, searching for something to say, finding nothing. Madame Bourdarias was back at once with a cloth to wipe the floor: 'The worst of it is the young people in the house. The thought of them troubles me. It doesn't help much to clean it up, see here. And one becomes modest as one gets older, Mademoiselle. Just as modest as when one was growing up.'

Alberta was alone again, shocked as if she had witnessed an act of cruelty. The next day she had made an awkward attempt to carry the bucket for Madame Bourdarias. A thin red hand, hard and rough, pushed her own away from the handle: 'I have four children of school age, Mademoiselle, and I help in three households. One bucket of water more or less ...'. And Alberta saw the naive, almost unnecessary intrusiveness of her action.

She had lived up here as one must with something that is more than one can bear, holding her breath and with her eyes shut. The red patches on the floor, the cough from the room across the passage, the man who lived there with his sad smile, always carrying something, milk bottles and dripping packages of food or long rolls of drawing paper, his skin yellow-white as silk above the black beard – these things had of course hurt her, as the whipped horse on the street did, or the ragged beggar with his outstretched hand. She remembered for a while, then thought about something else.

177

She had scarcely noticed the two elderly women who were her neighbours. With faded hair, clothes, eyes, on terms of enmity with each other and the whole house, strangely alike, they padded about like grey shadows, as frightening as everything life leaves behind unused. They reminded her of dusty old objects that nobody wants any more. It probably would not have surprised her if one day she had found them set aside in a corner out there.

Now it had all become horribly tangible. She looked round her room as if it were a chamber of horrors. And for the first time for a long period she again considered ways of escape.

There was really only one. She must see about writing something again. Even if Alphonsine found what she called a respectable type, it would be no use Alberta presenting herself just now. She looked like pictures she had seen of famine areas in India. Her ribs resembled a comb, her shoulder-blades protruded from her back like two abortive little wings. Her collar-bones, her childhood affliction, again stood out in relief. She was shockingly thin.

And now her body demanded food. Voracity suddenly possessed her. When she thought about it, it was quite a long time since she had eaten properly or even considered what she ate. What had she picked at recently? *Pommes frites,* boiled beans, chestnuts, spinach, bread. In her imagination she saw large plates of hot soup, steaming portions of meat. Her coat was thin, her shoes barely possible, her sandals out of the question in winter.

She owed money everywhere. In the dairy, at the *Epicerie* and the bakery. Soon it would be the rent. And panic seized her. Life had taken her by the scruff of the neck again, and was shaking her hard.

It was no use surveying her belongings. She owned nothing that would be accepted in pawn except the mattress on legs. Quite apart from other discomforts resulting from the transaction, her reputation in the house would sink to below zero if she allowed it to be carried away. It was unthinkable.

She would have to write again and borrow in the meantime, scrape material together as best she could, trim it and send it off. It had worked before, it ought to work now. Blue with cold, her fingers stiff, she set to, out of practice and reluctant, attempting to find the smallest thread that lay, thin and miserable, hidden somewhere in her mind. She ought to be able to tell the person from whom she was going to borrow that this was her article, here it was in her hand. In a few days the fee would arrive.

Instinctively she sought out the pleasant moments in the life about her, remembered the occasional glimpses she had had of Madame Bourdarias's room in the evening where four children, well cared-for and respectable, happily saved from all adversity, sat gathered round the steaming soup tureen on the red check tablecloth; while the enormous pitchpine bed, and the huge hanging lamp which all the poorer classes in Paris acquire as soon as they are able, seemed to fill the room. She included too the slender, clear-eyed young woman farther along the passage, the one from Auvergne, who always carried her baby in her arms and was always singing to it; monotonous, repetitious melodies, peasant airs to which one automatically beats time. That was the sort of thing people liked to read on Sunday afternoons after coffee, they liked above all idyllic scenes and the pleasant side of life. For a moment Alberta considered bringing in the bloodstains, but resolutely skirted them and contented herself with implying depravity in the character of the eldest Bourdarias, who was at the hobbledehoy stage and a worry to his mother. He always left a whiff of cigarette-smoke and an echo of ' *Quand l'Amour Meurt* ' in the composite atmosphere of the corridor.

The *épicier*? His colourful still-life on the pavement down in the depths brightened the grey street. It produced rather cheap effects, but was a relief for the eye. And it provided an opportunity for word-painting in a way that might give rise to an encouraging little remark in the editor's reply : ' Your last article was very entertaining. We look forward with pleasure to more from your pen.'

179

Cabbage, carrots, fresh wet lettuce, apples, oranges, eggs coloured with carmine, blue grapes, golden-yellow marrows; and as a realistic, but not too shocking addition, his trade in living and dead rabbits, small furry animals that he kept in crates under the tables outside. They nibbled lettuce, sitting on their haunches with one paw uplifted, snuffing the air with mobile, anxious noses. But fate plays with life and death, the *épicier* would come for them. He would look up and down the street, whistling and chatting with the passers-by while he squatted down and fumbled with his hand in the crate. And he hauled out a portion of life, a cowering bundle of terrified nerves suspended from two long ears, and disappeared with it into the darkness of the shop. Straightaway he was back again with a corpse, the thinnest, most pathetic of all small corpses, a flayed rabbit. He added it to his exhibition.

Here Alberta suddenly stopped. Paralysed by the superficiality, the one-sidedness and cheapness of her account, she sat, despondent to the core, hollow with cold and incompetence. She tore up what she had written and put on her coat. Liesel and Eliel were in for it. It was imperative that she have proper food. She went out into the drizzle.

From the outset it did not look promising. There seemed to be nobody at home. Alberta knocked several times and was about to go away again when the door opened suddenly. It was Eliel, looking unnecessarily surprised : ' Look who's here, Alberta! I thought I heard someone knocking.'

Alberta told him, somewhat astonished, that she had been knocking for a long time. ' Would you believe it?' cried Eliel. ' Here I am, sitting with Dr. Freytag. We were having quite an animated conversation, it's true, but still . . . ' And Eliel introduced Dr. Freytag, a tall, thin man with thick, tightly curled hair. He rose in the darkness of the studio and bowed coldly to Alberta, and, for no apparent reason, she felt an immediate antipathy towards him. He was the Austrian Liesel had mentioned occasionally, one of their acquaintances from St. Jean du Doigt.

Eliel did not invite Alberta in. He let her stand out in the rain while he informed her that Liesel was not there. He did not know where she was living. He turned to Dr. Freytag and asked him if he remembered where Liesel had said she was going? Was it not so, that someone had arrived whom she had to look after, someone travelling through? Freytag shrugged his shoulders and eyebrows apologetically as one who knows nothing and cannot help in the matter. The whole manoeuvre filled Alberta with a kind of unease, not solely derived from the fact that she was, to say the least, not wanted. Dr. Freytag's presence also prevented her from asking Eliel for a casual loan, which she otherwise could have done on the basis of much mutual assistance over the years. Confused and blank, she prepared to leave, full of inexplicable anxiety. It was not lessened when Eliel suddenly, quite at random and as if speaking over her head, made some bitterly humorous remarks about the rain: 'It's terrible how it goes on raining. It's shameful. Enough to make you pregnant.'

This old joke of Eliel's which Alberta had never found amusing, appeared downright macabre at this juncture. Was Eliel a little unbalanced? Was he a little drunk? It had not rained for more than a day. An old Parisian like Eliel should not get pregnant for so little. It could rain here for weeks and months at a time. She asked him to give Liesel her greetings and left. 'Yes, of course, indeed I will,' he called after her in an extravagantly bright and cheerful tone of voice. And Alberta was out in the street again. And everything was worse than before. There was treachery in the December day, pain rested crushingly upon the world.

Dusk was already falling. The winter darkness of the city comes gradually, grey as death. Alberta wandered down towards Montparnasse, uncertain as to what she should do, uncertain as to what had really happened to Liesel. Had she been up in the loft all the time, kept up there by Dr. Freytag? Or had something happened to her and Eliel? Had they fallen out? Had they been discovered and exposed? Was there really nothing the matter, or was something mysterious and inexplicable, distressing and inevitable, going on? Oh, it was probably only shortage of money and the weather that made Alberta see the black side of everything. Eliel had probably been the same as usual, a little thoughtless and scatter-brained, wrapped up in his own affairs.

Alberta wandered into Colarossi's. It was unlikely that Liesel would be there. But there was the warmth for the models. She could stand there pretending to look for her, waiting for her.

Correction was under way. A grizzled, friendly little gentleman in grizzled clothes with a red ribbon in his buttonhole went from place to place, began with an encouraging *pas mal, pas mal,* and continued in a lower, confidential tone, accompanying his words with rounded gestures across the paper, small curves of the hand, small shrugs of the shoulder. Finally he seized charcoal or brush, made merciless strokes right across the work, nodded benevolently and went on.

Alberta stood waiting as long as she decently could. The warmth streamed soothingly through her, while she made herself appear to be looking for someone across the thicket of easels, swinging palettes, skewed heads and brushes held convulsively at arm's length in a last hopeful assessment.

And she pushed her way out again, between ladies flocking eagerly round mediocre studies, past the fanatical German who interested himself solely in movement, and really had brought it to the point where his drawings resembled the jointed figures made of wood and wire one buys at the ironmonger's. Just then someone was accusing him of drawing sticks, not legs. He punched his painter's stool with clenched fist, declaring: ' *Es giebt überhaupt keine Beine nicht. Es giebt nur Stöcke.*' And Alberta suddenly felt what an elevated form of existence it was to be able to stand in a well-lighted, well-warmed place maintaining opinions of this kind; opinions of any kind. And

182

what a categorically low form it was to trudge along the muddy, rain-wet streets looking for her next meal.

In the Rue Delambre there was a little shop where for years she had indulged in culinary extravagances. It sold chocolates, sweets, coffee, spices. It was always a place where she could go and stand for a little in the light and warmth, looking at it all. A chocolate bar for three sous was sufficient excuse.

The air was always the same in here, heavy with vanilla and stored coffee. Behind the counter was one of the two deformed sisters who took it in turns to stand there. She interrogated Alberta with interest as to how she was, whether she still lived in the *quartier*? Oh dear, had she moved? But she remained faithful to her former purveyors. It was kind of her, very kind. Would she like Salavin's chocolate, or another brand? Her small purchase was by no means treated as of little account, on the contrary, it might have been a matter of importance. In the meantime sister number two, who was exactly like the first, their mother, also the same but older, and their father, white-haired, his pen behind his ear, were all called in. The father dealt with the paper work of the business and always carried a pen. They all gathered round Alberta, asking about the state of her health. Mademoiselle was still in Paris? Mademoiselle was happy in Paris? Mademoiselle had again spent the summer here? But there – one had Bellevue and Meudon, was it not so? One had the woods at Clamart. And near by were the Luxembourg Gardens. which were splendid.

The space was minimal, the view on to the grey street miserable and dull. A red cretonne curtain divided the shop from a dark little back room which served as sitting-room, dining-room, office. But each time the curtain was raised Alberta saw the hanging lamp illuminating a table set for a meal. A long shining loaf reflected the light, a soup tureen steamed on the check tablecloth, a bowl of salad looked newly tossed and inviting. And hunger for proper food again hollowed into her breast, while she kept

183

her side of the conversation going as best she could. Had not the family been to the country this year either? Was it not so that they had relatives in Brittany?

Oh yes, yes indeed. But everyone could not travel, it was impossible because of the business. So no-one did. They had each other, they did not know for how long. They kept together. Besides, they went on trips on Sunday afternoons, attended the open air concerts at the Tuileries Gardens in the evenings. They would really be very ungrateful if they were not satisfied.

When Alberta left them, knowing that they were gathering round the steaming tureen again, she thought of how she could have been like them, placid, industrious, frugal, friendly, easy to meet, closely tied to her children. How would life have turned out then? That year in Kristiania, for instance? There had not only been Engen Street. There had been the museums, the Abel statue and the Viking ships, the Deichman Library, uncle's bookcase which had been quite comprehensive. There had been two or three plays at the National Theatre. Above all there had been the National Gallery which she had visited often. But all this had only increased her dissatisfaction, creating fresh disturbance in her mind. And since? Reasonable conditions had been offered her time and again. She could have gone home with her knowledge of languages, and lived on them simply and respectably. She could have –

Alberta suddenly started walking quickly uphill in the direction of the Rue Campagne Première. She would not give up. Not yet. And she regretted nothing. She could not have acted differently on any occasion. There was something she had to do, she was searching for it. It led her on to painful and desolate paths through cold and loneliness. She could only wish she were someone else, that she need not be the person she was.

Now she wanted food. It occurred to her that if only she could get a couple of proper meals inside herself, if she could avoid, if only once or twice, the warmed-up beans, the half-cold chestnuts in the sad glow of the candle, she would get back her equilibrium again, find the courage to get to grips with something, even with her writing. To someone who takes the short view a meal can seem like a stage on one's journey, a new chance. If I get that far, I shall also get a little further. But with the sum she had in her pocket it was useless presenting herself anywhere, even at the Coachmen's Rest. She hurried on.

On the gloomy staircase of number nine she was stopped for a moment by a scene on one of the landings. A model with a man's coat slung about her was engaged in a cheerful tussle with a painter in a smock. They were fighting over a pipe, disporting themselves and laughing, then they suddenly fell silent and struggled on, their faces tense and serious. Alberta continued with their faces imprinted on her mind, blinded by them for a second, as if she had seen fire break out; empty and poor after the incident, as if left sitting in the ashes.

On the next landing she met Potter.

Potter was carrying an empty milk bottle, and transporting lettuce leaves and gnawed chop-bones packed loosely in a sheet of newspaper. In the wretched light from the gas-flame she looked older than usual, harrowed and sad. It struck Alberta that plenty of women of Potter's age were doing just this when evening came, their hands clutching the rubbish from a small, lonely household. It gave her the feeling of being condemned to death, with the mode of death demonstrated to her: to wither, to wither. Like Otilie Weyer at home. Like Potter and Stoltz and the old fools in the corridor where she lived. She began to feel desperate.

But Potter's face brightened, as lonely faces do when they meet someone. Was Alberta coming to see her? If so Potter would turn round and go up again. She was on her way to the garbage can, from there she had thought of going out to eat and then on to the evening drawing class. It was a long time since she had seen Alberta. Where was Alberta living now? What was she doing? She had got thinner. There was nothing the matter, was there?

' No, of course not.' Alberta attempted to laugh it off.

' I miss you,' said Potter. ' I like you. And I wish you would work. Work now while there's time. When you get old it's too late for everything, for that too. Don't let the men hinder you, dear. They hinder us at our best time, then leave us behind. I could tell you things, plenty of things. Won't you come up with me?'

Potter looked at Alberta hungrily, as if out of a long grey day's loneliness. And the painful question one should really only put with forced assurance to those who are in the same situation as oneself, and whose opinion does not matter, popped out of Alberta's mouth. Slightly appalled she listened to her own words: Could Potter make her a small loan? She happened to be in difficulties. And she muttered something about a letter that had been delayed.

She regretted it at once. Potter's expression changed, as if she had heard something shocking or scandalous. She said pityingly, ' I'm afraid I can't, dear.'

Her voice a tone too high, Alberta hastened to assure her that she was expecting it every day, it would be all right, and Potter's expression returned to normal. Oh, she was glad to hear Alberta say so. Delays in the mail were disagreeable, very disagreeable. She hoped it would turn up soon. *Au revoir* dear. And she went on down with her chop-bones.

Outside Marushka's door Alberta paused, and took a deep breath. Marushka was not the kind of person from whom one could not ask a favour, but money was money. Alberta should have been hardened, but she was not. She knocked.

Under normal circumstances Marushka would now either not answer or utter the traditional ' Who's there?' from immediately behind the door. Neither of these things occurred. From far away, as if from the farthest corner of the studio, there came a loud, clear and unreserved ' Come in '.

186

Astonished, Alberta opened the unlocked door, and remained standing in the doorway, uncertain, a little numbed by the heavy, spicy warmth that met her, a blend of perfume and heat that was almost paralysing. The curtains were drawn across the windows, the grey evening was shut out. There was a red glow from a small paraffin stove down on the floor, and above the divan a single gas-jet was lighted, with a rose-coloured silk shade over it. Under it Marushka was enthroned with her legs drawn up beneath her, supported by brightly coloured cushions on all sides like the inhabitant of a harem.

She was wearing a black kimono with gold embroidery, one of the expensive items of clothing one sometimes picks up and admires, but never thinks of buying. Her slender, short feet stuck out naked and childish from under the hem. Her pink toes were stretching themselves, as if pleased with their freedom. Alberta could not help being reminded of children she had helped with their clothes. In her lap Marushka had *Omar Khayyám* – recognizable from its soft leather binding – in her hand a cigarette. From the low table beside her an airy blue arabesque from an incense lamp coiled upwards. Half-blown Riviera roses were standing about, the silver vase with the cigarettes in it was shining. Books lay carelessly in heaps. The whole picture contrasted so strongly with the meanness of the staircase, the rain and early darkness out in the street, that Alberta needed to collect her wits. She was used to coming across Marushka in all sorts of situations: in a painter's smock, smeared with colour, or sitting on the edge of a table eating one of her extraordinary meals, the ingredients arranged round her in their respective wrappings and a jar of jam from Felix Potin in the middle of it all. This was new.

Marushka remained seated without moving. And indeed the light had been so well calculated to fall on her that it would have been a pity. Between the kimono and her short hair her face, neck and breast had something satisfied and creamy-white about it, a strange, thick fullness, here and there toning into the rose-coloured light from the lampshade. It was suddenly clear to Alberta what Liesel and Sivert meant when, with their heads askew and their eyes narrowed they agreed that there were possibilities in Marushka, that she ought to be built up in thick colour with a palette-knife. She was by no means free of smallpox scars, but this seemed to contribute to the richness. Just as astonished as Alberta, she asked without preliminaries: 'What is it?'

'No, nothing.' Alberta was thrown off balance by the circumstances, and felt herself to be as much out of place as she possibly could be in Marushka's studio at that precise moment. It was not she who should have come in. She prepared to withdraw.

But now Marushka rose to her feet and came tripping on naked toes across the floor, small, rather broadly built, above all buoyant: 'There *is* something the matter. I can see there is. Come back tomorrow. I – I'm expecting someone, to be frank.'

'Yes, I understand that.'

'Is it obvious? *Tant pis.*'

'I'll go, Marushka.'

'Listen . . .' Marushka seized Alberta by the arm. 'Is it money? I can see it's money.'

The flush rose in Alberta's face. 'I'll manage somehow.'

Marushka was still holding Alberta's arm. She rattled on quickly, as if every second counted: 'I've paid the cleaning woman, and had a parcel from Bon Marché, I haven't a sou. But tomorrow I'm going to the Rue de l'Arbalète to meet some of my fellow-countrymen. This evening – I'm prevented . . . .'

Alberta felt her shoulders sag. Marushka's many puzzle pictures on the walls around her, their colours deep and beautiful as carpets, but their construction such that one always felt like tidying and rearranging them, danced in front of her eyes. For a moment she glimpsed Sivert and Alphonsine, but they disappeared again at once. Something inside her gave way.

'Must you have it today? Listen . . . .' Marushka's face

188

glowed with a new idea: 'Hurry to the Mont de Piété with something or other. If you go now you'll get there before they close. It's not at all unpleasant, they treat you very politely. You can redeem it as soon as you have the money again.'

Alberta smiled bitterly: ' If only I had something to take there.'

' You must have something, a ring, a watch, a bagatelle. Preferably something on you. I don't think you'll have time to go home first.'

Then Alberta's weakness overcame her: ' All that I had, on me or at home, found its way there long ago.'

' *Comment*?' Marushka slapped Alberta on the back. ' Why didn't you say so at once? Look, take this!' And she fluttered on tiptoe across the floor, came fluttering back again, and hung her watch on its long chain round Alberta's neck. ' Here you are, *ma petite*. It's a good watch, twenty carats. You'll get at least a hundred francs for it.'

Blood-red, Alberta seized Marushka's hands, trying to prevent her, to take off the chain again. But Marushka held it in place with her strong little hands, stuffed the watch down the neck of Alberta's dress, and pushed her out of the door. ' Yes, yes, yes, why not? I don't need to look at the clock all the time. Alphonsine has a watch, and so have most of my friends. There are clocks in the street, at the station and the cafés, the world is full of clocks.'

' But Marushka, I don't know when I shall be able to redeem it again.'

' *Tant pis, tant pis*. While I remember, Liesel, go and see Liesel, I saw her the other day, she looked as if – there's someone on the stairs! Go now. Come again soon, *au revoir, courage*, off with you!'

Marushka gave Alberta a quick kiss on each cheek, span her round, shoved her out on to the landing, shut the door. Her tiptoe fluttering was audible for a moment, then there was silence. She was posing amongst her cushions again.

Far below the footsteps did not stop anywhere, but continued upwards. Simultaneously relieved and depressed,

189

Alberta went down to meet them. In a while she would eat warm food, soup, meat. She would be able to pay the rent punctually without having to take refuge in the little speech she had already begun to prepare and rehearse so as to be able to deliver it easily, in an off-hand manner: a misunderstanding, a delayed letter, pure mischance, a matter of a few days . . . .

She would be able to buy herself a lamp, something to read . . . .

The footsteps were just below her. Hastily she composed her face in case it was someone she knew and must greet. But it was one of the Americans, one of the many from Montparnasse. He looked searchingly at Alberta, as men do look at strange women, enquiringly, appraisingly. And she heard him knock at Marushka's door, heard a loud, clear ' Come in '.

A sensation resembling cramp seized Alberta's heart for a moment, a privation, raging as hunger. Then she went on her way with the watch, hurrying along the wet, glistening pavements, knowing she only had a few minutes left.

She arrived just in time to see the heavy doors swung to and bolted.

Back in her room she lighted her candle. The flame cast shadows up the walls and was reflected, thin and flickering, in the glass covering the reproductions.

She remained sitting with her coat on. This was one of the moments when she hated herself and everything about her, her wicker trunk and her worn soles, the whole of her shabby and purposeless existence. Reluctantly and with difficulty burning tears forced themselves out of the corners of her eyes. As if on its own account her mouth whispered defiantly: ' I *will* have a different, comfortable life, warmth, someone to be with, pretty clothes, fur round my neck, books that are mine and that I don't need to stand reading at the Odéon.'

An old and evil thought reared its head, watchful as a

poisonous reptile: I could go on the streets, earn ten francs, twenty francs, hide them in my stocking and earn more, I, just as well as others. I belong to myself, I can do what I please with my body. No-one can touch my soul. I could do it from cold, from the desire for human warmth. If I'm no good at anything else, I could always be of use on the streets.

Then her defiance melted. She sat there knowing that she would not do it, and that she wanted to even less now than before.

She must have a slight fever. Her ears were buzzing, she was cold inside and unreasonably warm outside. She had kicked off her shoes and her soaking wet stockings. With her hands tucked up inside her sleeves and her feet under her she remained sitting, while the packet of spinach she had brought home with her disintegrated from the damp and dripped greenly on to the chair beside her. And she dozed upright like the cab-horses.

When someone knocked she knew at once who it was. As if in a dream she opened the door, without changing her position and without saying anything, remaining sitting with her legs under her looking up at Sivert Ness, who stood there looking larger than usual in a new thick winter coat, his hat in his hand. She could not see his expression. The light did not fall that way. But she felt his eyes on her and met them haphazardly.

That was his hand, feeling her shoulder and her arm. She heard him say: 'But you're soaked, you're sitting here soaking wet. You mustn't do that you know. Nothing on your legs, and it's cold in here and everything – whatever next.' He leaned over, felt her saturated shoes, and shook his head: 'Everything wet through. This is sheer idiocy. It takes less than this to make you ill.'

That was his hand in her sleeve, drawing out hers, clasping it. It had hold of her, the strong hand she had gone half in fear of. She winced as if she had burned herself,

191

something inside her was shattered. Then it was over. She pressed the hand.

'Like a live coal,' commented Sivert. And he leaned over her and said in a tone of voice that she would not have believed him to be capable of: 'Well, there's only one thing to be done. For you have a fever. I can see it from your eyes.' He looked round for a moment, as if summing up the situation. 'You can't stay here, there's nowhere to set up a stove even.' And he leaned over her again. 'There's a red glow right across the floor in my room.' He began putting on her stockings and shoes as if she were a child, tying tight solid knots that could not come undone.

Alberta was filled with gratitude simply for his presence and for the warmth that flowed from him. Giddily she put her hand on his shoulder. Sivert looked up, held both her arms firmly for an instant, then released her. 'Now we must hurry,' he said.

❊ *Part Four* ❊

The north wind blew cold and hard, chasing clouds of dust
down the streets. When Alberta went from barrow to
barrow making purchases and saw the grey, frozen faces
crowding round her, Sivert's stove seemed an unjust
advantage with something of immodest upper-class luxury
about it. She noticed how many in the crowd smelt unpleasant, unwashed and stuffy and thought: No wonder – you
can't reproach poor people for being dirty. If you have few
clothes, live in cramped conditions and are always cold,
keeping clean becomes an insoluble problem. And she felt
a sensation that was almost deceit towards all those around
her who she knew would go home and continue to feel
cold.

When Sivert had raked out the embers in the morning
and riddled the ashes, the stove shone far out over the
floor, creating a circle of warmth. Into it was brought
Sivert's zinc bath-tub, heavy and unwieldy to normal folk,
but a bagatelle to him. Then all she had to do was get into
it, scrub herself red and warm with the heat from the
stove-hole glowing straight on to her skin, and curl up on
the divan in an aroma of coffee.

For the first few days Alberta had stayed in bed with
fever. She just sensed that two large, tranquil hands shook
up her pillow now and again and turned it, that she was
supported in bed and given something to drink; and she
dozed off again. Then came an evening when the fever had
gone. In rare high spirits she sat on the divan, wrapped in
Sivert's new winter coat for lack of a dressing-gown, ate

193

greedily, talked and laughed, all the time with the feeling that it was really another person sitting there, quite a different person from the old Alberta. Or perhaps it was that one life lay behind her, a new one was beginning. For better, for worse, it was so.

The weather was just as unpleasant as when she had arrived, with rain streaming over the panes in the skylight and dripping in several places on to the floor. Sivert had put dishes and bowls underneath. He himself sat in his usual manner, as if on a crate in the kitchen, listening to Alberta and putting in a word here and there. The stove burned as it should, casting a long red glow.

It was then that an ache took hold of Alberta, sorrow, longing, sympathy, fate, bitter necessity, all mingling and streaming towards her heart. Human loneliness suddenly became so clear to her. Here they sat, she and Sivert, as if drifted together, shut in by the rain and the darkness. How good Sivert had been to her! And she did something she had to do, it seemed predetermined that she should do it; she put her hand on the nape of his neck.

He sat turned towards the fire, so she did not see his eyes this time either. When he stretched out an arm and calmly drew her to him she felt an instant of tremendous distress, but made no resistance. And all that was mute in Sivert engulfed her.

Afterwards she smiled as best she could, the tears streaming down her face, a circumstance that did not seem to astonish Sivert in the slightest or put him at a loss. All in all, Sivert was easy-going about things like that. He made no enquiries about the past or the future, but took everything as it came. And it was good. There was obliteration in it. Shoots, that had once put out tendrils to no purpose and been singed off, were kept in check.

He would walk humming between his easel and his observation point in the middle of the floor, painting artichokes and other vegetables, making the utmost use of the grudging daylight. When Alberta had the meal ready on the table, he would rub his hands together with satisfaction, find it excellent, and, far from leaving the most boring part of it to her, would help with the washing up and clearing away.

She had begun mending his socks and repairing various garments that were lying about. He never asked her to do so, he had managed it himself very well and could presumably manage it still. The tidiness of Sivert's wardrobe was amazing. But when she sat down to it a second time he made no objection.

He had had a model the first few days. Alberta, lying dozing in the loft, heard at intervals his broken French as he talked to the model below. He did not attempt to hide the fact that there was someone upstairs, but went imperturbably up and down to see how Alberta was. 'Is that your lady friend up there?' asked the model. 'Yes,' answered Sivert. 'Has she influenza?' 'Yes.' 'Yes, it's the time of year for it now.'

Sivert finished his studies of the model in a few days. Then he began on the artichokes. Sometimes he made a quick sketch of Alberta, as she sat sewing. In the afternoon he went to life-class.

Then Alberta was left alone for a while, and it was a painful time, full of uneasiness. She ought to work as well, sit down and write something, see about earning some money. She had warmth, peace, someone to be with. She postponed it from day to day.

Once she went back to her room. It was comfortless and unlived-in, dusty and cold. She sat on the edge of the open trunk, looking for clothes she wanted, coming across loose sheets covered with writing, and also a little ring with an amethyst which she had taken from her finger and dropped into the trunk one evening that autumn. Now it lay there casually among so much else, a little stray object of pity. It looked at her upbraidingly, and she wept over it for a while. A thought that had sometimes brushed her mind fleetingly, reappeared: Death?

It can come like an icy wind striking down people like pawns with a single breath and bringing desolation to numbers of homes at one fell swoop. Having experienced it once, it remained for ever a reality to be reckoned with. She had never thought about it before.

But many of the circumstances of life were equally possible. A man comes to feel sorry for the little wife, red-eyed with weeping, who wants him back on any terms; perhaps he becomes fond of her again. It probably happens often. And La Bruyère certainly knew what he was talking about. What with one thing and another, there was no need to go so far as to think of death. Alberta had in any case arrived at the stage when she could bear to look at the whole thing in perspective; she was no longer a bundle of aching nerves meeting an endless series of painful moments as one might a whipping. She lived on, and wished to do so; and took what life offered, whatever it might be. Still, she would frequently see fragments of a face. The memory of a hand, a touch, a tone of voice, would strike her unprepared, as if from behind. The sound of Sivert's shaving in the morning – like someone peeling a raw potato – would perhaps continue to scrape her nerves for a long time, painful and too familiar as it was. But everything passes. She would not suffer like that a second time. A hard spot forms inside, that cannot be attacked again.

She read the sheets of paper for a while, since she was up there. They surprised her, they resembled small fragments of life piled in confusion. She thought vaguely that perhaps they could be threaded together into some cohesion. What would that look like? Then she packed them in again.

In the corridor she met no-one. It was the lunch hour and quiet on the stairs. Madame Caux looked out of her window: So Mademoiselle had moved to friends during the cold period? She was wise. Whatever one might say about the attic rooms, they were not warm. No, there were no letters. If anyone came asking for Mademoiselle, what should Madame Caux say? That Mademoiselle was away

196

for a short visit? Staying with a friend? Coming back soon. *Bien,* Mademoiselle.

And Alberta left with something of a guilty conscience. In a way she had abandoned her own existence, the cold, depressing house, the many people who were forced to go on living there.

Sivert's paintings consisted of landscapes, life studies, street scenes, still lifes. Their strength lay in their colour. Abundance as from a bouquet of flowers met the eye when Sivert propped his canvases along the wall, a collective sensation of flesh, clouds, green and stone grey all united, a sensation almost of scent. His technique was not new or unusual. He took an interest in the numerous contemporary experiments in that direction, but continued imperturbably to paint in his old manner, an uncomplicated simplification uninfluenced by any ' isms '.

' I must paint as I see it,' said Sivert. ' I can't do anything else.' In spite of this he often came home with books and brochures on new forms of expression, Cubism and Futurism, Orphism, Dadaism and Synchronism. He studied them seriously and reflectively, finding out what all these strange words really entailed. Where Eliel only sneered and poked fun, where Kalén became angry and aggrieved, Sivert sat and cogitated. ' I'll try to find out what those fellows mean, at any rate,' he would say, and stuff the pamphlets into his pocket until the next spare moment.

When he submitted a picture to Alberta's judgment, she stood a little embarrassed. It was the same with painting as with music: she was repelled or fascinated, strongly and decisively, but she found it difficult to say why. Besides much else she lacked critical ability. She wished she could find something to say besides ' It's beautiful, Sivert, it's excellent '. She was not good at that sort of thing.

On the other hand, she thought she did understand the total sum of strain and will-power that lay behind a complicated work. Now, when she watched Sivert painting every day, she could be stirred by his struggle with the motif, as

197

one always is stirred by masculine toil. He stood there, frugal, industrious, untiringly pursuing what he wished to reveal, sometimes from canvas to canvas. He had a peculiar way of suddenly painting with his thumb, of entering personally into the work, as if boxing with it. For him this was life's hard journey. And she was seized with a desire to be useful in her way, with carefully prepared meals, and so on.

One day when he was painting one of his still lifes, the eternal refuge of all impecunious painters, Alberta said almost at random – she was sitting thinking about one of Marcel Lenoir's pictures, a Golgotha scene with solidly composed, strictly simplified groups in a solidly composed, simplified landscape with shadows from great masses of cloud drifting over it: 'If I were a painter, I would paint life.'

She shut her eyes. There was a sudden flickering behind them. People were moving between groups of trees and high cliffs. Children played and ran, couples walked close together, or apart, as if they were strangers. Here was a woman sitting alone, weeping, here was another suckling her child, here was someone working, here sat a couple of old people . . .

'Life,' smiled Sivert. 'That's quite a tall order.'

Alberta opened her eyes. He was just going back from the picture, inspecting it, adding after mature consideration a new smudge of colour. 'Non-painters always want to do symbolic things,' he said. 'It's a certain sign of dilettantism.'

But Alberta, who still glimpsed a little of what she had seen, continued: 'Life. In the middle of it all I would put the tree of good and evil, full of apples.'

'Ouch,' said Sivert. 'Art is teeming with that kind of allegory. At home we have Vigeland, fortunately without any tree of good and evil, as far as I know.'

'That may be so,' persisted Alberta. 'I would put in people I knew, Alphonsine and Madame Bourdarias and you, Sivert, painting artichokes.'

It was good to sit and talk. It made the time pass.

' It would have to be kept strictly simple,' said Sivert after a while. ' Sculptural, almost.'

' Precisely. It would all have to be contained in the positions, the gestures.'

Sivert fell silent again, painted, moved forwards and backwards, went across to see to the stove. As he was squatting there, he said: ' Yes, the motif is really not so important. It depends on how it's done.'

The next day, when Alberta unloaded her purchases on to the table, he shoved a rough pencil sketch across to her. ' Look,' he said. ' Something like that?' And he explained the foreground figures to her: ' I haven't brought it off, but I thought this position should be thus and thus. And like this here. I've only drawn it straight out of my head.'

Then Alberta again did something she had to do. It hung in the air and seemed to be simply a continuation.

Quickly she took off her clothes, and posed in the warmth near the stove. ' Like this?' she said.

' Yes,' said Sivert eagerly. He had already taken out his sketch book and was drawing.

But when Sivert held her close to him and warm currents flowed through her from his hands, then they were two lonely, frozen people, who crept together beside the fire of life and warmed themselves as well as they could. It was neither wrong nor shocking, as some arrogantly insist. It was their simple right.

The spark kindled by two poverty-stricken souls somewhere in the darkness of infinity. Should they not be allowed to have it? A great affection for Sivert arose in her, a desire to give and give again. And a shadow of guilt towards him, as though there was much for which she had to compensate him. It was warm and safe in his arms, shut off from the world and the cold.

But then Sivert wanted to sleep. It was awful how quickly Sivert wanted to sleep. He yawned and gave the wrong answers, while Alberta still had a great deal on her mind, things which seemed to lie dammed up inside her and were waiting their turn to be said. She had them on the tip of her tongue . . . .

Suddenly Sivert gave a lengthy snore. He woke in the middle of it, sat up and said: 'What?'

'Good night, Sivert,' said Alberta, crestfallen.

But sometimes she would lie on her elbow watching him when he slept. He was handsome then, and looked like a child or a young boy. The thought that he would die one day occurred to her. She, too, would die. They would disappear from each other, sink down each to his own part of infinity, exist for each other no longer. The smell of his hair, the warmth of his arm, his even breathing, would all wither and be extinguished.

A boundless feeling of loneliness seized her. Her face was wet with tears. Sivert slept.

So she went from barrow to barrow in the mornings, multiplying and adding, had worldly cares and was not entirely useless. She was full of gratitude for it. When she came home she would sometimes feel she must go straight over to Sivert and say: 'How happy we are, Sivert.'

'I'm glad you think so,' Sivert would say, painting on imperturbably. Sometimes he would turn his head slightly and give her a quick kiss. And Alberta told herself that she had not expected him to put his palette aside, but he might have done so for a moment at any rate. She regretted having said anything, it would have been better not to.

They had come to each other each from his great loneliness. They had drifted together somewhere in time and space and accommodated themselves there as best they could. Sivert was no hero of romance, no conqueror in a Spanish cloak; but he was healthy and strong and capable. And she did not notice the glint in his eye, which she disliked, any more.

Without a collar and tie he looked like a shoemender. Alberta wished she did not have to see him dressed like that. On the other hand most men looked the same in that brief, ugly neckband with the nasty little round button. And Alberta was certainly no romantic heroine. The old, embroidered petticoat was far from being a thing of the past. It reappeared again and again, even at this time of year, and was by no means the only detail of her wardrobe that she wished was otherwise.

There was something mute about Sivert. Sometimes it would occur to Alberta that he had something of the enigma of an animal, a passivity of whose content she was ignorant and never became any wiser. And she realised that herein lay something of Sivert's fascination.

When they had been alone for some time, working together, chatting together, preparing meals together, everything felt extraordinarily inevitable and simple, as if it ought to be so. But when they met other people, or met each other again after being parted for a few hours, she would feel strangely disappointed and flat for a while. She might go over and straighten his hat or pull at his tie, as if she needed to correct her impression of him.

* * *

When Alberta knocked for the third time on Eliel's door and nobody answered, she remained standing for a while, perplexed. It was a long time since she had seen either Liesel or Eliel. They lived as if immured. Or they were living separately again. No-one knew anything about them any more. Alberta had been to Eliel's door in vain. Marushka's hastily interrupted words that evening in the Rue Campagne Première had sounded like a mysterious warning of danger. Even Sivert was strangely reserved about the matter. It almost sounded as if he could suspect anything when he said: 'They'll turn up again.'

One evening he was able to report that he had met Eliel at the Versailles. 'Well?' asked Alberta eagerly. 'Yes, well, Eliel could not understand why he was never at home when people came and knocked. It was a strange coincidence. Liesel was quite all right, she still had visitors in town.'

201

Do you believe that, Sivert?' asked Alberta. 'Yes, why not?' said Sivert.

Now Alberta was standing there, no nearer her object. She fumbled in her handbag for pencil and paper, intending at any rate to write a note and stick it in the door. Quite by chance she looked up, straight at the high little window, the window of the loft. And she caught a glimpse of Liesel's face, pale, large-eyed, before it disappeared again, so quickly that Alberta asked herself for a moment whether it was her imagination, something she thought she had seen.

'Liesel, she called, full of uncontrollable anxiety.

No answer. But now Alberta called again as if constrained to shout something down. It had been Liesel. She knew it with fearful certainty. And she knew more. A series of small circumstances she had scarcely noticed suddenly formed a straightforward sequence. What happened to so many women, what happened to others Alberta had known, what could have happened and still might happen to herself, had happened to Liesel. Now she had shut herself up there, in hiding. Alberta called again with all the intensity one can put into a call: 'It's me, Liesel. It's Alberta.'

The window opened quietly. Hoarse and thin, terrified of being heard, came Liesel's voice: 'Don't shout, Albertchen, for God's sake.'

'But what's the matter, Liesel? Are you ill? What's going on? Can I help you?' Alberta scarcely knew what she was saying any more. Liesel's thin voice cut her to the quick.

'The key is on top of the door,' whispered Liesel. 'You can come up for a moment. You must go again at once.'

Alberta opened it. The heavy smell of the clay made breathing difficult. Eliel's latest enormous work stood wrapped in wet cloths from top to toe, reaching such a height that the room was darkened by it. The winter damp lay clammily over everything, the paper was loosening from the wall beside the door. And an untidiness, that was unlike Liesel, prevailed everywhere. Clothes belonging to

202

Eliel lay about as if he had changed in a hurry. The washing-up from several meals spread itself round the primus and overflowed on to the floor. No cushion covered the hole in the basket chair, it gaped emptily and frankly. The stove was burning, but in a heap of ashes. From up in the loft came Liesel's hoarse voice: 'Don't look at anything, Albertchen. I haven't been down for some days, I know it's terrible there.'

Alberta went up the steps to the loft. Liesel was lying on Eliel's iron bedstead with the crooked legs, and it seemed to Alberta as if there was nothing left of her but thick plaits and large eyes, she looked so bloodless. Her hair was dishevelled, and she hurriedly hid her plaits behind her back.

'But Liesel!' exclaimed Alberta.

Then the tears rolled quietly down Liesel's face, many of them. She said nothing for a while. Then she lifted her head anxiously, and looked at the watch lying on the chair beside the bed: 'Eliel has gone out to get plaster. He's going to cast his big figure soon. He's in a hurry. It's to be ready in stone for the Spring Exhibition. ... As soon as I'm on my feet again, he's thought of asking Ness for some help with the moulds.'

Alberta felt a pang at her mention of Ness. But she said nothing. Everything in there was so oppressive, from the atmosphere to Liesel's tears.

'He won't be back for a little while,' Liesel decided, and dried her tears. 'Would you give me a drink, Albertchen? It's over there. It's difficult to breathe in here, don't you think?'

'I expect it's the clay,' said Alberta, relieved at every word she could say that had nothing to do with the situation.

'It is the clay. When you stay indoors for a long time it seems to end up here.' Liesel put her hand on her breastbone. She drank thirstily, and then lay down again with a sigh: 'Perhaps I shouldn't have sat up to look out of the window, but I couldn't help it. The time drags so when Eliel

203

is out, *aber so*. In the evenings, when he is at the Versailles, I sometimes feel I shall go mad. But of course he has to go.'

' I don't think he has to go at all. He could easily stay at home with you,' said Alberta, shocked. ' You have the worst of it, Liesel,' she blurted out, regretting it immediately, afraid of having gone too far and broached the subject too roughly.

But Liesel looked straight in front of her: ' It's important that he should put in an appearance and pretend there's nothing the matter. He *has* to go.'

' How long have you thought of staying up here, Liesel? I'm sure it's not good for you, you ought to ... '

' Until Monday,' said Liesel. ' Not a day more. I long to get out into the fresh air. I was down the other day, but it made me ill, so I had to come up and lie down again.' She looked at Alberta for a while. Then she said, smiling almost pityingly: ' You don't understand anything, do you, Albertchen?'

Suddenly she held out her hand: ' I'm glad you came. It's a good thing somebody came.'

Alberta squeezed her hand. All kinds of misgivings confusedly occurred to her, misgivings that hurt her physically. She dared not ask any more.

' But the worst is over, after all. I'll soon be better again,' whispered Liesel. The tears began to roll down her cheeks once more. ' But I'll never be the same again, Albertchen, never. I feel as if I was destroyed, disfigured, mutilated.' Liesel's lips trembled suddenly as if she had cramp, she wrung Alberta's hand, her eyes widened as if she saw horrors: ' The " duck's beak ", Albertchen – that's the worst of it. They have something they call the " duck's beak ". They *force* their way in with it. I cried each time, I cried the whole night beforehand.

' In the end all I wanted to do was to give up, but once you've begun ... It might have turned out a cripple, Albertchen!' Liesel hid her face in her hands and sobbed. ' It was so ... so humiliating – so degrading ... so ... To lie

204

there and let them do it to you!' she exclaimed with
loathing.

'But Liesel!' said Alberta helplessly. She only partially
understood, dimly sensing some ill-usage which appeared
to her to lack all reasonable dimensions. Liesel explained
a little more calmly: 'If only it helped at once. But I had
to go time after time. I was almost in the fifth month. It
was – it was a little child that came, a little body, naked,
bloody, with arms and legs and everything.' And Liesel
wrung and chafed Alberta's hand as if in delirium. 'I felt so
sorry for it, so terribly sorry for it, when they went and
threw it in – Albertchen! Don't *ever* do it, whatever happens!'
Liesel sobbed desperately. 'I shall see it for the rest
of my life, Albertchen.'

Her voice deepened with accumulated resentment and
scorn: '*They* don't understand anything. They go round
humming when it's over. A small operation, they call it.
Imagine – on a healthy person. I have never been so healthy
in my whole life. If only I hadn't been so desperate.'

Liesel clasped Alberta's hand with both her own, half
raising herself in bed. 'But have you noticed what awful
legs Eliel has, what large, tramping feet. And the way he
sniffs!' A look almost of evil joy suddenly passed over
Liesel's face. She fell back in bed. 'I was ill all night long,
I thought I'd die of pain and fever.'

'Liesel!' Alberta, completely at a loss, patted her, gave
her a drink, attempted to tidy up a little. She found no
words. Liesel lay there, exhausted, her forehead beaded
with sweat, breathing strenuously. After a while she said
more calmly, in a different tone of voice: 'The worst of it
is that I've become so spiteful. Yes, Albertchen, spiteful.
Malicious. I wanted to do it, and yet I feel I can't stand
Eliel any more. As if it were his fault. Yes, for you don't
think Eliel wanted to do it, do you?' She raised her head
and looked at Alberta intently.

'No –,' said Alberta uncertainly.

'*You mustn't think it was Eliel.*' A reflection of Liesel's
former pale flush passed over her face, and she said as if in

quick parenthesis: ' Naturally, he really would have liked nothing better than to have a little child. I ought to be ashamed of myself. It's been worse for Eliel than for me, worse for him, do you understand? And heaven knows what would have happened to us if we hadn't known Dr. Freytág. He helped us for nothing, although he was running a risk. Oh God, Albertchen – you won't say anything, will you? There's a grave penalty for it.' Liesel looked at Alberta terror-struck.

' No, Liesel.'

' I'm mad. I'm utterly unreasonable. Here I lie, getting wine and everything. Yesterday I had champagne. They are so kind to me. And it's not Eliel's fault he can't marry *und so weiter*.'

' You'll feel better when you're up and out of doors, Liesel,' said Alberta haphazardly. Tears were trickling down her cheeks as well. ' You'll get well again, of course you will.'

Liesel looked at her earnestly: ' Do you think so? Do you think I can become just as fond of Eliel again? When I get out and I'm not in here all the time? I do so want to. Can you forget the unkind things I said about him? He has suffered too. Over and over again we thought it was done. A long time goes by before you will admit that it is so, you try to believe all kinds of things instead. And Dr. Freytag was away for a while. And then – then it all became so terrible.'

Liesel glanced uneasily at the clock. ' You must go now. Eliel mustn't suspect that anyone has been here. To think that you never noticed, Albertchen.'

' I haven't seen you for a long time, Liesel.'

' No, and I am thin. I don't think anyone noticed. Are you still living in that horrid little room?'

' Yes,' answered Alberta a little hesitantly. ' But I'm thinking of moving,' she added, in order to come slightly nearer to the truth.

' I almost think you're lucky, not .... At least you don't have to be afraid of ... ' Liesel looked up at Alberta, who reddened at once. And Liesel's face reminded her for a moment of those of tired women, when they sit looking after young girls. ' Marushka,' she said. ' She's managing all right?'

' She's managing all right.'

' She's been married,' said Liesel. ' They always manage. Thank you for coming. Go now, hurry.'

And Alberta went. Out in the street she paused. Something told her to go back to her cold little room again, to her miserable, lonely existence there; a longing came over her to be the old, impossible and real Alberta, free in her fashion, free above all of the cold anxiety which she would not allow to come to the surface, but which was latent in her mind.

But she went down towards the Rue Vercingétorix as if drawn there.

When Sivert received a message from Eliel a few days later about the casting, Alberta decided to arrive as if quite by chance during the afternoon. ' Perhaps I shall meet Liesel,' she said. ' And they know nothing about us two.'

' Come, by all means,' said Sivert, imperturbable as always. ' I shan't give anything away.' With amazement Alberta felt a slight bitterness at Sivert's words. They were, after all, correct and appropriate, spoken with good intent, and yet wrong, wounding and spiteful. She thought what had occurred to her several times already : Sivert and I get on best when we have no contact with the outside world. As soon as we do, something goes wrong.

At the door of Eliel's studio she stopped short.

It resembled a place left in ruins after an earthquake. The plaster lay all over the floor, looking like collapsed houses, bulky and apparently immovable; heaps of large lumps and small lumps, heaps of rubbish and dust. A layer of white powder covered everything, lying on all the projections, hanging heavy in the damp atmosphere, clogging the throat and nose as soon as one entered.

Eliel and Sivert were moving busily about in it all.

Nothing appeared to be immovable as far as they were concerned; they were lifting and transporting great pieces, imprinted with gigantic fragments of the human form, which added to the impression of natural catastrophe, doom and destruction. Here giants had lived and moved.

In a tolerably clear spot stood Eliel's round bath-tub. To this the giant imprints were transported, and washed down with soapy water so that the cavities bubbled and shimmered with rainbow colours. Eliel and Sivert looked as if they had had a miraculous escape at a time when the destruction had long been under way. They were in overalls, covered with dry lumps of plaster, and had plaster lumps and dust in their hair. Sweating and hot, in full swing, they breathed deeply and rubbed their hands in satisfaction over a tremendous piece, wrested from chaos. Eliel splashed the sponge over it so that the soapy water shimmered like phosphorus. He called to Alberta: 'Look who's here! You've come just at the right time. Liesel is here, she's making coffee. Come in, if you dare, and join us.'

Sivert called: 'I've been given quite a job. I feel like a plasterer.'

Both of them gave the impression of being very much at their ease, lifting and carrying, washing and rinsing and tramping about ankle-deep in rubbish, with the same intense satisfaction as boys in a demolished building. They shared a wordless understanding, reaching agreement concerning their manoeuvres with the aid of glances and silent nods. Once Eliel said: 'This is awfully kind of you, Sivert Ness, let me tell you.'

In the corner by the door Liesel was keeping house. Dusty and wan, with her dress hitched up about her, she was setting the coffee-table. She sat down now and again rather suddenly and for no apparent reason. She seemed to slump down on the divan, while she continued to rub what she had in her hands, cups or spoons. It hurt Alberta to see her and she slumped down with her. She took the coffee-grinder, which Liesel handed over in an attack of weakness, and ground it unthinkingly, with short pauses and much wastage of coffee. The whole thing gave her the frightened feeling she used to get as a child, when a game that was being played around her suddenly, without anyone understanding why, became deceitful and dangerous, changing its character and going too far.

She felt a desire to seize the others by the arm and say: Let's stop now. The game's up.

Alberta had been in bed for a long time when Sivert came home that evening. He stretched himself as if after a good day's work, announcing with satisfaction that it was all finished. The figure stood there and only needed polishing. Then there was the cleaning of the studio. It was filthy. He supposed he'd have to give Eliel a hand with that as well.

' I think Liesel looks poorly,' said Alberta from up in the loft, not knowing why she said it. She had not mentioned Liesel to Sivert, she had not been able to bring herself to do so.

His reply made her suddenly pay attention.

' She'll get well again,' said Sivert. Alberta heard him walking about below, turning round pictures that were leaning against the wall, as he often did when he had been away from home for a while. He was greeting them on his return.

The words were not important. But his tone affected her strangely.

* * *

Alberta was sitting in the Café de Versailles, jammed in tightly, nervously turning the pages of the Norwegian newspapers. She had pulled herself together and written a couple of articles again. There had been nothing else for it. Without a word Sivert had so far borne their common expenses. In the long run this was impossible for many reasons, among others the fact that he was no Croesus.

Besides, Alberta had private obligations. She had kept on her room, needing it as a retreat and an alibi, and she had not pawned Marushka's watch, but had handed it in to her concierge a few days later.

She was tense and anxious. What she had patched together had been unlike her usual style, a little drastic, perhaps a little too realistic. Perhaps she had gone too far and it would not even be printed. Then she would be back where she started. She threw aside *Aftenposten*, there was nothing there, and looked round for *Morgenbladet*.

The café was packed. Tobacco and heat lay in the room like wool, hanging in layers beneath the ceiling. The contents of glasses glistened dully in the heavy air. The music, the voices, the tramp of dancing feet farther in seemed to come out of a mist. The whole atmosphere lay about one like a nauseating and used, but comfortable and protective old garment, good to turn to after draughty studios that lay on the bare earth or up under the sky, after rooms without stoves.

It was difficult to find the newspapers, difficult to read them. Norwegian voices exploded and Danish ones bleated penetratingly. An occasional Swede would also deliver an opinion after more mature consideration, and then shout down all those sitting round him. Kalén was wandering about, in the worst possible humour, provoked by *grippe* and spirits, causing a disturbance and giving offence wherever he went. At Alberta's side was the little Swedish woman, who had been keeping company with Kalén since the spring. Suddenly he began treating her worse than anybody else. She sat on the verge of tears, picking at her handkerchief, dabbing her face with it furtively and repeating: ' If only I could get him to go home. He's ill, his temperature was a hundred this morning. And now someone has offered him absinthe. That's the worst thing that could happen. If he were not such a splendid person when he's sober . . . '. And she snuffled.

Kalén stopped in front of a young woman, a painter,

newly arrived from Kristiania, and asked her aggressively
whether her name was not Frøken Olsson?

' No, far from it. Absolutely not.' The newcomer ignored
the drunkard demonstratively.

' But Frøken Olsson has in any case come here to try
to learn to paint? Is it not so?'

' My name is *not* Olsson,' came the reply in an offended
Kristiania accent.

' It's of no consequence, no consequence at all, what
Frøken is called,' persisted Kalén. He had taken up his
position supporting himself with both hands spreadeagled
on the table, and was not going to be budged. ' Frøken
can be called Olsson or Svensson or Karlsson or what the
devil she likes, that's not the point. Frøken must be called
something in any case. The point is that Frøken should go
home to Norway and have *children* instead of hanging
about here throwing Papa's money away learning to paint.
For Frøken will never succeed. She should go home tomorrow and get herself a *child*. Then Frøken will be as *useful*
as she could possibly be – '

' Now then, now then,' intervened appeasing voices from
several directions. Above them the Kristiania accent could
be heard, high-pitched and cultivated : ' What *sort* of a
frightful individual is *this*? He's not just drunk, he's *mad*.
Can't someone get rid of him?'

The Swedish woman squeezed Alberta's hand : ' If only
I could get him away from here. But I scarcely dare speak
to him.'

Someone had persuaded Kalén to sit down. They were
holding on to him, agreeing with every word he said : ' Yes,
of course, quite right. So very right.' And he slumped down
temporarily, dulled and pacified, as if the sting had gone
out of him for the time being. Alberta searched anew
through the pile of newspapers. She could still hear the
voice of the Norwegian girl : ' *Huff* – is that *gruesome* man
still here? I don't care in the *slightest* whether people are
drunk, I assure you, as *long* as they don't get vulgar.' It
reminded her so strangely of an unknown country a long

way away, called Norway. That was how they talked there, underlining the words heavily, eager to air *their* opinions, *their* views, in some way different from *everyone* else's. Alberta glimpsed blue hills, air grey with snow, scattered habitation that seemed to force you to shout loudly. Otherwise perhaps nobody would hear you. People there did not live close to one another.

Alberta also listened involuntarily for the Danish voices. Their cadences touched her in far too intimate a way.

But the Swedish woman suddenly commented with a repressed sob: ' It's my wedding day today.'

Alberta put down the paper. It was the least she could do.

' The terrible thing about marriage is that you wait the whole time for the other person to say something quite different from what he does say, and to do something quite different from what he does do. ... I don't suppose you understand what I mean ... '

' Oh yes,' said Alberta.

' You see, my former husband was a scientist, a zoologist. He spent all his time at the museum with the stuffed animals. While I ... '. And the Swede assured Alberta that she still had the revolting smell of the chemicals in her nose, and could recall them whenever she wished. And then the boa constrictor too, so utterly revolting. She had had to go past it on her way to the offices in the museum. It stood in a corner, quite a dark corner. The terrible thing was that you did not see it until you were right on top of it, so that it made you jump. It gave her such a turn every time, she never got used to it. Alberta could imagine for herself how disgusting it was with its enormous, thick body, coiled round a tree-trunk. It made you feel throttled.

' But did you have to go there so often? Your husband came home at night, surely?' Alberta asked haphazardly, mainly for the sake of saying something.

' Of course he did, but very late. Always too late to go out and see or hear anything. He sat late over his books.

212

he had so much to get through. I just went to bed, you see.'

' Oh,' said Alberta, embarrassed and helpless.

' So then I got the chance of coming down here and began to paint, which I had always had an inclination for. And I have made valuable acquaintances, I've come to know elegant people who have become of importance, real importance to me, people with tragic lives . . . .'

Kalén, thought Alberta mechanically.

' It doesn't stop one feeling a little sad on such a day. Memories come back. A fine man in any case, a truly fine man,' she snuffled.

' That's what you always say.' It was Kalén, who had freed himself again and now stood towering over the table.

' I beg your pardon? What do you mean?'

' Little angels always say, when they have left a man, that he was really so fine and sweet. Is it to improve your consciences or what? To be a bit noble afterwards? That's easily done.'

' Oh – !'

' What was your husband?' asked Alberta mistakenly. She had forgotten the chemicals and the boa constrictor, and merely wanted to show what interest she could, besides making it clear to Kalén that nobody was bothering about his tactlessness.

' A custodian,' came the quiet reply.

But Kalén exploded with the uncontrollable laughter of a drunkard: ' Custodian! Ha – ha – ha!'

' Is that so terribly amusing?'

' Rich. That's rich.' Kalén struck himself across the knees, seized a glass that was not his own, and swung it aloft: ' *Skaal* for the custodian! Health to him! I shall enjoy that for a long time . . . ha – ha – ha!' And he emptied the stranger's glass before its owner could stop him.

There was a stir. The owner of the glass, a quiet, bespectacled Swede, rose to his feet muttering something about educated people, ordinary manners. Well-meaning souls interposed themselves to explain. Meanwhile the little

Swedish woman got ready to go, pale and dignified: ' I
can't put up with that drunk fellow. I'm going now.'

Alberta said she would accompany her. There was an
atmosphere of catastrophe, of breakdown, in the fracas.
They helped each other with their coats. She nodded to
Sivert, who was sitting chatting to some Danes at the next
table.

Suddenly she heard a woman's voice in Danish: ' It was
a terrible accident. So frightful for his wife too. Yes, they
were divorced, but when she heard about it she went
straight down. But it was all over. He never regained
consciousness.'

Alberta stood as if petrified.

' A car accident, wasn't it?' That was Sivert, sympathetic
and careful as one is when asking about that sort of thing.

' A big lorry, one of those monsters that come at you
like a stone-crusher. Just as he was coming out of the
railway station in Cologne and was about to cross the
street. He was knocked down violently, fractured his skull
and suffered other injuries besides. I thought perhaps you
knew him. His name was Veigaard. He was an odd
person ... .'

Alberta supported herself against the table, a chance
table, with chance faces round it. They looked at her in
amazement. She looked back at them for a while.

Then something snapped. And she laughed out loud, a
hilarious, forced, unnatural laugh.

Everyone looked up, Sivert from the contemplation of
his two composed hands. He rose and came towards her,
speaking quietly and urgently, half jokingly: ' Listen
Alberta, have you had too much to drink? You can't stand
here laughing when the poor chap's dead. So help me, Kalén
doesn't seem to be the only one drunk here tonight.'

He took her arm, implying that he would accompany
her, that now they must concentrate on getting away. A
little farther off, between the tables, the Swedish woman
stood waiting for her, miserable and dispirited.

Then Alberta pushed Sivert away, went through the

swing-doors quickly, looked round for a moment, as if uncertain which way to go, caught sight of the tram-car that passed her street standing at the tram-stop, and ran to catch it. It moved off at once.

* * *

Each time Alberta woke in her comfortless little room with the comfortless sounds of poor people's grey lives seeping in through the gap under the door – the shuffle of slippers in the morning rush, the tap perpetually running, the slamming doors – she received a stinging, rough reminder that there is a worn, hard little path across the fog-bound marsh, where we can see no further than tomorrow. There is a ridge that one can grope for, hard to the feet, but safe: toil, honest toil, no matter what. Perhaps something will get frost-bitten on the way and shrivel up, but there is no need to lose one's foothold or one's way. And one's weakness will not become open to anybody who happens to be in possession of the small skeleton keys to it: tenderness in the voice, certain words that one craves to hear, that single one out from other people and run rippling through body and soul like a healing spring, kindness in a difficult moment.

She felt again, like the ache of an exposed nerve, the old longing to discover her own form of toil and to work at it. Hard, bitter, healthy toil, serving as a safeguard against all that was weak and hesitant in herself.

The rest was like playing blind-man's-buff; we rush about, our eyes blinded by our own longing. And death plays this game too, using his dagger quietly and from behind. Nothing seems to have happened. Or one has the impression that something quite different has happened. Until suddenly the cards are laid on the table in circumstances that make one laugh aloud as if in delirium. The game was up a long time ago.

Death can also amuse himself by reversing the fortunes

of the game in one throw. Alberta had seen that happen too.

A variegated web of violently contrasting light and shade was drawn unceasingly through her memory. A summer night in a haycock, the mingled scent of flowers over her face, dry, fleeting warmth from a hand touching her cheek, the secure feeling of being tucked in, just as when she was small.

A morning grey with dew and approaching daylight, a sudden play of new forces in her body, a face that looked at her, so tense with gravity that two small muscles appeared on either side of the mouth.

A misty morning outside open windows, the strange, new little sound of raw potatoes being scraped, the mixed scent of roses and freshly made coffee, the notes of *Santa Lucia* from a barrel organ near by.

The warmth of another person through a whole long night, the feeling of having reached one goal on a long, laborious journey, all that she had felt on waking, until the daylight and the street and a thousand glimpses of others' lives about her had succeeded in rousing old unrest to life again.

A moment at a railway station, when words she had not brought herself to say, decisive, strong words, forced themselves to her lips too late and to no purpose.

And a turbid dream that had taken hold, unreasonable, confused, until she was suddenly woken, roughly and mercilessly, by the cards being brutally turned up.

The rest she was only capable of seeing in relation to something old, something she normally kept locked well down inside her mind. Now it was unlocked for her, she lived through it all again. An icy wind seized her, whirling her with it through a piece of existence that seemed to be the hereafter, where day and night were one. Then she was dropped down into a churchyard in front of two large black holes in the snow. Stunned she stood watching coffins lowered into them and knew that now life would begin again, but otherwise, and beyond belief.

216

All thought of death, all conception of it, was indissolubly bound up with that first time, a winter evening at home in the small town, the wedding day of the new district physician from Flatangen. The arrangement had been that Alberta was to have tea ready when Mama and Papa came home. They would probably need something warm. Mama thought it would be cold down on the quay.

Alberta stood at the window in one of the dark sitting-rooms and watched them all go past, all the guests at Dr. Berven's wedding: Berven himself and his bride, who had come from Kristiania a couple of days previously and was so lovely, the Reverend Pio and his wife, the Governor and his wife, Mama and Papa, Beda and the Recorder, Dr. and Mrs. Pram, Dr. and Mrs. Mo, the Dean and his wife, almost twenty of them in all.

They came out of the darkness, walked quickly in procession through the circle of light made by the street lamps, and disappeared into the darkness again. The gentlemen walked with their coat collars turned up, Dr. Pram in a fur overcoat, his stick pointing straight up into the air out of his pocket as was his habit. The ladies fussed with their trains, pausing momentarily to get a better grip. The lace shawl, which the Governor's wife was wearing over her fur hat, slipped backwards. She stood still in the circle of light while Harriet Mo helped her. Mama looked up and gave Alberta a little wave.

Behind them came the street boys and youths, the maids who worked for various people, Lilly Vogel arm in arm with a girl from Namsos who had become her boon companion since Palmine Flor had married and become so respectable and superior.

Everything had been so ordinary. Alberta remembered clearly that Jensine had passed by the dining-room on her way up to bed. With her alarm-clock in her hand she had come into the dark sitting-room and stood for a moment in the window as well: ' Are they on their way down now? Look at the maids from the Prams' and the Recorder's. Beda's supposed to be not at all bad to work for. They want to go down and have a look as well when it's Doctor Berven who's leaving with a new bride and under his own steam. Well, nobody's going to get me down to the Stoppenbrink Quay at this time of night, thank you very much. I've lighted the spirit stove, the water's on.'

' Thank you, Jensine.'

Alberta was left to walk up and down in the cold, dark room. The light from the dining-room shone in across the floor. She walked across it from darkness into darkness, whimpering a little to herself, as she was used to doing when she was alone: ' I won't go on, I won't go on.' Her thoughts struggled with old, hopeless problems.

An evening like countless others when Papa and Mama were out without her. Only married couples had been invited.

She went out to see to the stove. It had been turned up too high. The kitchen was full of cold steam. On her way back into the hall something reached her, a hubbub from the street below, the hum of many voices, loud shouts that cut through them.

When she got to the window the street was black with people. They came running from all directions, from the alleys and down from Upper Town. Boys, old women who had scarcely given themselves time to throw on a shawl and were still fumbling with it as they ran, one or two men who cleared themselves a way by elbowing people aside, Mad Petra . . . . They converged in the middle of the street as if in a canal and streamed westwards.

Through the open window she heard Tailor Kvandal calling from his doorstep: ' Keep calm, dear people, keep calm!' Nobody listened to him.

A few short sentences freed themselves from the hum down below, a few impossible, brief phrases: ' Stoppenbrink's old quay – all the fine folk in the sea – they can't see to get them up again.'

The words affected Alberta like unexpected and unmerited blows, making her angry. That was her first reaction and the last she remembered clearly. Afterwards she

218

remembered in bits and pieces, as one remembers dreams.

She ran along the street with all the others, occasionally hearing shouts behind her: 'Alberta, poor thing . . . Miss Selmer . . . oh, don't let her pass, what if she . . . can't someone . . .'. A few tried to take her by the arm. She had to tear herself free.

Then there were all the lighted windows in Strand Street, normally so dark – it reminded her in an irritating fashion of Christmas Eve – and black groups of people who stood in the way everywhere so that she could not get through; from time to time a kind of procession, several men carrying heavy, mysterious burdens; shouts from down on the quay, lights moving down below, backwards and forwards.

Perplexed and seemingly quite outside it all Alberta drifted from group to group, shoved in the back by people trying to get through who did not see who she was. She remembered Jeanette Evensen's voice: 'Are they dead?' A man's voice answered curtly: 'They're dead.' Alberta's anger returned. The whole thing seemed to her like an idiotic, simple-minded joke, a tasteless performance, stupid beyond belief.

Somebody suddenly seized her by the arm and led her forward. A voice said with authority: 'Make way, this is one of the next of kin.' She went obediently and heard the voice say: 'You mustn't be upset. And you mustn't be frightened. It may not be so bad.' Alberta was given the feeling that now everything would be put to rights, soon the nonsense would come to an end.

They entered a passage. A small kitchen lamp hung on the wall. And suddenly it all became even more confusing. For the person holding her arm and talking to her so reassuringly was Ryan, butcher and radical, dripping with blood and a danger to society, one of the bogeymen of her childhood. The most fearful rumours concerning the slaughterhouse in his back yard were passed from child to child.

Afterwards she vaguely remembered untidy rooms, the small, simple, stuffy rooms of the poor, where people in

219

full evening dress and dripping with water were lying anyhow, on sofas, beds, wooden benches, tables, the floor. Some simply lay there, others were being attended to, having their arms worked up and down above their heads. She remembered Dr. Mo, so wet that he left great pools behind him wherever he went, but fully active, giving orders and feeling pulses, listening for heartbeats with his head on someone's breast – remembered that she seemed to find Papa lying quite still on a sofa, his face surprisingly young, manly and resolute – remembered that someone took her away, she did not know who.

Lie down for a bit now, Alberta, poor thing, please do.' The words were deeply imprinted in her memory, together with a hand that was lying on her knee when she opened her eyes. A working hand, red and rough, inured against everything and by everything. Confused, she looked into a heavy, masculine, leathery face, not familiar and yet not quite unfamiliar. It was a while before she realised that it belonged to Anna Sletnesset, a person seldom seen out of doors. She sat with the sick and with women in childbed. As if in a disordered dream this face from life's periphery was suddenly in the very centre of existence.

She was sitting at the other side of a small table, leaning over it to talk to Alberta. She seemed to have been talking to her for a good while already: ' What's the use of sitting here dozing off? It'll make you ill too, and what do you gain by that? Put down that fellow Dante and go to bed. I'm here, I'll tell you at once if there's any change.'

But Alberta would not go to bed. Giddy and sick she sat trying to collect herself after her brief nap, to read the book she had taken at random from the bookcase. It was Dante's *Inferno*, the old Danish translation. The table from in front of the window had been moved over here, one of the lamps from the sitting-rooms was standing on it with a handkerchief over one side of the globe. Everything was wrong or upside-down in one way or another: in the shadow, Mama's bedside table, full of medicine bottles and glasses with spoons in them, on a pillow further away Mama's immovable face. The air was heavy with illness and medicaments, and with a thick, even warmth which Anna Sletnesset, this innocent person from the street, carefully kept at an even temperature and controlled with a thermometer. Without hesitating she ordered magical quantities of coal and wood to be sent up, and Jensine brought them without protest.

Something inconceivable was happening. The dream went on and on, timeless, bound by neither day nor night. Down in the sitting-room lay Papa, white and still, his face young and manly, but sharper over the bridge of the nose from day to day. Out in the town lay several others who were dead, many dangerously ill, some dying. A couple of doctors had come from elsewhere, Dr. Mo was no longer on his feet, Dr. Pram was dead. A strange doctor came and went and told Alberta that it was providential that she had Anna Sletnesset; many more like her were needed now.

She remembered that Mama woke from her fever once when the doctor was there, that she lay there with her eyes clear and calm and asked whether she was in danger, she wanted to know the truth. The doctor's reply had burned itself into Alberta: 'You are in danger, Madam, but we are hoping for the best.' And Mama's lingering reply, as if given after serious reflection: 'It doesn't matter. I have been dead for a long time already.' And she asked after Papa, whether he was still asleep, whether he was always asleep now? 'The Magistrate is still asleep, Madam.'

'He needs to rest,' said Mama, her eyes already retreating again, as if on their way inwards towards something mysterious. Immediately afterwards she lost consciousness and did not return.

Much of this came to Alberta as knowledge she had to acquire afresh each time she woke after brief and unwilling slumber. Together with Anna Sletnesset she watched constantly, and would not go to bed, but sank from time to time into a painful, restless sleep in a sitting position.

Was it the same night that she had stood at the window

221

looking at Orion? She remembered getting to her feet, stiff with fatigue. In spite of the warmth in the room she felt thoroughly chilled as soon as she moved, her whole body trembling as she stood with the blind drawn to one side. There was a hard frost, the dark sky glittered with stars, Orion among them, easily recognizable. The belt's three suns glowed more brightly than everything else out there. Far off the church clock shone like a moon in the night sky. Which night out of many? The clock said five minutes past two.

It was then that Alberta was overwhelmed with anxiety on account of what was stirring deep inside her. She knew the feeling of old. It was like standing on the edge of deep water and fainting. What did she want, what did she desire, when she gave herself time now and then to desire and want?

Then she was sitting beside Anna Sletnesset again, trying to keep her head from nodding, refusing to sleep. She heard Anna say: 'Now you *are* going to bed, Alberta, poor thing.'

She was lifted, carried, put down. Her shoes were taken off, a blanket laid over her.

It was good . . . good.

Alberta, poor thing, you must get up now.'

It was Anna Sletnesset again, the doctor too. He was standing in the middle of the room looking sympathetic. Both of them took Alberta by the arm and helped her across the floor. Her legs felt as if cut from under her. She shook with helplessness.

' Have I been asleep?'

' Yes, poor thing.'

Anna's voice was different, so disquietingly mild.

' Is Mama dead?' Alberta heard herself say these strange words. She felt as if someone was standing beside her saying them.

' No, but the end has come.'

Then she was standing by Mama's bed. The face on the

pillow was still, white, tranquil, the eyes clear and shining. Mama said nothing, but she looked at Alberta with an open, pure expression, like a child's. And it seemed to Alberta that she had never seen Mama before; tenderness, regret, longing flooded into her as she knelt beside the bed.

An anxious, enquiring expression came into Mama's face, she moistened her lips with her tongue. Now she will ask for Papa, thought Alberta, agonized. What shall I say?

But Mama said slowly and indistinctly and as if with infinite longing: ' Jacob.'

Then it was terribly quiet. And her expression disappeared, withdrawing inwards and backwards. Two empty, staring eyes were left behind. Blinded with tears Alberta saw Anna Sletnesset's rough finger gently draw the eyelids down over them. ' A beautiful death, Alberta, a beautiful death to be sure,' Anna whispered, patting Alberta on the arm.

Alberta's tears suddenly stopped. She got to her feet, and accompanied the doctor downstairs. Politely and tactfully the stranger offered her his condolences and shook her hand.

She could still remember the sensation that had come over her when she had seen him out and gone in again through the cold rooms. It was like coming home from school and finding the curtains had been taken down: a sensation of something missing, of nakedness, of a cold wind that blew straight in unchecked.

Then she was in the kitchen. She could still see the lamp she put down on the kitchen bench, the cold meat she found, off which she suddenly began to carve slice after slice, her own blue hands doing it. A raging, ravenous, hunger had possessed her. She stuffed the slices into her mouth with her fingers, swallowing them without chewing properly.

And she went up to Anna Sletnesset and Jensine, who were busy seeing to things up there. They took her and put her to bed, undressing her like a child, and giving her hot-water bottles. For she trembled and trembled and could not get warmth into her body.

It was only when it was all over that Alberta found out what had really happened. Rotten, its piles and planks riddled with worms, the old Stoppenbrink Quay had suddenly been unable to hold up any longer. It had broken down beneath all those tramping, gay people. The tide was up, it was freezing and dark. The sequel she knew already. Some drowned, nearly all the survivors fell dangerously ill with pneumonia and all kinds of complications after the shock they had suffered. Several died. There was a mass burial with the flags flying at half-mast all over the town.

Uncle Thomas himself travelled north. He helped Alberta to make arrangements and decisions. With her full approval everything was sent to be auctioned. It had brought in a sum of money for herself and Jacob. Her share had been used up long ago.

When Alberta now woke in the little room in Paris and lay thinking back over her life, she felt as if she had really only been dreaming now and again, or that she had come into it by mistake. But they were dreams that left reality behind them.

There was Sivert, for instance. He was as real as could be. And he put in an appearance daily. He did not ask directly for any explanation, but sat there as if on his wooden crate with his elbows on his knees and his hands clasped, looking thoughtful. Sometimes Alberta would catch a hesitant expression on his face. He was probably wondering whether she was quite in her right mind.

He did not say much. He went so far as to imply that the timing of the crisis could have been better chosen. He was already in full swing with his composition, had almost come so far as to hope that he might be able to try it out at the Spring Exhibition. Strange that this notion of living in her own room should have come just now.

He would sit for a while, ask as if *en passant* whether she would not come out with him to eat at any rate. Then he would give her some packages he had put down by the door when he arrived. There would be bread, fruit, cooked vegetables, sometimes a grilled chop. Alberta felt terribly humiliated. On the other hand both her articles had been sent back to her with a few apologetic words. Unfortunately, the material was not quite suitable this time. However, something in the style in which she had written formerly would be welcome, and so on.

Mumbling with embarrassment she thanked Sivert for what he had brought. She would pay him back when she had the money. Sivert shrugged his shoulders: 'That doesn't matter,' he said. 'And I can't sit watching you starve to death up here.'

She went and posed for him now and again, in order to do something in return. But it was far from being the same as before or quite what Sivert wanted. If only she got up early in the morning. But she was tardy, and did not turn up until almost lunch-time. He had to hang about waiting for her without being able to start on anything else instead. Then they had to eat. Then perhaps the lunch did not suit Alberta. Occasionally she had to go and lie down on the divan for a while, seized by a strange and obscure indisposition. What with one thing and another Sivert sometimes wandered about a little impatiently, rattling his canvases and brushes. A sigh would escape him.

Nevertheless Alberta had put on weight since she had been eating properly again. Her figure was rounder than before. Every time she pulled herself together and posed again, unwilling in body and limbs, she caught sight of herself in Sivert's mirror. It was not as large as Mr. Digby's, but you could see quite a lot in it all the same. Every time she thought: I owe it to Sivert to pose; it's the least I can do for him. And she posed from old habit, until she trembled and swayed, feeling as if she were placating mysterious powers whose habit it is to force us into situations to which we are averse.

One day Alberta was sitting on the edge of her trunk,

rummaging amongst her scraps of paper. The window was open. The smoke of bonfires drifted in the air from the thousands of small allotments outside the fortifications. Warm sunshine alternated with cold wintry gusts, the clouds raced overhead with sudden depths of ultramarine sky between them. It was one of February's sporadic spring days.

She read them, put them down, read once more. Involuntarily she began to put some order into the muddle, sometimes finding several scraps about the same thing. In the course of time she had come upon new characteristics, had noted them and thrown them in. Laid out in small piles it almost looked like a collection of material. For some reason she knew more about people and their relationships than before, and could continue here and there. Where she had once broken off because she only glimpsed obscurity, full light now fell; where she had faced mute darkness, light began to dawn. She now suddenly saw through conversations, short exchanges she had written down hastily with the feeling that something lay behind them; she saw the people concerned coming and going before and after, moving in surroundings she had not known she could imagine.

Slightly astonished, half amused, she sat dabbling and reading, took a pencil and made a correction here and there, improved words and expressions, and then sat still, holding a little bundle of papers, her head resting on the window sill in a warm gleam of sunshine. Only then did she realise how tired she was. Tired of longing, making mistakes, being cold, pining, fussing about the wrong things. She closed her eyes, still seeing the sunshine as red light beneath her eyelids. It was good to sit like that, her body relaxed, to feel the sun and the air on her face, not to be cold.

And something dawned on her. All the pain, all the vain longing, all the disappointed hope, all the anxiety and privation, the sudden numbing blows that result in years going by before one understands what happened – all this was knowledge of life. Bitter and difficult, exhausting to

226

live through, but the only way to knowledge of herself and others. Success breeds arrogance, adversity understanding. After all misfortune perhaps there always comes a day when one thinks: It was painful, but a kind of liberation all the same; a rent in my ignorance, a membrane split before my eyes. In a kind of mild ecstasy Alberta suddenly whispered up to the sun: 'Do what you will with me, life, but give me understanding, insight and perception.'

She went over and lay down on the divan, making herself comfortable. The sun reached right in and shone on her as long as it was there, the red light still flickered behind her eyelids. New possibilities dawned on her, something more than the old newspapers on the table at home: *Morgenbladet* and *Aftenposten*. Other forms of writing were possible besides putting together casual articles for these two. New, bold ideas stirred in Alberta. Supposing she were to try! To try to find form for a little reality, not just continue to write horrid, well-bred essays about purely external events, eye-catching and easy to read – she, as well as so many others. When she was less tired she would do something about it, try to put something from the trunk into shape . . . .

Someone knocked. From acquired habit Alberta stretched out her hand, turned the key and sat up on the divan: 'Come in Sivert.'

But it was not Sivert, it was Liesel. She stood in the doorway, astonished, and said apologetically: 'It's only me, Albertchen.' Alberta, too, was astonished, and lay down again. Liesel had become so infrequent a visitor since she had moved out to Eliel. With her wan, small face beneath her thick braids she was not quite the old Liesel any more. 'I only wanted to look in,' she explained.

'That was nice of you.'

'Are you resting? Are you posing for Mr. Digby again?'

No. Alberta was only a bit tired, slept badly at night, had bugs and noise to contend with. One thing after another.

'Really?' said Liesel, sitting down and looking at

227

Alberta. Suddenly something strangely experienced came into her expression, and it struck Alberta as lightning strikes. For an instant she was made so giddy that the divan seemed to disappear from beneath her. Things that had and had not happened recently lined themselves up for inspection. Cold sweat broke out on her temples. She had asked life to do with her what it would. That had not been necessary. Life had begun exaggerating some time ago. This was impossible. At the same time she knew that it was so. Where had her thoughts been? Preoccupied with a series of old and new events, whose horror had bewildered her, which she could not keep apart from each other and still had not fully grasped. In the meantime rough reality had gone its way.

' Where can I find water?' asked Liesel.

' Out in the passage. Take a cup with you.'

Liesel came back with the cold water and Alberta drank thirstily. The roof of her mouth was suddenly dry and she felt as if her throat was parched.

' Is that better?'

' Yes, thank you.' Urgently impelled to chatter away the whole impression, Alberta asked after Liesel. How was she? How was her painting getting on? Was she going to exhibit again at the Spring Exhibition? She must certainly do so. Beneath her words the thought insisted: It can't be true, it's impossible, impossible, it's death . . . .

Liesel told her she could no longer paint. If only she could! She got so fearfully tired, did not seem to have the energy. Besides, she could not work on anything but still lifes, and even that was not feasible when Eliel had a model. She could go to Colarossi's, but – . And she confessed that she had become so incredibly lazy in the mornings. She found it almost impossible to get up, and then she would lie in the loft for the best part of the day because people were always dropping in. Eliel declaimed from the Edda : ' Things go from bad to worse if you sleep late in the morning. He who acts quickly is half rich already.' Could Alberta hear that she could speak Swedish?

Liesel smiled a little, and repeated the foreign tongue slowly, childishly stammering, marking the rhythm with her head. ' But it's no use, Albertchen. I'm quite impossible. And yet I must pull myself together. One day Eliel will go back to his own country, and I'll be left high and dry.'

He'll take you with him, surely, Liesel?'

Ach, he can't marry, Albertchen. Family life doesn't suit artists, especially sculptors. They must be bachelors, free of all ties.'

Alberta lay staring at Liesel. She had been through it all, the anxiety, the uncertainty, the continually teasing hope, the torture. Now she was pitiful and annihilated, an echo of Eliel. Suddenly Alberta hated Eliel.

At that moment there was another knock, and this time there was no doubt as to who it was. A faint hope of saving the situation flickered in Alberta for an instant against all reason; she put her finger to her lips, and Liesel sat tense and quiet as a mouse. But the knock came again, even the locked door was rattled: ' It's Sivert. Are you there, Alberta? Here I am with my hands full and I'm in a hurry.'

Crestfallen before the inevitable, Alberta opened the door. Sivert entered firmly, carrying dripping packages, a long loaf of bread sticking up out of one coat pocket and a bunch of celery out of the other. Liesel stared at him, clearly putting two and two together.

Sivert also looked overcome for a moment. Then he evidently thought he had mastered the situation splendidly : ' Look at that! I come up here once in a blue moon and kill two birds with one stone!'

Alberta's attention was caught by one of the packages. It contained boiled, white beans. She had disliked the look of it as soon as she saw it. Now it was lying on the edge of the table turning into a revolting blur of wet paper and thick, yellow pulp. She felt it slide into her, and began to sweat as if seasick. She clenched her teeth desperately, answering briefly with words of one syllable : ' Yes. No '. She would not look at the package of beans. But when she did not do so she saw them even more clearly in her imagination. They ought to have been wrapped up and not left lying about like that. But she could not go near them, and it did not seem to occur to either of the others. They were simply sitting, looking embarrassed.

Then she half rose: 'Go out, get out of here,' she shouted. And the worst happened. Sivert and Liesel instinctively shrank back as close to the narrow walls as they could. 'Oh,' groaned Alberta, and lay down. She turned her head a little: 'Please go, Sivert.'

And Sivert went. Liesel helped as well as she could, with towels she found hanging on the wall, cleaned up Alberta and gave her water, looked irresolutely at the result of the catastrophe. Alberta got up wretchedly, found the floor-cloth and tried to remedy the worst of it. Liesel took it away from her: 'Lie down again, Albertchen.'

In a short while she was back, sitting on the edge of the divan: 'Is it Ness?' she asked gently.

'Yes.'

'Perhaps I should not have come, Albertchen, but I didn't know anything about it. The whole thing is so unexpected. You didn't even like Ness.'

Alberta hesitated, searching for an answer. Then Liesel said: 'To be honest, perhaps it's a bit accidental who it is. But we want to love the person it happens to be, don't we?' She looked at Alberta almost entreatingly.

'Yes, Liesel, of course we do.'

But Liesel said eagerly: 'It mustn't turn out as it did for me, promise me that. You'll regret it your whole life, Albertchen.' She leaned over closer and looked into Alberta's eyes, her pupils dark as forest springs with repressed vehemence. 'You're never the same again, nothing is the same again. I want to love Eliel again just as much, but I can't. Now you mustn't be upset, you must talk to Ness about it.' She kissed Alberta on the forehead: 'Dear little Albertchen.' And Alberta suddenly felt that it was a great comfort and support that Liesel knew this.

'Only today I thought I could see some way in my

work,' she said, half to herself. ' I had such a desire to write, but in quite a different form from before.'

' Oh – .' Liesel gestured away from herself with her hand. ' That's precisely when it happens, when we think we're beginning to achieve something. Then it comes and interrupts it all. I was afraid of it the minute I came into the room, Albertchen. I could see there was something.'

Now life and death depended on Sivert. Now everything in her that was not him had to be hidden away, she had to cling to the person she loved. Liesel's words came back to her again and again: Perhaps it's a bit accidental who it is, but we want to love the person it happens to be. And she searched for every good feeling she had for him, trying to imagine that nothing had happened to make everything meaningless and impossible for her in one blow.

She went and posed for him as best she could, but she did not go as often as before. One day, standing at his easel, Sivert said: ' Why don't you come and stay here for a while again, Alberta?'

Not yet, Sivert.' Alberta suddenly burst into violent weeping.

She heard him behind her: ' Tell me what it is, Alberta. For I can't make head or tail of it all.'

But Alberta could not get it out.' It's nothing, nothing,' she said. Sivert sighed.

With new eyes she watched the small white bundles the working-class mothers carried with them when they were out of doors. They had nobody to look after them, they were tied by them from morning to night, forced to forget everything else for the sake of the white bundle, sacrifice everything for it. And Alberta felt mutinous. She thought: I'm not ready with myself yet, I haven't achieved anything, must I start thinking only about someone else, unable even to look in any other direction? At the same time she surprised herself noticing how such bundles were carried and dressed, and attempted instinctively to catch glimpses

231

of the tiny, well-wrapped faces. She vainly tried to imagine what her child would look like. It was all misty, she could see nothing.

But here again was one of the things she could not take in immediately.

Then she told him.

They were sitting on the fortifications in last year's grass, sitting there like other couples. Out above Fontenay the moon was rising. Smoke was drifting from the bonfires. It was a mild evening, far too early.

' We're going to have a child, Sivert.' It dropped from Alberta's lips like something ripe, something she had to say at that precise moment.

' What?' said Sivert. ' Are you sure?' he added.

' Yes.'

He sat tearing up the grass, looking down. Alberta's heart made a few painful, unaccustomed movements. She felt fate itself so close to her, so immediately above her, that for an instant she seemed to feel the thread being spun.

' We shall have to see about getting rid of it then, Alberta,' said Sivert quietly.

Alberta got up. She swayed slightly when she was on her feet. Sivert held her, intending to give her support. She drew herself away and began to walk.

He couldn't quite take it in, he said.

' It is so,' said Alberta roughly.

' Yes, yes, now don't get upset, Alberta, it's nothing to worry about. They say it's a trivial matter if you catch it in time. I know several people . . . '

Alberta felt her face turn white. Hurt and shame writhed painfully in her. If only Sivert had said something else she would really have loved him for it. She continued to walk, not bothering to answer. Now and then his hand touched hers. At a corner he took her arm, and she just missed being run over. She twisted away from him again, turning off near the Rue d'Alésia.

'Can't you come home with me this evening, at least? So that we can talk?'

'No,' said Alberta.

At the entrance to her street he attempted to kiss her and tried to hold on to her hands: 'Do you think I don't understand how upset you are? But surely we can talk about it. Perhaps it's a false alarm . . . .'

She pushed him aside, ran along the pavement, pulled the bell violently. Contrary to its custom, the door opened immediately. Without looking round at Sivert, whom she could hear coming after her, she slammed it behind her. She felt as if turned to stone in face and soul.

Sivert was there the next day. He sat on the divan in his usual position, his hands a little less tranquil than usual. One of them rubbed the other continually. And he admitted that, to be frank, he had wondered occasionally whether trouble was on the way, had been devilishly afraid of it, to be honest.

'Have you?' said Alberta.

Yes, after all, she had been rather strange lately, to put it mildly, as far back as the time when she became hysterical at the Versailles, and went off without saying a word.

'If you so much as mention it!' exclaimed Alberta.

'No, I needn't mention it,' said Sivert meekly, already complying with the situation to a certain extent.

He changed the subject to his future, his art. At home at Granli they could not help him much. They had no more than just enough. The farm was small, and there was still a debt on it. The money he had had from the sale of his pictures this spring was as good as finished. Now he was applying for a grant. But . . .

He felt damnably helpless. It was not a small thing for a man in his position to take on. Merely the responsibility! Had Alberta thought what a responsibility it would be? Obviously there was nothing a man wanted more, when he could manage it, than to . . .

He also referred to her future, her freedom and her work.

233

Had she realised what a tie it would be, considering how they were placed?

Alberta listened to him without altering her expression. Something inevitable had occurred to her. Its shadow lay cold across her life. Throw off the burden – yes, she would do it, if it were possible. But it was not possible. Sivert's solution was no solution.

He continued: If only circumstances were different! Alberta must not believe that he didn't . . . . Well, well, when she had thought things over a bit they would be able to live calmly and happily again.

Alberta got up, sat down, watched the movement of the clouds across the sky outside. She seemed to have difficulty talking. Her lips seemed to have stuck together and refused to co-operate. At last she said tonelessly: ' I'll take some hot baths, Sivert, very hot. It's supposed to help sometimes. As for the other – I won't do it.'

And she thought: If baths helped, the world would be a very different place.

Alberta had taken hot baths. In the Rue Delambre and the Rue d'Odessa and the Rue d'Alésia, so as not to attract attention by going time after time to the same place. She had almost scalded herself, had held out until her heart refused to do so any longer and everything whirled round her, had let the hot tap run so unreasonably long that she had been threatened with having to pay for two baths instead of one, next time. But the situation remained unaltered. Sivert said yes, but she must put herself in his position. Alberta continued to sit with her stony expression and said, ' Naturally '

She had a few words ready to the effect that he should leave her alone, that she could manage by herself, that he need not come again. But they were never spoken, they died unborn like so many of Alberta's words. Saying them would have been equivalent to cutting an anchor-rope and drifting out to sea alone in an open boat.

And Sivert repeated that as long as one did not let too

234

much time pass, it was not the slightest bit dangerous. That doctor Eliel knew was supposed to have said it was nothing, a mere trifle. Afterwards one was as free as a bird again. Good heavens, if only Alberta realised! It was an everyday matter.

'And Liesel?' Alberta heard a threatening note in her voice.

'Well, what about Liesel? Is there anything the matter with Liesel?' Sivert had seen Liesel in the street quite recently.

'Oh!' exclaimed Alberta in agitation. Like a caged animal she paced the two steps between the window and the door.

Then Sivert said: 'Well . . . what was Eliel to do, poor fellow? He was in no better position. Is a man really to let his whole future, all his opportunities, slip out of his grasp for the sake of someone unborn? Is that reasonable? I must say I more than understand him,' asserted Sivert. 'And he's had his share of trouble too, you can be sure of that.'

Alberta had halted. 'Eliel?' she said, holding her breath. 'But surely it was – ?'

Sivert looked at the floor uncomprehendingly for a long time. 'Yes of course it was this doctor who did it, naturally, that's obvious. It was certainly very fortunate for them that they knew him. He seems to be a nice fellow – human – '

'You must go now, Sivert,' said Alberta, her hands over her face. And Sivert, who occasionally behaved with surprising tact, got to his feet and took his hat and coat. He remained standing for a while, as if waiting for Alberta to uncover her face and at least look at him. But she did not do so. He sighed despairingly, and went his way for that day.

'But it means utter ruin, Alberta,' he said a few days later. And for the first time Alberta saw a pale, ravaged, almost contorted expression in his face. Then sympathy began to steal in on her, with a strange stubbornness and slowness. The hardness in her began to yield as if gliding away sluggishly, almost imperceptibly.

She said nothing. But she put her hand on Sivert's arm for a moment. To her, too, it seemed like utter ruin. But these forces catch up with you sooner or later. You may see an avalanche coming, or floods or other catastrophes, but nobody has ever suggested you can avoid them by so doing. One single, narrow, rough track was left to her and Sivert, difficult to follow, precarious and discouraging. She already felt her feet stumble many times, felt the weight of her burden. But the alternative was ruin too, and Sivert would not attempt it with her.

Suddenly his face was on her shoulder. He hid it there for a second or two. It was a boyish gesture – like that of a big boy who has done something wrong and does not know what the devil he can do about it, and has a moment of weakness with his sister or his mother. She bent her head and kissed the troubled boy's forehead for the first time for a long while.

As if by tacit agreement Alberta came again and posed for Sivert. Neither of them referred to it, they simply resumed the practice. It was the first time Sivert had worked on a large composition. He had come some way with it too, had made a number of sketches and begun to collect them on a large sheet of pasteboard. Sivert was not one to risk a canvas before he knew what he was doing, and that precisely. Alberta tired quickly and had to lie down on the divan, and this also took place tacitly, without discussion. One day it struck Alberta that perhaps she instinctively glimpsed salvation here – perhaps, deep down beneath everything else, she had begun to take thought for the morrow as well as she could, for someone besides herself. From now on she was more pleasant to Sivert, more talkative. The painful petrified feeling seemed definitely to have dissolved.

And then Sivert gradually arrived at a decision too,

without superfluous talk. Strictly speaking, he needed female models in this condition. They could carry themselves in proud triumph, or they could wander about, weighed down by anguish and distress. Life manifested itself in them in more than one way, and it was 'an ill wind' ... The proverb showed itself to be true now, as so often before.

She had begun to adopt hole-and-corner methods of reaching her room, making herself small on the stairs and choosing dark times of day, taking to the habit of throwing her coat round her shoulders, in and out of season, letting it hang loose and open. Nothing was very noticeable yet, but her dresses had begun to feel tight. She avoided conversation with the inhabitants of the house as far as possible.

One day Liesel came up.

'Have you talked to Ness, Albertchen? What did he say?'

Alberta was seized with fellow-feeling for Sivert, perhaps too a touch of feminine reluctance to admit to herself or to anyone else that, however much may have taken place, men are apt to see beyond women, to pay attention to other things besides them alone.

'He said – well, yes, not much. We must keep it dark for the time being, of course. You understand ....'

Did Liesel understand! With tears in her eyes she took Alberta's hand and held it to her cheek for a moment. 'Are you happy, Albertchen?'

'Happy? You know, Liesel, we have no idea how we shall manage.'

* * *

One hot August evening they were wandering down the Boul' Mich'. Alberta was now a little less cautious, and ventured more often down into town. At this time of year there were no dangerous acquaintances in Paris, and she had a nervous compulsion to move about.

The new St. Michel-Montmartre motor-bus was standing ready to leave. And Sivert was quite prepared to improve matters as well as he could. He did not flinch from promenading abroad with Alberta, by now considerably altered; he found things to do in so far as it was possible. He suggested a trip on the upper deck.

Sivert did not look at all happy. But he did look as if he had decided to struggle through. Alberta, on the other hand, had her petrified feeling, something frozen in the mind that only made itself felt at intervals. She seemed to congeal over and over again. Something was happening that was so overwhelming, she could not really take it in. It made her apathetic, almost indifferent. It would have to end as it might, preferably in death.

They bowled along through the oppressive streets. It was no longer the same as in the horse-buses that pitched along at a walking pace or a slow trot, according to contingencies, while snatches of conversation rose up from all the people sitting on chairs on the pavement. Now everything was drowned in the noise of the motor.

The air in the streets ascending towards the Place Clichy was worse than ever, a revolting brew of the stink of petrol and stagnant vapours. ' *Huff,*' said Sivert. ' Why did we come here? It would have been far better to take a tram-car out of town. It'll be pleasant to get back home.'

But further along the Boulevard Clichy something was happening. People were crowding round large tents pitched lengthways under the scorched trees on the walk in the middle of the street. The roaring of lions came from one of them. In front of another a Negro armed with a shield, arrows and a lance, tattooed and wearing a metal pin through his nose, stood on a platform above the crowd. The muffled sound of war drums arose, as threatening as distant thunder about him. Farther off a steam roundabout span round to loud music, and announced its departure

238

with a shrill whistle, very up-to-date of its kind. A switch-back was in full activity to the accompaniment of clattering and shrieks. Enormous posters announced that here man-eating tribes from Central Africa were on exhibition. The smell of fried apples, pancakes and wild animals cut through the heavy air.

' Come on, let's go in,' said Alberta suddenly. They were standing in front of the Negro's tent.

Sivert demurred for an instant: ' I'm not sure that it would be wise for you to go in,' he said. ' I've heard that . . . '. He would like to see the blacks himself. ' Even if it is only trickery, they can be very picturesque.'

' I *want* to go in,' said Alberta curtly. She felt the cold stubbornness that often had the upper hand in her now. If it was ill-advised, so much the worse.

Once inside the tent Sivert wanted to take her out again. ' The smell,' he said. ' It's enough to finish you.'

But Alberta could stand it. A deep sympathy, something compelling, had seized her as soon as she entered. These Negroes squatting round simulated camp-fires or wandering round on flattened, naked feet, grinning at each other and exchanging comments on the sightseers which were certainly not flattering, perhaps exceedingly coarse – she felt a warmth for them, a searing pity, similar to the pity one feels for inefficient jugglers and performing animals, for all poor things that have to put themselves on show.

They were all ages, old people, young ones and children, the majority men and young boys, but an old man and a couple of old women too, looking like the mummified heads one sees in museums. In one corner a war dance was taking place to the accompaniment of the drums, people were gathering there, standing on tiptoe to see over each other's heads. Sivert jammed himself in with the rest, sketchbook in hand, asking Alberta to wait for him and to go outside if the smell was too much for her.

She wandered round the big tent, watching the weaving and other handwork that was being shown in the corners, and then stopped in sudden surprise. In the far corner there was a separate section, a smaller tent raised inside the large one. Illuminated by a hanging lamp a young Negress was kneeling inside it. She was holding a child in her arms. and had pushed her sleeveless red dress down from her shoulder and taken out her breast to give to the baby. He was loosely wrapped in a brightly coloured cloth. Alberta could only see the back of his head and one strong little hand which struck again and again at his mother's flesh, gripping it with pleasure. Just as Alberta approached, he relinquished the breast. The mother put him down on a blanket on the floor while she put her dress straight. Then she bent down and loosened the cloth, and remained looking down at the child, who stretched himself, satisfied, while his eyes slowly blurred with sleep. He was a sturdy baby, probably a few months old, round and firm as a little baroque angel, in spite of the city air, the dust and all kinds of wrong conditions.

The mother wrapped the cloth round him again, picked up the child and rocked him gently, watching him intently. Behind her the walls of the tent gave continually under the pressure of the crowd outside. She seemed to be unaware of anything but the child she was holding.

Alberta had never seen such sweetness in a face, such placid, infinite tenderness, such tranquil, intense happiness.

The child was asleep. The mother looked up. Her eyes were as frank and soft as those of a gentle, beautiful, shy animal. They glittered moistly, blue as enamel round the large, brown pupils. The mouth beneath the small, flat nose was paler than the face, scarcely red, but generous with the same animal goodness, making Alberta think of the dumb devotion of dumb creatures, their instinctive and primeval expression of it. She was reminded of the doe that licks its calf, of horses nuzzling each other.

The Negress looked at Alberta. The large, moist eyes looked her up and down. Then the lips parted in a smile full of understanding, she nodded delightedly a couple of times from Alberta to the child and back again. And she slid carefully down into a sitting position on the floor of straw and branches with small woven mats scattered here and there over it, leaned once more over the child in her arms and remained sitting thus, as if lost in patient, joyful submission. She did not move again.

But something was released in Alberta's heart. For the first time she felt without defiance and coldness that she was to become a mother. The approaching enemy was a little naked child, infinitely defenceless, with only herself to turn to and trust. Boundless sympathy for it streamed towards her heart and eyes, and was released, warm and wet on her cheeks.

Sivert arrived. He was full of the war dance, which had certainly been genuine enough, by Jove. But it was high time they went, it was a wonder Alberta had not even felt sick. Was she crying? Well, what was the matter now?

'I'm only a little tired,' said Alberta.

People were filling the tent, hiding the young mother. There was nothing more to wait for. Sivert led her towards the exit: 'We'll find something to drink somewhere,' he said. 'Something cool and refreshing.'

That evening Alberta went home with Sivert. She accompanied him to the door and went in with him, without either of them referring to it.

But when they were inside the studio and he had lighted the lamp, he said half jokingly: 'Are you still there? Well, I think that's the best thing, don't you? It can't be very pleasant going up and down those stairs any longer, I imagine.'

He looked about him: 'We shall have to arrange things as best we can here.'

Then Alberta went over and took Sivert's hand. And she did as Liesel had done with hers, laid it against her cheek.

AFTERWORD

by Linda Hunt

Reversing the old adage about a prophet not being honored in his own country, Cora Sandel's *Alberta Trilogy* has long been a classic in her native Norway but is nearly unknown in the English-speaking world, especially in the United States. *Alberta and Jacob, Alberta and Freedom*, and *Alberta Alone*, first published in 1926, 1931, and 1939 respectively, were not even translated into English until the first half of the nineteen-sixties when they appeared in England; a one-volume American edition (which contained all three novels under the misleading title of *Alberta Alone*) appeared in 1966 but drew few reviews, little attention, and soon fell out of print. A look at the *MLA Index* for the decade of the seventies shows that numerous critical articles on Sandel, and especially on the *Alberta* books, appeared in the Scandinavian languages but none in English. The card catalogue of the New York Public Library's main branch reveals no holdings in English on Cora Sandel.

For American readers, Ohio University Press in publishing the *Alberta Trilogy* is making an important contribution to what Germaine Greer has called "the rehabilitation of women's literary history." These three feminist novels are so good that along with hailing their recovery one cannot help but feel angry that we in the United States have had to wait so long for the opportunity to experience their excellence.

Alberta and Jacob (1926) is an evocation of one year in the life of a shy, repressed adolescent girl living with her family in a stuffy, provincial town in the most Northern part of Norway during the last years of the nineteenth century. Alberta Selmer's family and their neighbors could be characters out of Ibsen in their bourgeois concern for sexual respectability and the importance of keeping up the appearance of material prosperity. Alberta despairs at the prospect of a life like that of any of the women in her town. If spinsters, they are objects of pity and, actually, objectively quite "odd"; if

242

sexually rebellious, pregnancy tames them. Respectably married, their lives are bounded by food and servant worries, gynecological troubles, and envy of their neighbors. This grim destiny is appropriately emblemized for Alberta by the figure of Nurse Jellum the midwife who keeps reappearing throughout the novel (and indeed recurs in memory in the sequels), "with her terrible bag and her quiescent know-all smile."

Alberta's options are contrasted to that of her brother Jacob who functions as a foil lest we make the mistake of not recognizing that Alberta's troubles are related to gender. While his life in this environment is far from enviable, he is encouraged to stay in school (although he is a terrible student and she is an excellent one), and he is able to find some relief from the stultifying life of the family by carousing with a sailor friend and coming home late, sometimes drunk. His decision to go to sea is a calamity for his caste-conscious parents, but they accept the unavoidable and he makes his escape. Alberta cannot follow Jacob's example and simply leave or even plan eventually to leave because she has internalized the family's assumption that as a dutiful daughter she will sacrifice her own well-being to be a buffer between her wretchedly-married parents.

Sandel expertly uses the frozen landscape of this Arctic town and the frigid interior of the Selmer house as an externalization of Alberta's inner life. The strange, brief summer of Northern Norway with its twenty-four hours of daylight functions as a metaphor for the protagonist's first furtive recognition that there is a world outside of her experience which can offer light, warmth, and happiness.

Alberta and Freedom (1931) begins with its protagonist standing nude, in Paris, posing for an artist. Lest the reader think Alberta has found the freedom and warmth she longed for as a girl and which the title of this volume seems to promise, we are told immediately of the terrible vulnerability Alberta feels, of the physical and mental discomfort of standing in one position for so long, and, inevitably, of the cold-

243

ness of the studio. (External cold and heat are metaphors for Alberta's emotional condition throughout the trilogy.) The Norwegian young woman's parents had died, and she has at last been able to flee to the Bohemian fringe of Paris; it is the period before the first world war when the Left Bank became a symbol of youthful release from restrictive conventions, but, as this novel and its sequel show, the pursuit of freedom is not easy for a woman.

Alberta and Freedom is framed by images of a woman's physical vulnerability and susceptibility to bodily exploitation. The opening scene of Alberta posing, compelled to earn her bread by making a body into a commodity since she has been trained for no profession or occupation, is matched by the closing scene of the novel in which Alberta, unmarried and pregnant, wanders around an exhibition of "man-eating" tribes from Central Africa which has come to Paris. She comes upon a young "Negress" nursing a child; the African woman recognizes Alberta's condition and nods in delighted affinity. The experience releases in Alberta previously pent-up maternal emotions, and yet it is clear from the imagery that for Alberta, both she and the Black woman are, like animals, captives of their bodies, reduced to a bodily existence. The fact that the African mother is being exhibited to crowds for a price serves to underscore the theme of sexual exploitation.

Between the first and closing scenes we read of Alberta's life in Paris: perhaps the most striking thing about this life is its apparent purposelessness; she does make occasional undisciplined, almost furtive attempts to express herself creatively through writing, but it is impossible for her to take herself seriously enough to have genuine literary ambitions. She spends her time wandering around Paris half-starved— on the Metro, on foot, on trams—taking in the human drama all around her but always a stranger at the feast. Unwilling to accept any of the roles society has assigned to women, Alberta, at this stage, is a kind of Underground Woman, "an outlaw" as one character calls her. She is the female counterpart to all those male anti-heroes of modern literature who define themselves in terms of their marginality. Alberta has no analysis of what is wrong with the position of women in society, but all of her instincts are to keep herself a marginal member. As the narrative voice tells us, "She still had only negative instincts just as when she was at home. They told her clearly what she did not want to do. . . . she was left free to reject what she did not want and without the slightest idea of what she should do with herself."

Sandel depicts the circle of Alberta's Montparnasse friends, men and women who have come there from all over the world to be artists. Alberta's closest friend is Liesel, a struggling painter who always spoils her paintings just when they are very good by putting a dab of color where it does not belong or painting in some lines that mar the overall design. Like Alberta but several steps ahead of her since at least she is able to define herself as an artist, Liesel cannot trust her inner vision. She succumbs to a young sculptor, and initially her love affair is joyous, a reproachment to Alberta's loneliness. But Elial, Liesel's lover, determines the conditions of their life together so that his work always takes precedence over hers. Sandel is certainly making a point about the obstacles to artistic success for women since none of the women in Alberta's and Liesel's Paris circle achieve artistic fulfillment, but both Elial and Sivert, Alberta's lover, become quite successful. The women painters as they get older are evoked as "trudging around Montparnasse. . . . they had wrinkles and untidy grey hair, and they dragged themselves around with large bags of brushes over one arm . . . fussing and wearisome, they filled the academies and life-classes . . . they lived on nothing, making tea with egg water. . . ."

In the final volume of this trilogy, *Alberta Alone* (1939), the protagonist's existence is much less marginal as a result of a marriage-like relationship and motherhood. Alberta has backed right into a life not too different from the one she sought to escape. In this book Sandel shows that integration into society for women too often means oppressive burdens: Alberta is encumbered by the endless work and persistent worry that being a mother entails; weighted down by her lack of love for the father of her child, on whom she is financially dependent, and by her developing love for Pierre, another woman's husband. But the relationship with Pierre is different from either of her previous entanglements with men in that he encourages Alberta to take seriously the pile of papers in a folder that Sivert has always demeaningly referred to as her "scribbling." For the first time she begins to think in a positive way about what she might want to do with her life.

In the course of this third novel Alberta becomes increasingly aware that she must find a way to be financially self-sufficient. In the last scene she walks along a road in Norway carrying the completed novel in a suitcase, her aim publication and the beginning of an autonomous and purposeful existence. Because she has left the child behind, everything she sees along the road, a mother and a baby, mare and foal, seem to tell her she is at odds with nature. Sandel defines Alberta's emotional state at this juncture in her life by an image of external cold which by accretion through the three novels has become increasingly powerful: "the mist had risen now, there was clear visibility and it was cold. No arms around her anymore, not even those of a child; naked life as far as she could see, struggle for an impartial view."

Throughout these books Cora Sandel is a fine stylist with a keenly-observant eye and a good ear; she has been well-served by her translator. Sandel's mastery of precise detail and fresh imagery allows her to bring place and character to vivid realization, endowing both with the emotional meaning she seeks. Thus, the coffee pot in the chill, cluttered Victorian dining room in the Selmer home "stood there like a revelation, its brass well-polished, warming, steaming, aromatic . . a sun among dead worlds." Seen through the window of the office where she works, Beda Buck, the girlhood

246

friend who is as free in spirit as Alberta is repressed, "shook her fist through the window at Alberta, because she was wandering about . . . while Beda had to sit indoors." In Paris the cafe awnings, the dry leaves in a hot summer square, the "rusty" voice of a night club singer, the shrouded shapes in a sculptor's studio, all suggest Alberta's melancholy at being alone in the nearly-deserted city in August. In Alberta's down-at-the-heels hotel room mice drown in the wash-bowl. As Alberta and Sivert become increasingly estranged, his eyes are "much too blue," his presence on several occasions experienced as "a wall." Sandel's ear for dialogue is equally evocative.

Moreover, these novels are structured in such a way that form imitates substance. Instead of chapters, we have a series of scenes separated by blank space or blank space with asterisks. Each time the scene changes the reader must struggle, without expository narration, to re-orient herself, to figure out where Alberta is, who the other characters are, what is happening or what the conversation is about. The effect, especially because Sandel's writing is so visual and reliant on dialogue, is almot cinematic. For example, in *Alberta and Freedom*, an early scene opens in a carefully-described studio in a Parisian hotel. Alberta is lying on a bed talking to Liesel whom we are meeting for the first time. The reader wonders: is this where Alberta lives in Paris? Who is this friend? (The room turns out to belong to Liesel.) In having to work out the situation, the reader is experiencing what Alberta continually goes through as she struggles to make sense of a world which is not welcoming and where nothing is easy for her. Like Alberta, the reader feels peripheral to the life which unfolds.

Sandel's skillful experimentation with formal innovation along with her command of language and the importance of her themes certainly should have ensured her an audience and a reputation outside her native Norway. The question remains: why were these novels not recognized for their quality earlier, at least in the sixties when the Elizabeth Rokken translation appeared in England and America? An examination of the reviews from that time reveal some clues. It is apparent even from the positive reviews (and on the whole the novels were well-received) that the specifically female reality Cora Sandel mined, the answers she found to problems of plot and structure endemic to women's fiction, and her feminist themes made sufficient and appropriate appreciation unlikely in the first half of the sixties in England and America. The work done by feminist critics in the last decade has made Cora Sandel's achievement accessible to us in ways it simply was not earlier. (It would be fascinating to know what Scandinavian critics have been saying about her work all along.) The sixties' reviews also show the extent to which bias against feminism and even downright sexism was an obstacle to a fair literary assessment of Sandel's work.

In 1966 an American reviewer (a woman), writing for the *Saturday Review*, enthusiastically compares Alberta with Philip Carey, the protagonist of Somerset Maugham's *Of Human Bondage*. Like Carey, she says, Alberta emerges from a dreary small-town childhood into "pre-war Paris and the brief years of freedom, art, and love, no money, and infinite possibilities." Since this is not what happens at all, we can only assume that the reviewer processed what she read to suit her preconceptions about what the artistic life in Paris was like in those years, preconceptions that had been formed by reading both the literature and the literary mythology produced by men.

Sandel has written these books in part to show us that while Bohemian Paris may have been a moveable feast to male writers and painters, there was no way that Alberta and her friends could have had the same joyous experience. While they do possess talent, they lack the self-confidence, the money, and the freedom from both conventionality and heterosexuality that made it possible for some few women— the likes of Gertrude Stein and Natalie Barney—to establish a woman-loving artistic culture in Paris in this period. As Liesel says in a letter after she has returned home to her family, "The artistic poverty-stricken life isn't much fun in the long run. The men can do it, but not us."

The reader today finds herself nodding, 'Yes, that's how it would have been for most women.' She is likely to think of Virginia Woolf's hypothetical story, in *A Room Of One's Own*, of what would have happened to Shakespeare's equally-talented sister (if he had had one), if she had tried to go to London to become a playwright. Shakespeare's sister, in pursuit of freedom, adventure, and creative fulfillment, falls victim to, among other things, her lack of control of her reproductive life—as do Alberta and Liesel. But back in 1966 when the *Saturday Review* piece on the Alberta books appeared, few people were reading *A Room Of One's Own*, and literary minds, even female ones, were not sensitized to the fact that reality gets dangerously distorted when we try to fit female experience into a framework of literary conventions made by and for men.

Almost all the reviews from the nineteen-sixties complain that in Sandel's trilogy "nothing happens." The reviewer of *Alberta & Freedom* in the *Times Literary Supplement* (July 26, 1963) asks, "But what about development, action, drama?" Because of the work of such feminist literary critics as Joanna Russ, Annis Pratt, Nancy Miller and Gubar and Gilbert, we understnd that Cora Sandel is avoiding the patriarchal plot-structures that have been recognized as a major obstacle to women writers seeking to express an authentic female point of view. Since women in stories inherited from the male literary tradition have limited alternatives regarding what they can do (fall in love and marry, fall in love and die), Sandel chooses plotlessness, but in doing so she is not choosing lack of form. Joanna Russ would describe the structure of the Alberta trilogy as "lyrical" in that images, events, passages and words are organized around an implicit emotional center, that center being Alberta Selmer's repressed soul and its yearning, as it gropes in the cold and damp of life, for freedom, warmth, and security. Virginia Woolf structures her novels along similar principles.

These three novels read together also have another kind of structure which comes from the working out of certain mythic patterns which feminist criticism such as Annis Pratt's *Archetypal Patterns in Women's Fiction* and Carol Pearson and Katherine Pope's *The Female Hero* show us are recurrent in fiction by women. Both of these recent studies stress the importance of the mother-daughter relationship, symbolized in Greek mythology by the story of Demeter, the goddess of the harvest, and her daughter Persephone who is stolen from her side. Just as in the myth the season of cold when nothing grows initiated by the ruptured relationship between mother and daughter can only end when the two are returned to each other, a female hero in fiction often requires reconciliation with her mother or a mother-figure in order to get in touch with her own power and achieve her creative potential.

Alberta's relationship with her mother is already deeply estranged when *Alberta and Jacob* opens. Mrs. Selmer, self-doubting and disappointed with her life, is incapable of nurturing a daughter. Although Alberta is so cold that her skin is perpetually blue, she has to sneak the hot cups of coffee she craves. At the breakfast table Alberta must help herself to food as surreptitiously as possible while Mrs. Selmer loads Jacob's plate with piles of cheese. Alberta's mother is similarly ungenerous on the level of emotions. She tells Alberta repeatedly that she is a disappointment because of her lack of beauty, her shyness, her inability to interest herself in domestic accomplishments, her inexplicable interest in reading "learned tomes," and her refusal to encourage the attentions of her father's clerk.

Mama's inability to provide warmth is largely responsible for Alberta's guilt-ridden and anxious personality; she is so constrained that she feels "she was without the use of speech, she would die of muteness." Always afraid of eliciting her mother's scorn or anger, Alberta can never feel relaxed in her mother's house.

Given the youthful Alberta's fear that she will "die of

250

muteness," we can understand why in later years her writing becomes the key to life for her. Given the lack of ease she feels in the house in which she spends her childhood, Alberta's discomfort in a series of dingy, even sordid hotel rooms and then in Sivert's crowded studio takes on greater poignancy. Even in a pleasant summer cottage in Brittany she is unable to enjoy the beauty of her surroundings because she is terrified that the sea air is dangerous to the health of her delicate little son. Alberta can never feel at home anywhere.

The inhospitability of her environment, wherever she is, is a factor in her failure to impose coherence on her manuscript. We see Alberta wrestling with her "muddle of scribbled papers" in poorly-lit hotel rooms and on the slopes near the beach in Brittany where she must "struggle . . . with the wind for control of her straying papers."

Towards the close of the last volume Alberta is sitting in a wood in rural Norway uncomfortably balancing her manuscript on her knees, desperate to finish, when she is discovered by an old woman with a "kind, wrinkled face tied up in a handkerchief." The woman, Lina, invites Alberta to see her house on a nearby farm. They go upstairs to a room where "the sun poured in on a large table standing between the windows . . . . There was simple furniture . . . Some dried wreaths above the sofa gave out a strong sweet scent. . . . Alberta had, without thinking, put her folder down on the table. There it lay as if it had come home. She almost felt at home herself." The farmwoman allows her to use the room to work on her manuscript, and in it, over the course of a beautiful Norwegian summer, she completes her novel.

Lina's psychic function is to be a surrogate mother to Alberta and, appearing just when the younger woman needs her most (exactly when Pope and Pearson, in their book on the archetypal "journey" of the female hero, say this figure appears), is able to heal the damage done by Alberta's actual mother who had functioned as a "captor." Lina's description fits that of the "wise old woman" whom Annis Pratt tells us is often in women's novels an archetypal guide for the soul as it

251

pursues its spiritual quest. Lina is surrounded by plants and animals and, as the sweet-smelling wreaths in the room demonstrate, has a knowledge of herbs. Married, but very much her own woman, Lina provides a model of calm autonomy. Most important, she not only provides Alberta with the sanctuary in the form of a simple room which Pratt reminds us so many women characters need to get in touch with their power but, like any good mother, she affirms Alberta's gift by recognizing it: "I understand enough to see you're a kind of author too, it's just that you don't want anything to interfere." Again like an ideal mother, she compels Alberta to impose discipline on herself by telling her firmly she must vacate the room by the date summer visitors are due to arrive. In finding a spiritual mother who both nurtures and yet encourages separation, Alberta becomes capable of saving herself through mastery of language, overcoming the "muteness" which was her biological mother's inadvertent legacy.

Alberta can develop as a person only through the kind of inner, psychic experience that reconciliation with a mother figure represents. As the reviewer of *Alberta and Freedom* quoted before complains, she does not develop psychologically very much in the course of the novels. For example, when Jeanne, Pierre's wife, orders her to send him a telegraph terminating their relationship, she simply complies, as much a slave to an authoritative voice as when she was a child who had internalized her parents' values.

Reading Annis Pratt can help us to understand that Alberta fails to develop much psychologically until the very end not as a result of weakness in Sandel's narrative skill but for the same reasons that female heroes in general don't progress towards maturity through action in the social world. The female bildungsroman cannot demonstrate "*bildung*" in the way that male novels of development do because in patriarchal society adulthood for women means neither authority nor autonomy. Unlike the male hero who develops by achieving an adult social identity, for Alberta increasing integration into society only means further entrapment. Like so many protagonists of women's fiction she can "break through" into true adulthood (as she is told to do in a very Jungian dream by the "young girlish figure" who is her guide) only by asocial moments of epiphany such as she experiences in her almost clandestine first visit to Lina's room.

Alberta's reconciliation with the symbolic good mother links the last volume with the bad-mother motif in the first book, *Alberta and Jacob*, providing unity to the trilogy as a whole. Since Lina is encountered in summer, and Mrs. Selmer tyrannizes over the adolescent Alberta predominantly in the dark, freezing depths of winter, it seems possible that Sandel may even have had the Demeter-Persephone myth consciously in mind. Certainly the extraordinary emphasis on the soul-withering Arctic cold in *Alberta and Jacob* suggests the endless winter that results, in the myth, from the rupture of mother and daughter.

Other criticisms of the *Alberta* books in the reviews from the sixties require no response but are interesting because of their naked anti-feminism and sexism. An unsigned review of *Alberta Alone* in the *Times Literary Supplement* (February 25, 1965) dismisses Sandel's concern for the emancipation of women as outdated and complains about the "female narcissism" in the book. This same reviewer finds the character of Alberta insufficiently deep to warrant her position as the center of interest in a trilogy, an opinion he is entitled to, but one is forced to think about his biases when he observes, "This is not *just* to say that women are less interesting than men, and that this is the flaw" [emphasis mine].

The resurrection of feminism in the years since the *Alberta Trilogy* was first published in English has encouraged literary minds both to develop the interpretative skills necessary to understand women's literature and to be on the alert for "lost" books by women. The appearance in America of these three novels by Cora Sandel should be regarded as an important event of literary archeology. However, literature by women has been retrieved in the past only to slip again into obscurity. It is important that people be told how good the novels in this series are and be urged to read them singly and/or as a unit; it is important that these novels be taught and written about. Readers are ultimately the ones who keep worthy "lost" books alive.